T0195555

Broomstick Tales

The Cryptic Secret of Zweig's Magic Wand

Told by Wazoo the Wizard

Written and illustrated
by Arnie Grimm

authorHOUSE®

AuthorHouse™
1663 Liberty Drive
Bloomington, IN 47403
www.authorhouse.com
Phone: 1 (800) 839-8640

© 2020 Arnie Grimm. All rights reserved.

No part of this book may be reproduced, stored in a retrieval system, or transmitted by any means without the written permission of the author.

Published by AuthorHouse 02/29/2020

ISBN: 978-1-7283-4899-5 (sc)
ISBN: 978-1-7283-4897-1 (hc)
ISBN: 978-1-7283-4898-8 (e)

Library of Congress Control Number: 2020904077

Print information available on the last page.

Any people depicted in stock imagery provided by Getty Images are models, and such images are being used for illustrative purposes only. Certain stock imagery © Getty Images.

This book is printed on acid-free paper.

Because of the dynamic nature of the Internet, any web addresses or links contained in this book may have changed since publication and may no longer be valid. The views expressed in this work are solely those of the author and do not necessarily reflect the views of the publisher, and the publisher hereby disclaims any responsibility for them.

To Ken, Dave, Tim, Jeff, and Alex the master craftsmen who built my retirement home in Colorado.

Contents

Chapter One
George and Gracie

It was a bright day this June when the Magic Book Seller opened his booth at Broomstick's Renaissance Faire. He arrived at the annual renaissance faire unnoticed with his booth appearing at an empty grassy spot that was actually set aside for faire goers to sit and relax in the shade of a large tree.

This day began like the other days at the fair. Faire goers were dressed for the festivities in period clothing with their paid tickets in hand.

The jousting tournaments were getting underway with experience riders ready to slam their lances into the shields of their opponents. Light soft wood splintered and flew in all directions giving the spectators a great show.

School was out for the summer and the young teenagers had their month long passes to the faire.

Standing at the castle like stone entrance was first time faire participant George Düben. He was a young boy that was a month away from being fourteen with freckles across his nose. His Chestnut brown hair was parted down the middle and swept over his ears.

The reason why George had never been to the renaissance faire before was he and his sister Gracie had recently moved to Broomstick from San Francisco, California.

He was dressed in a handmade wizard's apprentice robe that was sewn along the sides from the lower ends of the sleeves to the bottom. George wore a wide imitation leather belt around the middle with a plastic Celtic style belt buckle.

Sewn on the robe was a circle patch with symbols that represented the Moon, the five planets and the Sun. In the middle of the patch was the Earth. Neither George nor his sister knew what the patch symbols meant. It just looked cool.

On top of George's head was a cone hat without a brim and on his feet, were soft leather Peter Pan style shoe coverings over his sneakers.

George's sister Gracie made the entire outfit for him with assistance from the local craft store. It didn't cost much to make although Gracie had to skip a few lunches to pay for it.

George and Gracie were not part of the magical world. They were in fact one hundred percent knotem as in magic to them was in fairytales. George and Gracie didn't have a clue that they had move to the largest population of magical folk this side of the Atlantic. So why was George dressed as a wizard apprentice, you ask?

That is what brings me to my story. Oh, and who am I you ask? I'm your story teller. I am Wazoo the Wizard and this Broomstick tale is called Zweig's Magic Wand.

George and Gracie Düben had been temporarily living with their parent's longtime friends in San Francisco, California after their parents were killed in a private plane crash exactly a year ago to the date.

Gracie knew her and her brother couldn't live with their parent's longtime friends until she graduated from college. George was a handful with his lack of acceptance that their parents were not ever coming back. He slipped into an imaginary world of his own to cope with the loss.

Life was dull for Gracie. She was going to school full time and trying to work part time jobs. None of those jobs fit with going to school. Gracie wouldn't last long because of showing up late and calling off to attend a class.

George was failing all his classes in junior high school. He was repeatedly sent to detention for disobeying teachers or ignoring them altogether. Gracie couldn't pull George out of this imaginary world to even talk to him. Gracie knew things had to change.

Gracie said to herself, when she was really frustrated, "I wish I had a bit of magic in my life to change my whole life."

A fairy happened to overhear her wish and decided to grant that wish. You may think this was an act of kindness. It wasn't. You see this fairy, had her own agenda. You will find out later in the story what her motives were.

Gracie decided to move to Broomstick after seeing a cutout ad from a certain magazine we are familiar with in the magical world called 'Once in a Lifetime Job Opportunity'. The ad was pinned up on the college bulletin board. It offered students a free scholarship if they would transfer to Benjamin Candlewick Law School.

"This is it, our chance to start a new life," said Gracie to herself as she wrote down the information.

Gracie didn't notice right after she wrote down the information for transcript submission and walked away, the ad began to smolder and burn as it dropped to the floor. On the back of the ad in white contrasting letters on the blackened ash paper one could have read, "Gracie Düben, you have been accepted to Benjamin Candlewick Law School".

George and Gracie were orphans, so to speak. Sadly, that left Nineteen year old Gracie to raise her brother.

For the present, they were struggling financially with Gracie going to Benjamin Candlewick Law School on the free scholarship. Gracie didn't have to worry about a mortgage payment as she had bought a nice house near the college with what little insurance money the courts allowed to be paid out.

It was all the other bills that kept her living from paycheck to paycheck. Property taxes, utilities, food and gasoline were piling up as the probate court dragged its feet to release their parent's bank accounts.

Gracie was glad the last day of school came and she could work full time for the next three months. She had a job working at the Ex-press Coffee shop on the north side of town. Gracie worked double shifts and any weekend shift she could grab.

George liked the idea of dressing up for the renaissance faire. He wanted to be a wizard's apprentice. You need to understand George was taking his parents death pretty hard. He was dealing with it by slipping into an imaginary world in his head where everything was just the way he wanted it. The renaissance faire gave him another route to travel in this imaginary world of his. George pretended to do magic.

George was old enough to know the difference between his imaginary world and the real world. He didn't share this knowledge with anyone. George put on this act to stop people from talking to him about how he felt about losing his parents. He just let people think what they wanted about him, including his sister.

At the renaissance faire George was walking through the booths looking at all the strange things that were for sale.

Just around the corner was the Magic Book Seller's booth. George saw a very tall man standing at the booth with a table lined with old magic books of all shapes and sizes for sale. The price range was from cheap to very expensive.

George thought to himself, "I don't have a magic book."

"Young man, yes you, young man come over here. I have something to show you," said the seven and a half tall man wearing a very long bluish green robe with unusual symbols embroidered in a small circle.

George cautiously walked over to the booth. He looked up at the very tall man not saying a word. The man looked down at the freckled face of the chestnut haired boy that stood no higher than the man's knees.

"What's your name?" asked the man.

"George."

"Your full name," asked the man.

"George Düben."

"George Düben, I see you are a wizard's apprentice. You do not have a book on magic. Let me just say this is your lucky day," said the man.

Now George wasn't old enough to see a scam coming. However, that line of this is your lucky day didn't sit well with him.

"I think I'll pass, thank you," said George as he started to walk away.

"Whoa, hold on there. I didn't mean to scare you away, George Düben," said the tall man.

"Sorry, not interested," said George.

"Come on back, just for a minute, George. Let me show you a very special book," said the man.

George hesitated, and then he took a couple of steps back toward the booth.

"Only a minute," said George.

"I am Karman the Magic Book Seller," said Karman as he waved his hands over his old books.

"What would you do if you had a book on magic that could tell you anything about magic?" said Karman.

"Uh, I don't know, maybe make people happy," said George.

"Exactly what I had in mind, and much more," said Karman.

"I can't afford a magic book," said George.

"And I'm not trying to sell you one either," said Karman.

Karman pulled from behind his table a leather covered book. He opened it to show George the old hand written diary of a wizard that lived long ago.

"Go ahead, hold the book George," said Karman.

"I can't, I don't have much money," said George.

"What would you say if I made it a gift to you," said Karman.

George knew the renaissance faire was all make believe. George stood there for a long moment staring at the magic book.

"I could play along just for today then give the book back before I go home," thought George.

The Magic Book Seller said, "It was once owned by a very powerful wizard that lived many centuries ago."

"I was told that wizards are a myth and are only in fairytales. So how could this magic book be centuries old?" said George.

"Oh, I'm afraid what you said is a myth. Wizards do exist even today. I stand here before you as a Master Wizard waiting for you to accept my offer," stated Karman with a deep voice.

"Will I learn what a wizard's apprentice does?" asked George.

"Whatever this wizard wrote, you will be required to use this magic book to find his lost magic wand," stated Karman.

George thought this was a good game. He will read the book for clues and look around the fair for this missing magic wand.

George carefully took the leather covered book.

"Go ahead and opened it and start reading the magic journal," encouraged Karman.

George turned the pages with his hand. George felt uncomfortable holding the magic book. The sensation of a hot flame ran down his arm to his stomach causing a queasy feeling.

"Ah, no I don't think I want this book," said George.

George went to put the magic book down on the table. But Karman quickly pushed the book back at George.

"By taking the magic journal you have accepted my irreversible offer. There is no turning back," stated Karman.

George could see the very tall man wasn't going to take no for an answer.

"Take care of this journal and don't allow anyone to take it away from you. Read it carefully and follow the instructions closely. Inside you will find a clue needed to finish the task. Find the magic wand. When you have completed your task of finding the magic wand, you have everything you need become a great wizard, except one important piece of magic. And that piece of magic will come in its own time," said Karman.

"Wouldn't I just bring the book and wand back here to you at the end of today? It shouldn't take me very long to play this game," asked George.

With red outlining the whites of his eyes, Karman's eyes grew very large as he stared at George. His nostrils flared. Karman held out his hand in a firm manner and grabbed George by his robe.

"This isn't a game, boy. By taking the magic journal, you have committed yourself to the magical world. Failure to complete your task will be dealt with severely. Do I make myself clear to you, boy?" said Karman.

Karman let go of George's robe with a slight push. "Now go and find that magic wand," Karman said to George.

Suddenly George was standing there staring at an empty grassy space with a shade tree where the magic book booth was just a second ago.

Miranda the fairy snickered to herself as she sat up on a tree branch above George. "I got you, you are mine forever," laughed Miranda.

A girl with strawberry blonde hair, freckles across her nose, and with large front teeth wearing a web inset-bodice dress with a leathery bat-neck collar walked up to George.

"What are you staring at?" she asked.

George was still in a trance like state of terror wondering what just happened.

The girl tapped George on the shoulder. "Hey, are you alright?" asked the girl.

George came back to reality and looked at the oddly dressed girl. To him she looked about eleven. She was cute in an awkward spooky way. George thought her nickname could be beaver teeth.

At first George answered, "Yeah, I'm alright," then quickly changed his answer. "No not really. I don't think anyone would believe what just happened to me."

"I might if you told me," said the girl.

George didn't want to tell his fantastic story to a stranger especially to a 'girl'. George expected her to laugh at him if he told her about the magic book booth disappearing.

"Naw, it's okay. I think I'll just go home," said George.

"Please tell me. I'll believe you no matter what you tell me," said the girl.

George relented and told her about the seven and one half foot tall book seller and the booth that was there where the grassy space is now.

"He gave me this old magic book. I'm to find a magic wand by finding clues in the book," explained George.

The girl stood there not saying a word peering straight into George's eyes. She had a devilish look to her that brought goose bumps to George's arms. He knew she didn't believe him.

"It's been nice meeting you. I'll see you around the faire sometime," said George.

"Wait, don't go. We really haven't met. I mean to say, we don't each other names. I'm Kizee," said the girl.

"Kiz-ie. Is that your real name or a made-up name because you don't like your real name?" asked George.

"It is actually supposed to be pronounced Key-nay. It's Swahili. Everyone pronounces it the way it looks. I like it that way also," said Kizee.

"I'm George. Okay we met I'll see you around," said George.

"Wait, please don't go. I don't any friends," said Kizee.

Kizee hit a nerve with George. The boys at school stereotyped him with hurtful assumptions about orphans. He learned quickly who his friends were. Nobody was the answer.

What could George say? He couldn't walk away now. If he did walk away, it would be exactly like throwing away a twenty dollar bill you just found on the ground. Mentally, George kicked himself for even thinking of walking away after Kizee said she didn't have any friends.

"Alright I'll stay. Just for today though," said George.

"I believe your story about the book seller and his disappearing booth. Earlier, before I saw you standing here I passed by the booth. I saw the very tall man," said Kizee.

George looked at Kizee with a suspicious expression. "You're just saying that to make me like you."

"No really I did see the man. He was wearing a very long bluish green alchemist robe with the four element symbols earth, wind, fire and water around the alchemy symbol embroidered in a small circle," said Kizee.

Surprised, George took a step back from Kizee. "You know what those symbols were on the man's robe?"

"Well yeah you should too, being a wizard's apprentice," said Kizee.

"Why would a girl know about these unusual symbols like knowing the alphabet?" thought George.

Then the obvious hit him, "She saw the book seller!"

"You, you saw the booth that was right there. And, and the seven and half foot tall man?" said George pointing at the empty spot.

"I told you I did. Now let me see the old book he gave you," said Kizee.

George pulled the old journal close to him. "Karman said not to let anyone take it away from me."

"Alright don't show it to me. It won't change my feelings toward our friendship. I'm tired of standing here. Let's go and play some games or something," stated Kizee.

For the rest of the day George and Kizee hung around together and played games like throwing darts at the planet dartboard with the earth in the middle and shooting plastic balls out of air cannons at pirate ships.

When the end of the day had come, both George and Kizee agreed to meet the next day at the fair. George had found out he was wrong about her age. Despite what age she looked to George, Kizee was thirteen and four months.

"What a strange girl," thought George as he walked home.

Kizee learned of George's parent's tragic death and that his sister was his guardian. She thought it was odd that his parents were on a plane and not using magic to travel.

When George got home he went straight to his room and hid the old journal under his pillow. He changed out of his wizard's apprentice robe and got ready for dinner.

Gracie was in the kitchen making a quick dinner of canned chicken, frozen vegetables with Alfredo sauce over noodles.

"How was your day at the fair?" asked Gracie.

George was thinking of an answer to this question all the way home.

"I made a friend today," said George.

"You made a friend. That's good. What's his name?" asked Gracie.

"It's a she," said George.

"OooH, so what's 'her' name?" asked Gracie teasingly.

"Kizee," answered George.

"Kizee who?" queried Gracie.

George sat there at the table for a moment before answering. "Uh, I don't know. She didn't tell me. I guess I'll find out tomorrow when I see her at the fair."

"You already have a date with her?" teased Gracie.

"Come on Gracie stop you're teasing. She is just a girl I met today," stated George.

"Can I assume she is a real person and not one of your imaginary friends?" asked Gracie.

"She's a real person," answered George.

"Not knowing her last name has me concerned. You know I want you to stop pretending everything will go back to the way it was before…" Gracie trailed off not wanting to start an argument.

Gracie changed the subject to make dinner go easier for the both of them. "Do you want to hear about my day?"

"Sure," said George as he circled his fork around his plate.

"I started working full time at the coffee shop. I made some new friends also," said Gracie.

George was half listening as he ate another blah meal. He was thinking of what really happened to him this day. If he told his sister she would surely think he was in his fantasy world.

George couldn't have made up a fantasy this elaborate. George wanted to get to his bedroom and take a look at that old book.

After dinner was over and the dishes were done George made his way to his room while Gracie worked on bills and probate court requests.

With his door shut, George pulled out the old leather journal. George sat on his bed and opened the journal to the first page.

Bold black ink lettering stood out from the page.

"The Quagmire Journal of Magic," read George with certain puzzlement of the name.

George turned the page. "Rules of Magic," read George with excitement.

George continued to read, "Thirteen principles of Magic."

Each principle had a section that explained how to use the rules. He skipped that chapter.

Next were the rules of astral plane travel. "Wouldn't that be wild to travel to other places in and out of the universe," though George.

After scanning that section George turn to the rules for wizards to live by.

George read them aloud, "Watch your back. Be smarter than the magic you are doing. Dream until your dreams come true."

Suddenly, the bedroom room door hinge squeak.

"That sounds like sound advice," said Gracie standing at George's bedroom door.

George looked up as he attempted to hide the journal under his pillow.

"I heard you talking to someone. I thought it might be your new friend. Is that something you picked up at the fair today?" asked Gracie.

"It's just a book someone gave to me because I was dressed as a wizard's apprentice," stated George.

"Strange, that you were trying to hide it from me. May I see it?" wondered Gracie.

George was very hesitant to give it to his sister because he was told not to allow anyone to take it away from him.

In this case, he may have no choice. George did think of a way to avoid it.

"It has a protection curse on it. No one else is supposed to touch it except the Master Wizard and his apprentice," explained George knowing it was lie.

Gracie knew when George was in his imaginary world and this sure seemed like this is one of those times. "Hem I see, if you hold it and opened the book as I looked over your shoulder, the curse shouldn't affect me," said Gracie.

George was stuck. He knew there was no way to get his sister to leave him alone until she had a look at the journal.

"I guess if I show you the very first page nothing will happen," said George.

George stood up from the bed with the journal in his hand. He opened it to the first page. Gracie peered over his shoulder.

"The Quagmire Journal of Magic, that sounds quite exciting considering quagmire can mean a perilous predicament or an unsolvable dilemma. It could even be a quandary of inescapable sticky situations," suggested Gracie playing with George's overactive imagination.

George went to close the book when Gracie reached over and put her finger in the book.

"Where were you reading when I opened your door?"

"Um, under rules of magic," said George as he pulled the journal away and down.

"Oh, I'm sorry I touched the book. I suppose I have a curse on me now?" said Gracie.

"Maybe not this time, next time though you may not be so lucky," said George.

"Okay I'll watch myself. I know as a wizard's apprentice you will protect me from any evil curses that may come our way," joked Gracie.

Gracie closed the bedroom door leaving George standing there half relieved and half concerned.

George sat back down on his bed and continued to examine the magic journal "Collecting Fairy Magic," read George at the top of the page.

Below the title were these three rules.

Rule number one: Always bring a gift to a fairy and be very polite.

Rule number two: Never touch a fairy unless she touches you first. Then and only then, touch her very gently with an open hand.

Rule number three: Never fall in love with a fairy. You will lose your heart and possibly your magical powers.

"Fall in love with a fairy. That sounds silly," George laughed lightly.

George then noticed in the back pages of the book was a thicker than normal page. One corner of the page was separating. George peeled the page apart. It was blank.

"Is it blank or does it have a message on it?" asked George to himself.

Chapter Two
Pinky Swear

George was up early and already dressed in his apprentice outfit. What he didn't have was something to carry the magic journal in.

George went to the entrance closet where Gracie kept some stuff of their parents. He found a box with purses and various handbags.

George pulled out a hard leather bag. It had a single flap that covered the bag. The leather strap was long enough for him to pull over his head and carry it on his side. George looked in the mirror and the hard leather bag actually went with his outfit as if it was made for a wizard's apprentice of the sixteenth century.

George put the book in his new wizard's apprentice bag. Gracie had already left for work. On the kitchen table was a breakfast bar and five dollars for lunch with a note.

Don't spend this money on something and not eat. We cannot afford a medical bill. - Gracie.

George grabbed his wallet from his hiding spot. He put the five dollar bill in it with the other money his sister had given him for food. He put the wallet back.

George stood in line with his renaissance faire pass in hand. He was looking around for Kizee. After George passed the stone entrance he stood at the wild smelling incense cart where they had agreed to meet.

Kizee tapped George on the shoulder. "Good morning," said Kizee.

George jumped out of his skin as there was no way she could have walked up to him without seeing her.

"Where did you come from?" asked George with a startled voice.

Kizee giggled but did not answer George's question because to her it was a moot question.

"That's a nice leather bag. It makes you look like a full fledge wizard," said Kizee.

George perked up with Kizee's compliment, although George didn't understand why her compliment made him feel good. He didn't know how to respond.

"Uh, okay, so what do you want to do first?" asked George.

"Let's catch the first jousting tournament," said Kizee.

Kizee hoped to get seats close to the Queen. The arena filled up quickly leaving George and Kizee at the top of the bleachers.

Disappointed, Kizee reverted to what she liked to do best, and that was to talk.

Kizee asked, "So what are you going to do with that old magic book?"

George wasn't sure how much information he should tell Kizee. Nothing was said about not showing anyone the book.

"Let's go somewhere quiet where we can talk in private," said George.

In the far corner of the faire was a quiet spot near the lake. Kizee sat down on the grassy slope. George removed his bag from his shoulder and sat down next to Kizee.

He held out his hand with his pinky finger extended. "Do you promise not to tell anyone what I am about to show you?"

"You're confiding in me? You trust me with your secret?" said Kizee.

Kizee grabbed George's pinky finger with hers and said, "I promise to keep all secrets as long as you swear to be my friend forever."

George felt something strange almost like when he received the magic book. Only this time it was different. It was a calming feeling. For some reason, George felt like he could trust Kizee explicably.

"I swear," said George.

"And I swear to keep all your secrets and be your friend forever," swore Kizee.

They shook their pinky fingers like a handshake then let go.

George pulled out the journal and opened the book to the separated page. He handed the journal to Kizee.

"I think this is supposed to be a clue to help find the magic wand. But it is blank," said George.

Kizee felt the page. "The paper was added on top of the separated page and it has a magic spell embedded into it."

"What does that mean?" asked George.

Kizee stared at George for a long moment. "It means silly, we need to some very powerful magic to make the clue visible to us."

George just said, "Oh."

"I might be able to help you," said Kizee.

George was curious what she meant by she could help him. He gave a quizzical look.

"The wizard was collecting fairy magic, most likely to put into the magic wand. Maybe you are supposed to find the wand and finish what he started. So, we need to finish the list of collecting fairy magic. It may help us find what this blank page is all about," stated Kizee.

"And how do we get fairy magic from a fairy?" asked George.

"I know you always bring a gift and be polite when you want to talk to fairies and never touch them," said Kizee.

George was curious about Kizee. He read that in the magic journal last night. "Why would she know this crazy stuff?"

"You are a strange girl. I'm beginning to understand why you might not have any friends," said George.

"You're not exactly Mr. Popular either. Are you going to let me help or not?" commented Kizee.

George knew he couldn't do this alone. He thought, "No one would have to know I got help from a girl."

George opened the journal and showed Kizee what he read the night before. "Look here, what you said about fairy magic is in this book."

"It isn't a secret."

"Okay then, why would, do not fall in love with a fairy be one of the rules. That seems silly don't you think?" queried George.

"Oh, that is very important. I was taught that both fairies and pixies have magical powers to control men and make them do anything. Mermaids are the same way. They enchant men with their beauty. Sailors have drowned trying to swim down to them," explained Kizee.

"You sure do know some strange things. Why do you know what is written in this old book. What school subject did you learn this in?" asked George.

"I didn't learn any of this in school," answered Kizee.

George shrugged his shoulders and turned the journal to the first few pages with the other rules of magic. "Do you know about the thirteen principles of magic?"

"Of course, didn't you learn them when you were seven?" asked Kizee.

"Uh no, why did you?" questioned George.

"I learned them before I was five," bragged Kizee.

"Yeah alright," said George.

"I'm sure there isn't anything in that wizard's journal I haven't heard of. Are the rules to live by in there?" queried Kizee.

"What rules are you referring to?" quizzed George.

"Watch your back. Be smarter than the magic you are doing and dream until your dreams come true," said Kizee with confidence.

George gawked at Kizee. Then he said, "Alright you made your point. You know what is in this old journal. So, looking at the list of fairy magic which one do you suggest we start with?"

"I think the first one should be the Yellow Fairy. We'll have to plan a picnic," said Kizee.

George looked up the Yellow Fairy in the journal. "It says here, The Yellow or Golden Fairy has the Midas touch, so to speak. Everything she touches turns a yellow or golden color. Don't worry about her touching you. You will not turn to gold or change color."

George kept reading aloud, "This fairy brings the brightness of the Sun to any gloomy situation. She is accredited for the wonderful yellow flowers in nature. Her magical power is joy. If one had this magical power one would light up a room as they entered. If one would shake hands or receive a hug from you, happiness would be transferred to them."

George got to the part about the picnic. "To obtain this magic, invite the Yellow Fairy to a picnic. Lay out a yellow blanket with yellow cloth napkins, yellow plates and polished flatware. Do not use any items that make trash."

"Fairies can be very picky. They want things just right with nothing out of place," stated Kizee.

George read, "On the yellow blanket place a glass pitcher of fresh squeezed lemonade with expensive crystal glasses." George stopped reading. "When I go on a picnic I'm lucky to get a juice box with a straw and this fairy wants crystal glasses?"

"You're dealing with magical creatures here. They have something you want. You have to treat them with the upmost respect," explained Kizee.

"Have you done this before?" asked George.

"I was allowed to go find a garden fairy once. I had to sit very quiet and not move. We waited for an hour for the fairy to appear. When she did, it was for a minute or two," said Kizee.

"What did you get from her?" asked George.

"Nothing, we were just visiting," stated Kizee.

George shook his head and read more from the journal. "Next we place an expensive crystal bowl with lemon gumdrops and a lemon meringue pie out on the yellow blanket. If she accepts the invitation to the picnic she will sit down on the yellow blanket. Cut her a slice of pie and offer it to her with a smile. If the picnic was successful she will offer you a small potion bottle filled with yellow crystals. Use them sparingly."

"Can you get the picnic stuff by next Saturday?' asked Kizee.

"That's three days away. I doubt it. What about you? Can you get any of this?" asked George.

"For this to work you must supply everything," said Kizee.

"I guess I don't have much of a choice," said George.

George put the journal back into his bag. They both got up and went back to having fun at the renaissance faire. When they turned down a particular row of merchant's booths Kizee got excited and grabbed George's hand.

"Come with me. I want you to meet my Mom and Aunt," said Kizee.

George stopped dead in his tracks and pulled back his hand. Something suddenly didn't feel right. He had a burning sensation circling within him. It was the same feeling from the magic book.

"I'm not so sure this would be the right time. They might be busy helping faire goers buying…whatever they are selling or something," said George not understanding what has come over him.

Kizee stood there staring at George angrily. "I thought you were different from everyone else. You want to know why I don't have any friends. This is why. All of you in this town are scared of my Mom and Aunt."

Kizee began to cry right there in the middle of the faire. George didn't have a clue what Kizee was really crying about.

"You even pinky swore to be my friend forever," choked out Kizee.

"How can I be afraid of your mom and aunt when I don't even know who they are? I really don't know you very well. We just met yesterday. I don't even your last name," said George.

"You know who I am. Everyone knows who I am," yelled Kizee waving her hands around wildly.

"I don't know who you are," shouted George.

"I'm a Wisestone," cried Kizee.

"What's a Wisestone?" asked George.

"Stop teasing me. You know it's my last name," shouted Kizee while continuing to cry.

"No really, I didn't know what your last name was. If it will make you stop what you're doing, I'll meet your Mom and Aunt," relented George.

Kizee slowed down her crying and looked at George. "You... you really don't know who I am? Maybe you are really the friend I wished for."

"If I'm your wish come true, you wasted a good wish. I'm no one special," said George.

"I don't want anyone special. I just want a friend that likes me, just me and not judge me by my family name," explained Kizee.

George knew exactly what Kizee was referring to. Being raised by his big sister without parents just didn't sit well with other kids and teachers in school when they learned of his last name. It was plastered all over the news when his parents died being entrepreneurs in the fashion world. The Düben clothing brand was in every retail store in America, up to a year ago.

"I really understand that, I'm sorry. Let's go meet your mom and aunt," said George.

Kizee wiped her eyes and showed a little smile that showed her two large front teeth. "Their booth is right over there at the end."

Kizee once again grabbed George's hand and led the way. George could see the booth was large and wide with racks of clothing and accessories on one side. On the other side were shelves with old fashioned candy jars that had the three inch opening on the side with chrome lids. They were filled with strange herbs, roots and other dried up things that had eyeballs protruding out of the dried skin.

Kizee pointed, "That's my mom bagging up a customer's purchase and that is my aunt assisting that lady with an outfit."

A queasy feeling rushed over George. He thought it might be that he hadn't eaten anything except for that breakfast bar. George took in a breath and kept going as Kizee pulled him along.

At the booth Kizee didn't let go of George's hand. George felt Kizee tightened her grip. He thought it was just in case he had second thoughts of running away.

Kizee was holding onto George tight because this was the first time ever she could introduce a friend to her mom.

"Mom, are you busy?" asked Kizee.

"Never too busy for my little witch," said Harriet.

Chapter Three
Conflict of Interest

George was sitting at the dinner table staring at his plate of food which was spaghetti noodles with heated up canned tomato sauce on top.

Even though he hadn't eaten anything all day except that breakfast bar, George wasn't hungry.

"How was your day with your new friend?" asked Gracie.

"I met her mom and aunt today. They have a merchant's booth at the renaissance faire," said George.

"So, you must have found out her last name," said Gracie.

"Yeah, but I don't understand something. Kizee said the reason she hasn't got any friends is because of her last name," stated George.

"What's her last name?" asked Gracie.

"Wisestone," said George.

Gracie sat straight up in her chair with wide eyes staring at her brother. The blood drained from her face.

"Wisestone, as in Winston Wisestone Mayor of Broomstick?" questioned Gracie.

"Uh, I don't know. Her mother is Harriet Wisestone and her aunt is Agnes McDermit. That is all I know. They're very nice. By the way, Mrs. Wisestone would like to meet you," said George.

"No! Not only no, and this no means you can't see this girl again," said Gracie with parenteral overtones.

"Why?" asked George.

"Conflict of interest," stared Gracie "To start with, the law school I am attending on a free scholarship is named after Benjamin Candlewick the Supreme Court Justice. It is her great grandfather on her mother's side. Her father is the mayor of Broomstick. He is the one who decided who got scholarships. Do you see the picture? If you do anything to upset that little girl we could lose what we are trying to build here," explained Gracie.

George made a very sour face while he twirled his fork in the noodles.

"I see by the expression on your face you still don't understand. We are on the wrong side of town so to speak. We are pour orphans struggling to make a living. She is from a very rich and powerful family in this town. That is why your friend doesn't have any other friends. You don't mix socially with who is paying for your food and education," further explained Gracie.

George put down his fork and pushed away from the table. "They're not paying much by what we have been eating since we moved here."

"Don't change the subject," glared Gracie.

"You can't stop me from seeing Kizee. We'll see each other in school," said George with a little raised voice.

"You're still in your imaginary world. She doesn't attend public school. Think George, did you ever see her at school in the spring?" stated Gracie loudly.

George thought to himself, "That could explain why she knows strange stuff."

"If you're through eating, put away the food and clean up the kitchen. I have to go into work for a partial third shift. I'll be back by ten," said Gracie ending the conversation.

George was left alone to his thoughts. He was thinking about the picnic on Saturday. "I don't care who Kizee's father or great grandfather are. I'm not going to stop being her friend. This Saturday we are going on that picnic to talk to the Yellow Fairy."

George pulled out the magical journal from his bag. From the journal, George made a list of things he needed.

Out in the garage were boxes that Gracie hasn't unpacked. Most of it was just stuff their mom and dad collected.

George went in through the side door into the garage. He turned on the overhead lights only to see there wasn't any room to move around.

George managed to get over to the garage door and unlocked it from the inside. He grabbed the bottom of the rollup door and lifted it up.

The door rolled up and to George's surprise on the outside of the garage standing there was Kizee. She was dressed in Victorian blouse and a ruby wine maxi skirt and black slippers. It was completely different from what Kizee had been wearing at the renaissance faire.

"Hello George, I knew you would be home alone so I thought I would come over and see if you needed any help on getting the things you need for Saturday's picnic," Kizee said with a big smile.

"How did you know I would home alone?" asked George.

"My cousin Peter owns the Ex-Press Coffee Shop. He told me your sister was working tonight," stated Kizee.

"Oh, there's another conflict of interest she'll be yelling about," George said more to himself than to Kizee.

"What do you mean a conflict of interest?" asked Kizee.

"I told Gracie what your last name is and she told me I couldn't see you anymore because of a conflict of interest. She said the college she got the free scholarship from is named after you great grandfather. Gracie also said that your father is the mayor. I'm not supposed to socialize with the one that is paying for our food and education," explained George.

Kizee stood there a little annoyed at what George had told her. "I guess you want me to leave then since we aren't supposed to socialize. This breaks our pinky swear of being friends forever," complained Kizee.

"No, don't leave. Our pinky-swear is a promise I made with you, not my sister or your relatives," said George.

Kizee cheered up and her smile had come back which made George feel better. In between the boxes Kizee noticed two ghosts. She assumed they were George's parents as they resembled him.

"What are you doing out here in the garage?" asked Kizee to the two ghosts.

George reading the side of three boxes said, "I'm looking for stuff I can use for the picnic. Here, these boxes marked China Cabinets should have the expensive crystal glasses in them."

Kizee looked at George puzzled as she wasn't really talking to him.

George opened a box and pulled out gold plated flatware. "What do you think, three gold plated forks and a pastry server," said George.

"Gold plated flatware is an excellent choice," said Kizee.

From another box, George retrieved three crystal glasses, a glass pitcher and a crystal bowl.

"I don't know if these crystal items are expensive enough. They should do, don't you think?" queried George.

Kizee looked at them closely. There from Waterford, Ireland. That is exactly what you need," agreed Kizee knowing how much magic is in Waterford Crystal.

George put the items he found into another box and hid them in the back of the garage for safekeeping until Saturday.

"I still need a yellow blanket, three yellow cloth napkins and three yellow plates. Nothing in here is yellow. I'll have to buy them somewhere. I just don't have much money," noted George.

"You could try a liquidator retail store like the Less Than a Buck or Big Deal Discounts. I think they stay open until nine. We could go there now," suggested Kizee.

"No, if Gracie found out I left home she would ground me for who knows for how long. How about tomorrow we meet at the renaissance faire and go from there?" asked George.

"Okay. What do you want to do for the next two hours?" questioned Kizee.

"Isn't your Mom going to be mad if you stay out after eight?" asked George.

"You're kidding, right? Most of the cool magical stuff happens at night," stated Kizee.

"I'm not allowed to talk about make believe worlds. I can play, as my sister calls it, under strict supervision. She thinks the renaissance faire is a good controlled environment for me to let out my imagination," stated George.

"She's right you know. You shouldn't live in a made up world when the real world is full of surprises," said Kizee.

George was curious as to what Kizee was referring to. "What kind of magical stuff and surprises are you talking about?"

"Come on I'll show you and you don't have to go too far from your house," said Kizee.

Kizee held out her hand to George. He wasn't sure about all the hand holding she likes to do.

Kizee shook her hand at George. "Come on I won't give you cooties," said Kizee jokingly.

George took Kizee hand and she led the way down the driveway. "Wait, I have to close up the garage," said George.

"I already took care of it," said Kizee.

George looked back as Kizee pulled him along. He couldn't believe his eyes. The garage door was rolled down and side door was closed.

"How did she…?" George dropped it not wanting to know the answer.

Kizee brought George to an open field and stood in the middle of the high grass. "Now help me stamp down the grass into a circle."

"Are we making a space alien field pattern?" asked George.

"No, we are making a magic circle," said Kizee.

When they finished, the circle was about thirteen feet across. Kizee stood in the middle with her arms stretched out. George stood off to one side.

Kizee began to turn slowly around as she said, "I conjure you Circle of Magical Power, to be a rampart and protection against all negative forces this hour. May you be cleansed of all impurities. May this Circle preserve and contain the Power I raise within."

Kizee stopped turning and put her arms down. To Kizee's surprise George had move to the edge of the circle away from her.

"Don't step out of the circle, we don't know what is out there yet," warned Kizee.

"I'm not sure what is in here. That was the weirdest thing you've said since I met you. How many other kids our age have you done this with?" asked George.

"No one else, just you," said Kizee.

Then Kizee waved her hands around and said, "Invisibility dome."

"This friendship is getting on the spooky side," thought George.

"Now what do we do?" asked George.

"We watch," said Kizee.

After a few minutes, Kizee pointed at an area of little glowing lights flying toward them. George said, "Okay, fire flies."

"Not fire flies. Fire flies do not travel in a formation. Those are Nezbats. They travel in a formation very much like world war two bomber squadrons. Some believe they are imitating them," explained Kizee.

At first George thought Kizee was making it up until they flew around their circle. He could see the little strange bugs with huge glowing eyes and long rounded noses. Their bodies extended back with large wings and a tail rudder much like a plane.

George could hear them as they flew by. It wasn't their wings making the sound. The sound was coming from their mouths. The Nezbats had their mouths open with clenched teeth making a roaring sound just like the world war two bombers.

George watched as they flew around the circle then sped away. Over in a bare area of the field was an ant hill. The Nezbats began to dive and were dropping something George couldn't quite make out in the dark until they hit the ground. Little flashes of light burst upward with the sound of old fashion caps from a cap gun.

"They're doing a bomb run on that ant hill!" shouted George.

Behind them George heard the rustling of bushes. He turned to see walking in a single file, five very short and very ugly people.

"What are they?" asked George.

"Those are Trolls. They live under the old bridge at the creek. This is their time to hunt for food," explained Kizee.

"Not us I hope," said George.

"No, they prefer rodents and anything that lives underground," said Kizee.

In the next hour, Kizee pointed out creatures with names like fundlebunds, schnicks, and thrumhammers. There were other assortment of magical creatures that passed by their magic circle.

"Hey what time is it?" cried George.

"It's almost time to go home. I won't let you get into trouble. You have to learn to trust me, George. After all I am your best friend. And best friends don't let their best friend get into trouble," stated Kizee.

"Well if I'm not home when Gracie gets home our friendship will come to a complete halt," said George.

Kizee smiled as she waved her hands around. "Magic Circle, be gone!"

George expected something to happen. He didn't know what exactly, but something was different. Kizee stood there in the circle smiling at George. George just looked around.

"Come on its time for you to get home," said Kizee with a sigh.

Kizee reached out and took hold of George's hand. They walked back down the road to his house. At the front porch Kizee let go of George's hand.

"I'll see you tomorrow in front of the faire entrance. And by the way, you and your sister are invited for dinner tomorrow night," said Kizee again staring at George with a smile.

Kizee turned and walked off into the darkness leaving George standing on his front porch. Gracie's Headlights lit up the driveway and the front of the house as Gracie drove into the driveway.

"Funny," thought George. "How come I couldn't see Kizee walking down the driveway?"

Chapter Four
Downfall of the broom company

Ever since McDermit Brooms merged with that corporate vacuum company things haven't gone well. Very recent the stock price plummeted to an all-time low. Even the magical broom sales have dropped off over the years.

Franklin McDermit wasn't too concerned about it. Agnes McDermit had the Hidden Quiddity Potion Shop to keep money coming in. Their three nineteen year old daughters didn't have any interest in their father's business.

Cyndi worked at the Moonlite and Spiders Glow in Dark Cross Quarter Festival supply store. Wendy stayed working at her mother's and aunt's potion shop. Mindy on the other hand worked for the Bermuda Triangle adventure cruise line where they take tourist on a plundering pirate adventure.

Mindy sailed on the galleon ship the 'Wanted Pirate' as one of the crew, captained by Anne Bonny. As the crew interacted with other pirate cruises Mindy would pick up stories, buy old treasure maps, and sometimes she would get a look at sailing charts and memorize co-ordnances. Mindy kept a journal of all the bits and pieces that should lead her to treasure. There was one particular hidden treasure Mindy was interested in. Half was in a dark elf realm and the other was in a sunken ship in the Bermuda Triangle.

On occasions, the cruise would travel over the equator for the old sailor tradition of Shellback day.

On these cruises they would come in contact with the doomed ship Purgatory captained by Davy Jones the grim reaper of the salty deep. On one of these cruises Mindy McDermit met a doomed sailor by the name of Searat.

Searat has been on the Purgatory almost forever, or so it seemed. He didn't look old. He was weathered, but not old. More like twenty nine or so. Searat was a bit on the skinny side. Mindy could pick up Searat with one hand if she had the mind to.

At first, Mindy felt sorry for Searat. As time gone by, her feeling changed to a comfortable friendship.

One day Mindy whispered something very strange to Searat. "I know a secret about these waters."

"A secret about the Bermuda Triangle?" questioned Searat.

"There is a vast collection of treasure in those ships down there. Their bowels are full of gold chests just waiting for someone to snatch it away right under the nose of old Davy," said Mindy.

Mindy looked around to see if anyone else was listening to their conversation. She also took noticed as to where Davy Jones was.

"Why you be telling me this?" asked Searat.

"Because, I like you and I think I can trust you with my secrets," said Mindy.

After that cruise Mindy thought of ways she could retrieve that treasure. "I need Searat's help to locate the ships. But how can I get him off of Davy's ship?"

Mindy went to Captain Anne Bonny. "Captain, the summer solstice is in a few weeks. I request time off to attend my family's gathering."

"I'm sure we can handle the summer influx of vacationers. Permission granted for shore leave," said Captain Bonny.

"I do have one more request. It is a difficult one. I'm sure you'll understand and help me with it," said Mindy.

"What is it Lieutenant?"

"I would like the sailor Searat of the Purgatory to accompany me. I know he is a doomed sailor and there isn't any chance of a relationship. But I feel I owe him one small segment of happiness that he can take with him to the end of time," requested Mindy.

"That is a very tall order to ask Davy Jones to allow a doomed sailor to leave the ship even for a short time," said Captain Bonny.

"Yes sir, I understand. I had to ask."

"Not so fast sailor. I didn't say it was impossible. I do have some favors to call in from Davy. Let me see what I can do," said Captain Bonny.

Mindy allowed extra time for travel in her request for shore leave. Searat was allowed shore leave as well. Mindy knew she and her sailor friend were on a tight schedule.

"Be him back before the next new moon or you will serve me for a century," stated Davy Jones when Mindy had taken her sailor friend.

The liberty launch from The Wanted Pirate was filled to capacity with sailors. Mindy and Searat sat at the back of the boat. Everyone was staring at Searat.

"Bosn' can you let me off just on the edge of the triangle?" asked Mindy.

"Out here in the middle of the ocean?" questioned the Bosn'.

Mindy pulled out her magic wand and pointed at the choppy water. "Put up a sail, and fix a rudder forward and aft. Conjure up a floatable raft."

Mindy and Searat got on the raft and hoisted the small sail. Mindy called out to the Bosn'. "We'll be back before the next new moon."

When the liberty boat was out of sight, Mindy twirled her wand and put the raft in an air tight bubble. "Down, down, dive below," Mindy ordered the raft.

The bubbled raft submerged under the ocean water going deep into the depths of the treacherous unforgiving triangle of Bermuda.

It was a rough ride going down. It was like a class four river rafting trip with some class five thrown in for good measures.

"Hold on the sail rig, keep it steady," called Mindy as she double handed the rudder with her feet wedged in between two raft boards.

"Over that way on your portside, do you see it?" yelled Mindy over the rushing water passing the bubble.

There to their left was a wreak ship. The bow was jammed down into the ocean bottom. As they passed the stern the name of the ship was on the back.

"The Angel?" said Searat.

"She was carrying gold from the crew's hard earned labor. They worked a mine until they couldn't carry anymore," explained Mindy.

"How do you know this?" asked Searat.

"I have been collecting sea stories, old charts, and hand drawn treasure maps since I was ten years old," explained Mindy.

Searat lowered his head and began to cry. "The Angel was my ship. I was the Captain. Davy Jones claimed I made the decision to turn into the storm to catch the wind in the sails. All on board, including me went to our watery grave down here," stated Searat.

"And for that you are a member of Purgatory's crew?" asked Mindy.

"Davy Jones said death was too easy of a punishment for my mistake," stated Searat.

"I'm…I'm sorry, I didn't know this was your ship," said Mindy mournfully.

"But that is in the past. Let's get the gold," counted Searat.

Mindy and Searat brought the raft down to the sunken ship. She pulled out her magic wand. "Plummeted down, sank to the ocean floor. Make a hole, fill it with air. Give me a door."

The ocean at that depth should have been dark and dismal. Since it was the mysterious area of the Bermuda Triangle, the water was clear and the sun's rays barreled all the way down to the bottom.

From the sunken ship's portholes, dingy water and dead sea-life propelled out like water cannons until the air bubble filled the void and encapsulated them and the ship.

Searat led the way down into the cargo hold where there were five chests of pure gold nuggets, and forty clay jars of gold dust. Searat and Mindy struggled moving the five chests to the raft. They were heavy and Mindy was doing most of the work.

"It might have been easier to move the whole ship," said Mindy as they pulled the fifth chest onto the raft.

Mindy waved her magic wand around and shouted a very strong spell. "Waste no time or drop a dime. Carry us to the bright blue sky. Let us fly to the prevailing wind, take us to our journey's end."

The bubble was again just around the raft. The wood creaked with the extra weight as it lifted away from the sunken ship. The water around them spun like a water spout as the raft headed to the surface.

"Hold tight that sail, Searat. We're about to break the surface," yelled Mindy over the noise of the rushing water.

"Aye, aye Captain," Searat yelled back.

The bubbled raft popped out of the water and flew straight up into the air where the wind grabbed ahold of them. Mindy looked at the stars and steered a course to the Magical Bank.

Mindy pushed the bank door opened. She and Searat sat down a chest to keep the door open. Four trips later Mindy and Searat were standing in the middle of the Magical Bank with five sea chests of gold nuggets and forty clay jars filled with gold dust.

Mindy had opened one and propped her left boot on the lip of the chest. "I wish to make a deposit!"

Chapter Five
Summer Time

For the first time in George's young life he had experienced extremely irrational things that he couldn't tell his sister. Before, George would spout off about being in his imaginary world. Now, if George would say anything of what he had experienced in the last two days, Gracie would have him back at the crisis management counselor in a heartbeat.

George sat in his room wanting to tell someone. So, he started a personal diary on his computer. His first file was named 'Magic Circle'.

George wrote, "I'm not understanding exactly what I saw standing in the Magic Circle with Kizee. I think maybe it was partly the darkness maybe wanting to see what Kizee wanted me to see. I don't know."

George got up real early the next morning and went down the road to the open field. He stood in the circle he and Kizee had stamped down with their feet remembering what had taken place the night before.

"Over there should be a bombed-out ant hill," said George.

George walked over to area where the ant hill was and saw a completely destroyed mound with bomb craters surrounding it.

Next George found the dried up muddy footprints of the Trolls. Their footprints were not normal for people that size and only had four toes. George followed the dried up muddy footprints. They crossed the road and disappeared into the brush.

"I need to get my camera and take pictures of this," stated George.

George ran back to the house and grabbed his camera. First, he went to the bombed-out ant hill. What he found there this time was a normal thriving clean ant hill with large red ants going about their business.

"Wait this is not what I saw a few minutes ago," said George.

Then George looked around for the dried up muddy footprints of the Trolls. None were to be found. He even went over to where they had crossed the road.

"I can't believe this. The footprints are gone," sighed George.

Disappointed, George walked back home. By the time he got there, Gracie was up and getting ready for work at the Ex-press Coffee Shop later in the morning.

"What got you up so early?" asked Gracie.

"Nothing really, I saw an animal last night and was going to take pictures of its tracks," said George disappointedly.

"Well here is five dollars for lunch. Breakfast bars are in the cupboard. I got to run. See you tonight and don't hurt that girl's feeling too much when you tell her you can't see her anymore," said Gracie as she was scrambling out the door.

"There is something I forgot to tell you..." started George.

"Tell me tonight," called Gracie from the door.

"Yeah it's about tonight…" George's words were lost as the front door closed behind Gracie.

"We're invited for dinner," George's voice trailed off.

George was walking up to the entrance to the renaissance faire. George didn't wear his wizard's apprentice outfit as Kizee and he were to go shopping for the rest of the picnic items.

George jumped again when two arms grabbed him from behind. "Hey, what's got you on edge?" asked Kizee.

"Nothing, it's just I never see you walk up."

"Do you have your list?" asked Kizee.

"Right here in my pocket," said George feeling calmed down.

"Alright then let's get going," said Kizee.

"Oh, I didn't get a chance to tell Gracie we were invited to dinner tonight. I don't think she is going to take it too well because she told me again I am supposed to break off our friendship," said George.

"Let's go and tell my mom. Mom can pop in to see your sister today when my mom goes to meet Dad for lunch," said Kizee.

"How about this, you go talk to your mom and then meet me at Big Deal Discounts," suggested George.

"Alright, I shouldn't be too far behind you," said Kizee.

George turned away from Kizee and headed toward the road. It wasn't too far of a walk to the bus stop. After standing there for a minute the bus turned the corner.

The bus pulled up with the air brakes making a slight squealing noise. The door swung open right in front of George.

"Does this bus go down to the shopping mall?" asked George.

The bus driver said with a smile, "It sure does, right to where you want to go."

George dropped in the exact change and sat down just behind the bus driver.

George watched people get on and off the bus. One thought George had about them was, "It doesn't seem like anyone is going anywhere."

The bus pulled up to the bus stop at the shopping mall. George stepped off the bus to see the large sign 'Big Deal Discounts'.

Gracie had just sat down in the back of the coffee shop for her break when a hand carried message arrived. She didn't know it was delivered by a SNARF fairy.

Gracie stood up to look around. "Wait, who is this from?" asked Gracie to no one.

Gracie sat back down and opened the envelope. She pulled out the letter and unfolded it. It was handwritten in beautiful script.

Gracie read, "When you have the time please come to the manager's office." It was signed Winston Wisestone.

"Well that just does it. I'll apologize for George's behavior and hopefully keep my job," said Gracie staring at the hand-written note.

Gracie folded the note and put it in her pocket. Gracie grabbed her bag and went to the lady's room. She quickly worked on brushing her unkempt wavy brownish red hair. It didn't matter how much she brushed it, her hair still looked the same.

Gracie stared at herself in the mirror. "George, why of all people did you have to go and make friends with…"

Gracie realized she wasn't alone in the lady's room and stopped talking to herself.

Once in front of the manager's door, Gracie tried to compose herself.

It wasn't easy as the door opened. Standing there to greet her was Winston Wisestone.

"Good morning Miss Düben. I was about to have a cup of coffee can I have them get you something to drink?" asked Winston.

"Ah, no thank you. Listen Mr. Wisestone I will have a talk with my brother George and he will never bother your daughter ever again I assure you. I apologize for anything he may have done to… (That's not the right word.) I mean, has said to her that may have offended her," bungled Gracie.

Winston just smiled as he sipped his cup of coffee. "Are you sure you don't want something to drink? There are other beverages."

Gracie stood there not knowing what to say that would rectify the situation she thought George had caused.

"No thank you Mr. Wisestone. Did George cause this big of a problem?" said Gracie.

"There's no problem, Miss Düben. I asked you in here, oh where are my manners, please sit down," offered Winston.

Winston offered Gracie a chair at a round table where Winston sat down his coffee. Winston sat down right after Gracie.

"I asked you in here because I got a message this morning that you haven't received our invitation to dinner tonight. We relied on our daughter to deliver our request when we should have done it ourselves. I apologize for that," said Winston.

"I haven't met your daughter, Mr. Wisestone. I only heard of her through my brother and he didn't...Wait, he said he had something to tell me this morning," said Gracie thinking out loud.

"Mr. Wisestone I can't accept," said Gracie.

"Please Miss Düben, Harriet and I really want to get to know you and your brother since Kizee is excited about having George as her best friend," said Winston.

"Best friends? They just met only a couple days ago Mr. Wisestone. I'll accept they are newly acquaintances, which brings me to my problem about this. If I may, I'll come right to the point, this isn't a good situation for me. I'd rather George not be friends with your daughter. It makes me very uncomfortable. I am attending college here on a free scholarship of you're, um, well you understand we just aren't..." stumbled Gracie.

"I here you loud and clear Miss Düben. Kizee told me what you told George about not socializing with the one who is supplying your educational grant money," stated Winston.

"Well then you understand why I have to decline your offer for dinner tonight. Thank you, Mr. Wisestone for understanding, I will let George know to stay away from your daughter for now on," said Gracie as she stood up to leave.

"Wait a moment Miss Düben aren't you forgetting someone in your decision to decline my offer of dinner? I am on the other side of this new friendship. My daughter's happiness is a great concern to me as you are trying your best to raise your brother as best you can. We both have responsibilities as a parental figure," explained Winston.

Gracie sat back down. She felt she wasn't excused just as yet. Winston sipped his coffee for a long pause. He sat the cup back down when it was empty.

"Kizee has a hard time making friends as she has a very special talent than the rest of us. To some it is a little unsettling. So, when Kizee brought George to meet her mother, well you could imagine how her mother felt when Kizee said this is my friend. Now I can't let you take away Kizee's only friend from her because you have a class level stigma," explained Winston.

"Are you using your political position to force me to let George be your daughter's playmate?" questioned Gracie.

"No, Miss Düben, as a father I am requesting you to allow George and Kizee to be friends and accept an invitation to dinner to discuss their friendship. Over dinner we can talk about how to proceed with the conflict of interest you seem to have," said Winston.

Gracie saw no way out. Winston had played the game very well. "Alright what time and where?" relented Gracie.

Winston pulled out of his pocket an envelope and passed it over to Gracie. "It's completely informal. Don't wear anything you wouldn't want to get barbeque sauce on. Do bring something warm to wear for later."

Gracie left the manager's office and went back to work making espressos. Whispers from customers and other workers filled the air as Winston Wisestone left the coffee shop.

Gracie wanted to scream.

George was in the dishware aisle looking for anything yellow when from behind Kizee hugged him and said, "Hiya Georgie."

"Don't you ever just walk up to people? And don't call me Georgie," asked George.

"Alright… George. Mom talked to Dad and he will fix everything. I was reminded to tell you to bring something warm to wear for tonight," said Kizee.

"I really don't think Gracie would want to stay long. Most likely we'll leave after an hour," said George.

"You have to stay for the party," said Kizee.

"Is it someone's birthday or something?" asked George.

"No silly, it's Solstice Eve," stated Kizee.

"Solstice Eve, what's that?" questioned George.

"The evening before Solstice obviously," answered Kizee.

"I got that part, but what is a Solstice?" again questioned George.

"The beginning of summer," answered Kizee.

"Summer started on Memorial weekend. Everyone knows that," said George.

"Don't you know your astronomy calendar?" asked Kizee.

"You're a strange girl. What is an astronomy calendar?" asked George.

"The lunar and solar events that mark the changes of the seasons and tomorrow is the summer solstice marking the longest day starting at sunrise," explained Kizee.

"Is that why you selected the Yellow Fairy for tomorrow?" asked George.

"Exactly, now let's get the yellow tablecloth," said Kizee.

Gracie was waiting for George when he walked up the porch carrying a large paper bag with 'Big Deal Discounts' printed on the side.

"Strange bag for the renaissance faire," said Gracie.

"I can explain. Kizee and I are going on a picnic tomorrow to celebrate summer solstice," said George.

"Yeah about that, you knew all along you weren't going to end this friendship," said Gracie.

"After meeting Mrs. Wisestone I knew there was no way I could. She gave me a look with a smile that frightened me. Kizee had the same kind of look when we pinky swore," said George.

"Pinky swore about what?" queried Gracie.

"Uh, about being friends forever," said George.

"Something tells me there more to that pinky swear than you telling me. For right now I'll drop it because you have to get ready for dinner with the Wisestone's. Dress for a barbeque and bring a warm jacket," said Gracie.

George sat quietly in the car as Gracie drove trying to follow the direction she received from Winston.

"There aren't any street names or numbers in this area. How am I supposed to find their house?" said Gracie.

A feeling came over Gracie that made her turn right at the next corner. Looking at the pristine yards and houses, Gracie picked one out and stopped in front.

"Are you sure this, is it? I thought being the mayor of Broomstick they would be living in a mansion," said George.

"I would think that also. However, look at these houses, the gardener must be paid very well," said Gracie.

A familiar voice called out, "Hello George, glad you and your sister could make it," said Agnes.

Agnes gave George a hug. "Hello Gracie, I am Agnes McDermit and this is my husband, Franklin. And coming up the walkway is our daughters."

Gracie shook hands with Agnes and Franklin being polite.

"This is Cyndi. Right next to her is Wendy," said Agnes.

Coming up behind them was Mindy who was carrying a weatherworn sailor on her shoulder.

Agnes being a little surprised. "And… this is my middle daughter, Mindy."

Gracie and George stood there as Mindy carried her date up

the walkway. Gracie and George noticed the three girls all looked alike.

Mindy stopped and said, "I work on the galleon ship the Wanted Pirate as one of the crew, captained by Anne Bonny. The Wanted Pirate is part of the Bermuda Triangle adventure cruise line where we take tourist on plundering pirate adventures."

Agnes and Franklin were looking at the weatherworn sailor.

Mindy said, "He'll be alright. He's on leave from Davy Jones's ship."

"This be the boy you've talked about?" asked the sailor to Mindy. He turned toward George. "Run boy, run as fast as ye can."

"Come on Popeye, let's find you some coffee," said Mindy.

Gracie and George followed them into Winston's and Harriet's house. The first thing Gracie notice was the décor. It seemed a little unnatural, like walking into a late night horror movie hostess recording studio.

"They must be horror movie memorabilia collectors. Don't touch anything," said Gracie.

Gracie and George continued out to the backyard where Winston and Harriet were. Winston was dressed in a barbeque apron and hat pouring a sauce over a large piece of meat the size of a full steer that was revolving on a chain driven skewer.

Over on a long table Harriet was setting down bowls and platters of food, none of which Gracie had ever seen.

"Just take what you think is safe and smile as you eat it. Don't ask what it is," instructed Gracie.

"Hiya Georgie!" yelled Kizee as she ran over to him.

"I asked you not to call me that," said George.

Kizee smile diminished a little when she said, "I'm sorry George."

"Cute pet name, you should get it tattooed across your chest," said the sailor sitting off to one side holding a cup of coffee.

Gracie guided George away from the sailor. Kizee did one better. She grabbed George's hand and led him over to her father. Agnes rescued Gracie from the sailor that was coming up behind her. Agnes also knew from meeting George they were knotems and all this is strange to them.

"Let me point out over there being a poor hostess is my sister, Harriet," offered Agnes.

"And that must be Kizee who just took off with my brother," said Gracie.

"Yes, she is a very gifted...child for her age. Don't let her special talent creep you out," said Agnes.

"Mr. Wisestone said she sees thing different than the rest of us. I thought he was referring to her imagination," said Gracie.

"We had the same idea until we had her tested recently," said Agnes.

Gracie asked, "So how is she gifted?"

"I'll let you discover that on your own as you get to know her," said Agnes.

Then Agnes shouted out to Harriet nodding her head toward Gracie. "You should stop what you are doing and tend to your guest."

Agnes then looked deep into Gracie's eyes with a hypnotic stare. "If you are ever in need of help, call me."

"Daddy, this is George. He is a wizard's apprentice," said Kizee.

Winston stared into George's eyes as he shook hands. He already knew that George was not from a magical family.

"A wizard's apprentice you say? Apprentice to anyone I might know?" asked Winston playing along.

George thought about his answer before he said, "I just dress the part for the renaissance faire. My sister made my outfit."

"A wizard's apprentice that is a very noble profession," said Winston all the time smiling at his daughter who is still holding onto George's hand.

Harriet came over to Agnes and Gracie. "Thank you for accepting our invitation to dinner. I've wanted to meet you since the day I met your brother George. He is a very interesting boy to talk to."

"Your husband made things pretty clear this morning that I should accept your gracious invitation Mrs. Wisestone," said Gracie.

"Please call me Harriet."

"No, I think under the circumstances I had better stick with Mrs. Wisestone," said Gracie.

After Kizee had taken George around to all her cousins she went back over to Gracie.

"I'm sorry. I was so excited to have my cousins meet George I forgot to introduce myself to you. I am Kizee Wisestone."

"It's nice to finally meet you, Kizee. At first I thought you might be an imaginary person until I learned your last name," said Gracie.

"Please don't let my last name come in the way of you getting to know me," asked Kizee.

"I will try not to let it bother me. Your Aunt Agnes says you have a special talent and I should discover what it is as I get to know you. Would you like to tell me what it is?" asked Gracie.

Gracie and Kizee conversation was interrupted by someone carrying a tray of drinks. "Hello I'm Bee. Would you care for something to drink?"

"Water, please," said Gracie.

Bee pointed to a tumbler with a clear liquid and ice. "If you want anything else to drink just ask me." Bee smiled and wondered off.

Gracie noticed other people had shown up. They were not exactly dressed as casual as she was. Then again Gracie wouldn't dress in crazy clothes like that either.

"Did Kizee say anything about a costume party to you George?" asked Gracie.

"She said it was a solstice eve party. I didn't know what that meant," said George.

Kizee was once again holding George's hand.

Someone passed by Gracie and said, "Those two need a piece of rope tied around their wrists considering it is solstice eve…"

Gracie tried to see who had said that when she spoke out. "Considering it is solstice eve what?"

Gracie looked down at Kizee and asked, "What is a solstice eve party?"

"The day before the summer solstice, tomorrow is the first day of summer," said Kizee.

"You celebrate the summer solstice with a party," said Gracie. "George we're leaving…NOW!"

"But Gracie we haven't eaten," said George.

"I'll buy you a hamburger on the way home," said Gracie.

Gracie was dragging George toward the front door all the while Kizee was still holding onto George's hand.

"Kizee please let go of George. We have to leave," said Gracie.

"But why, the party hasn't even started. George, please don't leave," cried Kizee.

Winston was right there. "Is there something wrong?"

"Yes, very wrong Mr. Wisestone. I will not allow my brother to witness this…this blood sacrifice cult ritual you are having here," said Gracie waving her one free hand around.

"A blood sacrifice cult ritual, is that what you see here? I assure you this is just a barbecue to ring in the first day of summer, nothing more," said Winston.

"Kizee, give me a minute alone with Miss Düben. Take George with you," said Winston to his daughter.

Kizee led George to the backyard. Gracie stared in horror. She could not stop him from going with Kizee.

"Miss Düben, I asked you to come here tonight to see for yourself. As strange as we may seem to you, we are not your enemy. You would have found out eventually through Kizee…"

Gracie interrupted Winston. "That, that you're, you're a, what is that name? A…a druid of some sort, that follows the sun and stars like at that circle of rocks?"

"Miss Düben, please sit down. How well do you know legal history here in America?" ask Winston.

"I understand your freedom of religion under the Bill of Rights," said Gracie.

"That is not what I am referring to. Do you know how our legal system was developed?" asked Winston.

"The Supreme Court decides Constitutional law," answered Gracie.

"I'm referring much father back. What caused a major change in our pre-constitution colonies that led up to our Bill of Rights?" queried Winston.

"The Salem witch trials. They were without due course of process of law and a writ of habeas-corpus. What does that have to do with what is going on here tonight?" questioned Gracie.

"You must promise not to tell your brother what I am about to tell you. He will learn it on his own and will accept it better that way," said Winston.

"What am I promising not to tell my brother?" questioned Gracie.

"I must have your promise first," said Winston with concern.

"Alright for now I'll give you a temporary promise I won't tell. If I feel he needs to know I will let you know that I am taking back my promise," said Gracie.

"You're going to make a very good lawyer, Miss Düben. Our families moved here and started Broomstick to avoid the witch trials," said Winston.

Gracie stared at Winston and then looked out at the backyard. Blood drained from her face as the history of Salem and the word 'WITCH' sank in.

"And...and Kizee I suppose is a little witch?" asked Gracie.

"Just like her mother," smiled Winston.

"What exactly do you see in allowing this friendship to continue?" asked Gracie.

"Kizee thinks George is a young wizard because of his outfit he wore at the renaissance faire. Looking into George's eyes, he doesn't know Kizee is a witch. Let them discover on their own the truth. One or both will see this friendship will not work and will end it. And we go our separate ways living contently in Broomstick," explained Winston.

Gracie thought it over while watching George and Kizee out in the backyard. Kizee hasn't let go of George's hand and now she is holding onto his arm.

"I'm not so sure Mr. Wisestone may be right about this," Gracie thought to herself.

As she stared, it also looked like more people have arrived for the party entering from some other entrance than the front door. To Gracie amazement some people were dressed normal.

"Miss Düben, please rejoin the party. I assure you, you will have a wonderful time," said Winston.

Gracie followed Winston back to the backyard where people were already standing and sitting with plates of food including what was on the barbeque.

Gracie stopped Bee who was still walking around with a serving tray of liquid filled glasses. "Do you have anything to relieve my anxiety?"

Chapter Six
Rocket Man

It was very early on Saturday morning when everyone at the Wisestone's Solstice Eve party made their way in a ceremonious procession toward the center of town.

It was not known to most knotems of Broomstick that the town square was actually laid out with reference points similar to ancient sites like the Medicine Wheel in Wyoming or Stonehenge in England and henges in Ireland that marked the equinoxes and solstices.

When the Wisestone party arrived, there were other groups of people already at the town square. Gracie was not convinced nothing would happen to her brother George and his friendship with Kizee Wisestone would end. She had met many people of the magical community that night which didn't ease her nerves.

Gracie met many knotems with frightful stories about the magical world they were drawn into. One person was Jay Münter.

Jay Münter told frightening stories that curled the hair on the back of Gracie's neck. She made a mental note of how his son was turned into a wizard at the age of thirteen.

Another person Gracie met was Ivan, a knotem that was with Mary Pride. He claimed their souls were joined together by a magic spell and was hidden away in a magic wand for a very long time.

It was almost time for the sun to rise. Everyone was looking east at the horizon waiting for the first glimpse of the Sun. Suddenly the entire town square got very quiet. Gracie had a creepy feeling as if the air suddenly became deathly still. Not a single leaf on the trees moved.

There it was, the first single ray of the morning sun searing across the open area through a V cut into the top of a polished marble stone pillar. Everyone except Gracie let out a great roar of excitement. Horns began to blare with people rhythmically banging on drums.

When the excitement settled down and people meandered home, Winston brought George over to Gracie with Kizee holding onto George's hand. Next to Winston was a young man with short neatly trimmed hair. He was dressed casual with stonewashed blue jeans and a cotton button down shirt.

"Mr. Braun will take you home and drop off your car later. I hope you had a good time this night Miss Düben. Kizee, you can let go of George now." said Winston.

Kizee released George's hand but not before she gave it a healthy squeeze. "I'll see you this afternoon," said Kizee.

As Gracie and George were following Mr. Braun to his car, Gracie started asking him questions.

"How are you related to Mr. Wisestone, Mr. Braun?" asked Gracie.

"I'm not. I work at City Hall for Mr. Wisestone. Please, I'm only twenty two. Call me Eric. To me my father is Mr. Braun," said Eric.

"Are you one of them?" continued Gracie asking questions.

"If you referring to being a wizard, no," said Eric.

"Married to a witch?" asked Gracie.

"Nope," said Eric.

"Married?" queried Gracie.

"Nope," answered Eric.

"Then how are you involved with...these people?" asked Gracie.

"I told you, I work for Mr. Wisestone. I also happened to live here in Broomstick," said Eric.

"Well so do I except I'm not involved..." Gracie stopped in mid-sentence. She stopped asking Eric questions.

"Get up, it's almost time," said Kizee standing at the foot of George's bed.

George ruffled his hair to clear the sleep cobwebs from his brain. "Kizee, what ...how did you get in my room?" asked George.

"Now that's a silly question. Come on we'll be late and we'll miss her if you don't get a move on," said Kizee.

"Miss who and late for what?" asked George still not fully awake.

"We'll be late for the picnic and miss talking to the Yellow Fairy," exclaimed Kizee.

George rolled out of his bed. Just before he started getting dressed George realized Kizee was still in his room.

"Hey, a little privacy while I get dressed," said George.

Kizee just looked at George with a questionable expression.

"Wait for me in the kitchen. I'll be out shortly," said George.

George turned to his dresser to get out clean clothes. In the mirror, he didn't see Kizee behind him. George turned around and looked at his bedroom door.

"It squeaks when it opens," George said to himself.

George met Kizee in the kitchen where she had already packed up the picnic stuff. The lemonade was already made and was in a sealed plastic container. The lemon meringue pie had a reusable protective cover over the glass pie plate.

George grabbed the handle on one side of the picnic cooler and Kizee picked up the other side. When George got to the front door he found the door still locked.

George was about to ask to obvious question. Instead he just unlocked the door and opened it.

"Where are we going and how are we going to get there?" asked George.

"There are some things that aren't written down on how to approach fairies. One thing to keep in mind is never use magic around fairies as they can feel intimidated by others magical powers," stated Kizee.

"So, what does that mean to us?" asked George.

"We are walking to where we are going," explained Kizee.

"Walking, and carrying this big cooler. Hold on let me get my wagon from the garage," said George.

Kizee and George took turns pulling the wagon as they walked down the road. At one point Kizee directed George to take a trail into the woods.

George could see the trees had been there a long time. "This is a very old forest. I can tell by the slow growth of new trees. Not much Sun gets past the larger trees."

As the two traveled deeper into the woods, George thought he was seeing the trees move as if they were watching them. It seemed to George he could see faces in the bark of the trees. He explained it away as streaks of Sunlight through the leaves and shadows from branches.

George felt something grab his foot. He fell down face first on the trail. As he was picking himself up, George heard Kizee talking, but it wasn't to him.

"Now that wasn't nice at all. All of you just stop it. And as for you, I should chop you down and make you into a coffee table where people can put their feet up and spill drinks all over you," said Kizee.

George stared at the tree Kizee was talking to. Nothing seemed out of the ordinary except he thought he saw two eyes blink.

"Come George these trees aren't worth out time. The clearing we're going to is just up ahead," Kizee pointed out.

Kizee grabbed the wagon handle and led the way. George walked behind the wagon. On occasion, he would look back at the trees.

At the clearing the Sun shone down, lighting up the area with vibrant colors. The tree leaves were various shades of green contrasted with the browns of bark and compost carpeting the ground. Out in the middle of the clearing was a patch of soft green grass waving in the light breeze.

"We'll lay out the yellow blanket here George," said Kizee.

George sat out the glass pitcher and filled it with the squeezed lemonade. Next to the pitcher he placed the three crystal glasses. The plates were next to the pie with the gold flatware.

"We're all set. Now we wait," said Kizee.

Kizee's timing was very good. The birds began to sing and other ground animals started to come around. George could see many of them hanging on branches as if to catch a glimpse of their favorite movie star walking the red carpet.

Through the trees came wondering a beautiful woman with golden blonde hair and yellowish orange lipstick that matched her fingernail polish. She was wearing a two piece yellow chiffon dress with yellow silk stockings. Her yellow painted toenails shown through her open toed yellow slip on platform shoes as she gracefully walked through the forest. Yellow winged butterflies fluttered all around the Yellow Fairy.

George leaned over toward Kizee's ear. "I thought fairies were little winged things."

Kizee whispered back, "Fairies come in all sizes. It is pixies that are only four inches tall."

"What do I do now?" asked George.

"Greet her and ask her to join us for a summer picnic," advised Kizee.

"Good afternoon Your Fairyness would you like to join us for a summer picnic?" asked George bowing slightly.

"Good day to both of you. What a wonderful first day of summer. Yes, yes, I will join you in your summer picnic," said the Yellow Fairy.

The Yellow Fairy sat down on the blanket with grace and poise. George poured three glasses of lemonade and offered the first one to the Yellow Fairy. George handed the second glass to Kizee.

George proceeded to cut the lemon meringue pie. He served a slice to the Yellow Fairy on a yellow plate with a gold dessert fork. He did the same to Kizee.

Once they were served, George sat down and took a sip of lemonade. Kizee nudged George with her foot.

"Make conversation with her," whispered Kizee.

"Uh, that was a wonderful Sunrise this morning, did you by chance catch a good view of it?" asked George.

Between bites of the lemon meringue pie, the Yellow Fairy answered George. "I had a wonderful view sitting here on top of the trees. Where were you for Sunrise?"

"I was in the city square in Broomstick…"

The Yellow Fairy wasn't even listening. She asked the question, but didn't wait for an answer. The Yellow Fairy just kept talking about nothing at all. Yellow this and gold that with glistening and dazzling thrown in for extra emphasis. It was amazing that the lemon meringue pie even stayed in her mouth and she didn't dribble the lemonade down the front of her dress.

"…with my best friend Kizee," said George gesturing toward Kizee.

George noticed the Yellow Fairy's crystal glass was empty. He lifted the pitcher up. "Would you care for more lemonade?"

"Yes please," said the Yellow Fairy.

George also poured another for Kizee and himself.

The Yellow Fairy finished her pie and second glass of lemonade. Suddenly the Yellow fairy stopped talking and gracefully stood up.

"I had a wonderful time. I wish I could stay longer. However, I must be somewhere else soon to oversee a seedling sprout," said the Yellow Fairy.

From her waist, she pulled out a small bottle filled with yellow crystals. "Please do me a favor and spread some happy summer sunshine around," requested the Yellow Fairy.

George accepted the small bottle with a smile. "Thank you and have a good summer day," said George.

After the Yellow Fairy had walked back into the woods George turned to Kizee. "I can't believe it, we did it."

George and Kizee finished the lemon meringue pie and drank the rest of the lemonade.

They laughed and giggled when talking about the Yellow Fairy. "She certainly was stuck on the color yellow," said Kizee laughing out loud.

With everything packed up on the wagon George and Kizee headed for home. George kept a close eye on the trees as they went down the same path they used to get to the clearing.

When they got to the one tree that tripped George, it had moved into the center of the path. Sitting there on a stump was a tree fairy with long stringy brown hair swinging her legs back and forth. She had on a sheer white toga. Her skin was almost as white as her toga. She wore a very light pink lip gloss on her lips with eye shadow to match.

"Wouldn't you agree it's a nice day for a walk in the woods?" said the White Fairy.

"If one was allowed to walk without being bullied by a tree fairy," said Kizee.

"What are you doing? I thought we were supposed to be nice to fairies," whispered George.

"There are certain fairies one must avoid, like her. She is a tree nymph that abducts people, mostly males and keeps them inside trees for her personal entertainment... forever," Kizee whispered back.

"What do you want, Maranda?" asked Kizee not being too nice.

"I'm a little disappointed that you didn't invite me to your picnic," said Maranda as she stood up from the tree stump next to George.

"Would you have come?" asked George.

"Absolutely, I would have loved to sit next to you on a blanket in the woods," said Maranda rubbing her finger down George's nose.

"We'll include you at our next picnic, now if you don't mind, move your tree so we can get home," said Kizee.

"Not so fast, little girl. You know George, I could help you find that lost magic wand. Why don't you tell this Raggedy Ann witch to go home and stay with me for a while to discuss it?" said Maranda.

"Don't look at her eyes George. She'll put a spell on you," Kizee said to George. "Be gone fairy before someone drops a tree on you," said Kizee to Maranda.

"You have the saying wrong little girl. It's you that should be worried about a falling house. And I'll leave right after little Georgie shows me the clue he discovered in the journal. And no help from you," said Maranda as she pinched George's cheek.

"If that is what your wanted to see in the first place why didn't just say so," said George.

George reached into his leather bag to pull out the magical book.

"Don't show it to her. She will destroy our only clue," instructed Kizee as she pulled out her magic wand and pointed it at the White Fairy.

"You don't have to resort to threatening me," said Maranda.

"Then I suggest you move your tree and let us pass," stated Kizee.

Maranda gave in and moved the tree off the trail allowing George with the wagon to quickly scoot by. Kizee followed George's lead.

"You haven't seen the last of me. I will get what I want, and I want you little Georgie," yelled Maranda.

Maranda laughed to herself as they walked on.

After they got back to the road George asked, "And how did the fairy know I was to find the magic wand? Why do you suppose she wanted to see the blank page?"

"I don't know. Perhaps Maranda is working with the wizard that gave you the journal," said Kizee.

Gracie was up when George and Kizee returned from their summer afternoon picnic. Gracie still had a concern appearance to her face. She couldn't help thinking about what she had learned about the town of Broomstick the night before.

"Hey George, I don't have to work tonight. What do you say we go to a movie this evening?" asked Gracie.

George didn't answer right away as he was thinking about how Kizee could help him find the magic wand with the Yellow Fairy's magic. He peered over to Kizee for some help.

Kizee could feel it was an awkward time to be there. "This is family night. My family always gets together on Saturday evening for family night."

"Yes, that is a very good tradition your family has and we should do that also, just the two of us together. And tomorrow we'll go for a drive to see some houses in the surrounding towns," said Gracie.

"What about money, Gracie?" asked George now concerned with the change of Gracie's attitude.

"We got a check from San Francisco. I think we deserve a weekend getaway," said Gracie who was not telling the truth.

Kizee turned her head a little to the side and looked past Gracie at the two ghosts that were there. They were sadly shaking their head no.

Gracie could feel Kizee's eyes staring at her. It was like the feeling of a child's sticky hands after eating a peanut butter and jelly sandwich.

Gracie shivered at the feeling. Somehow Gracie knew Kizee could sense she was lying. She quickly tried to shake off the eerie sensation that was in the house.

"Go and get cleaned up George while I get my purse and car keys," said Gracie.

"I guess I'll see you at the renaissance faire then?" said George to Kizee.

"Okay, I'll be at my Mom's potion booth," said Kizee.

Gracie grabbed the front door and opened it smiling pleasantly at Kizee. "Have a good time at your family night," said Gracie.

Kizee smiled and walked out the front door leaving George and Gracie standing there just smiling awkwardly. After Gracie had shut the door Kizee flipped her two fingers around and disappeared.

Gracie was driving slower than normal with George sitting in the passenger seat. She was thinking of ways to start a conversation that would lead into George telling her things about Kizee.

"I bet Kizee is fun to be with since she seems to have a strong imagination like you," asked Gracie.

George sat there not yet saying anything.

"Of course, I've noticed you haven't said too much about your imaginary world lately. Is there something you would like to share with me?" queried Gracie.

George felt the strange sensation inside him that started from the touching of the magic book that also occurred just before meeting Kizee's mother and aunt.

George thought of the consequences that might happen if he told his sister of all the events that had happened since the first day of the renaissance faire.

It was this time a year ago, right after the funeral when George first dropped out of reality due to the loss of his parents. The crisis counselor kept asking him question that didn't make sense.

One piece of information that stayed with George was what he overheard the crisis counselor telling Gracie.

"If he doesn't accept the reality of your parents not coming back, you may have to seek professional help at this facility," said the crisis counselor as he handed Gracie a business card.

George looked over at his older sister and said, "Kizee told me that I shouldn't live in a made-up world when the real world is full of surprises."

"And I agree as long as it is in the real world. So, what kind of surprises in the real world has Kizee shown you?" asked Gracie with the loaded question she wanted to ask.

"Kizee and I went to the field just down the way from the house and observed the wildlife for a couple of hours. It was very surprising to see how many creatures are around us," said George.

Gracie thought for a long instant of small rabbits, squirrels, and flying insects of the sort. "Hem, maybe this girl isn't a bad influence after all if she is showing George simple local wildlife in the real world."

"George, are you through with your imaginary world? Can we talk about our parents?" asked Gracie.

George sat there silent as a ghost whisper in your ear. "I still miss them," he said with a soft voice.

Gracie pulled the car over to the curb. She turned to George. "It's okay to miss them. I miss them too. I also hurt inside and that hurt will never leave. But George, we still have each other. We are still a family you and me together. And we must go on living."

"Can I still be friends with Kizee?" asked George.

"Yes, yes George, you can still be friends with Kizee as long as you want," said Gracie as she hugged her younger brother feeling that she has finally brought him back to reality.

After a long moment, Gracie wiped her eyes and started the car. "Let's go see a movie."

In the parking lot of the movie theater Gracie noticed a man walking alone toward the ticket window. It was Eric Braun.

Gracie called out, "Eric Braun, hello."

Eric turned his head in the direction where his name had come from. He changed his direction slightly to intersect with Gracie and George as both were walking toward the ticket window.

"Good evening Miss Düben and also to you ah, don't tell me, George?" said Eric.

"Yes, that is correct. My brother George," said Gracie with a newfound smile as she gave her brother a one arm hug.

Awkward silence was present waiting to squash the conversation and let them go their separate ways. It was Eric that conquered the killer of human interaction.

"What movie are the two of you going to see?" asked Eric.

"We haven't decided just yet. We're starting a new tradition of Saturday family night," said Gracie.

Eric took that statement as a brushoff line. Again, awkward silence stepped in.

"Any suggestions of what would be entertaining?" asked Gracie taking a swipe at the awkwardness.

Eric scratched his head. "Well, a superhero movie is always good."

George spoke up for the first time and asked, "What are you here to watch?"

Eric peered down at George with a smile wanting to thank him for completely breaking the awkwardness between the three of them.

"I was coming to see the new space adventure movie," said Eric.

Gracie smiled before she said, "First impression I would have figured you for the dark occult vampire movie."

"That is a good one considering where we met. Ah, would you and your brother honor me in being my guests tonight at the movies?" asked Eric.

"Thank you but no. I promised George this would be family night. Maybe some other time," said Gracie.

"Gracie, it's alright. Look Eric is alone on family night," said George.

"Well okay. But we will buy the popcorn. And this is not a date," stated Gracie.

Eric held up his hands. "That never even crossed my mind. Officially on the record, this is not a date."

Eric Braun was a young man with short neatly trimmed hair. Outside of work he dressed casual with stonewashed blue jeans and a cotton button down shirt. He was twenty two years old already with a Master's Degree in engineering, primarily in rocket guidance systems. He was recruited to work in the research and development department at the vacuum company. Then came the downsizing and Eric was let go.

At the end of Saturday family night when they were walking out of the movie theater, Eric asked, "Do you have any plans for tomorrow? If not, we could go on a picnic."

Gracie stopped just before her car with George at her side. "Eric if you want to be friends, you are going to have to accept that I and George are a package deal. If I go anywhere with you, George comes along."

"I wouldn't have any other way. I really want to be friends with both of you. What do you have to say about this George?" asked Eric.

"I think my sister needs a boyfriend. But I'll accept the three of us as just friends for now," said George with a smile.

"So, what do you say, the three of us go on a picnic tomorrow?" asked Eric.

Gracie held out her hand. "No official dating. This is all just as friends."

"Just friends," agreed Eric as he and Gracie shook hands.

Eric showed up early on Sunday just as Gracie and George were getting ready to eat breakfast. On the table, Eric saw a box of breakfast bars and a quart of nonfat milk half empty.

"Hold on here a minute. This is Sunday. Sunday's are when all diets go out the window and a hot filling breakfast is made," said Eric as he picked up a breakfast bar shaking it at Gracie.

"Let me cook you two, breakfast," said Eric as he went over to the refrigerator.

Gracie tried to stop Eric from opening the refrigerator, but it was too late. To Eric's surprise when he opened the refrigerator there was nothing in it. He opened the freezer only to find two frozen containers of water and a box of frozen peas.

"What is going on here?" asked Eric staring at Gracie.

Gracie sat down at the kitchen table and put her head in her hands. Eric didn't stop at the refrigerator. He went around the kitchen opening the cupboards.

"A couple of cans of soup and a box of crackers, that's it?" stated Eric.

"Eric, this is really none of your business. Perhaps you should leave," said Gracie not looking at Eric.

"No, I'm not leaving. I want to know what is going on here. Why don't you have any food in the house?" queried Eric.

"We haven't gone to the store yet. A check came from San Francisco yesterday," said George.

"A check… what kind of check?" asked Eric.

"From our parent's bank account," answered George.

Gracie started to quietly whimper. "There isn't any check. I lied to you George."

Eric sat down at the kitchen table next to Gracie. "Would you like to tell me what is going on. Maybe I can help?"

"The probate court has our parent's bank account locked up working on an IRS audit. Düben Fashions is under investigation for money laundering. We are living on what I make from the coffee shop. I lied about the check because of Kizee talking about family night," said Gracie.

"Okay there is something I can do today. We are going shopping," said Eric.

"No Eric I don't want to be your charity case," stated Gracie.

"Do you realize that we shook hand on a deal last night that I will not allow you to get out of?" stated Eric.

"What deal, oh to go on a picnic? I don't feel like going now," said Gracie.

"For someone that wants to be a contract lawyer you don't handle agreements very well. We shook hand to be friends, remember that part? We are friends," reminded Eric.

Gracie just stared at Eric with contemp. "What are you getting at?"

"I know," said George. "Friends don't run out on friends no matter what."

"That's right George. And I am not going to run out on both of you. Now let's go and get some food for breakfast and our picnic," said Eric.

"I hate you. You know that? You twisted our agreement about not dating into...into... Oh what's the use? Let's go shopping," said Gracie.

"Now that's the spirit," said Eric.

In the afternoon sitting on a blanket in a park surrounded by waterfall fountains and trees Gracie asked Eric, "So how did you wind up here in Broomstick?"

"After I graduated I wanted to work for a rocket company. It's a hard field to get into now days," said Eric.

Gracie joked, "You're a rocket scientist?"

"No, I'm an engineer. My cousin was the rocket scientist. My Grandfather dropped the Von when he immigrated to the U.S." said Eric.

"That doesn't answer the question of how you wound up in Broomstick," said Gracie.

"Isn't it obvious, a job," said Eric.

Gracie quipped, "So Mr. Rocket Engineer, what is your latest design for a dust sucker?"

"Oh, it is very top secret. If I told you I would have to lock you away in my dungeon," laughed Eric.

While Gracie and Eric were talking, George wondered around the park looking at the fountains and watching the water tumble over the rocks when out of the corner of his eye George spotted a small figure.

At first, he thought it was an unusual colored butterfly. He slowly turned his head as not to scare away the butterfly. That was when he saw her.

She was about two to three inches tall with bright green colored wings with a hint of yellow around the edges. She was wearing a very skimpy lime green bikini bathing suit. She wore above the knee white and green stripped socks with green wedge shoes. Her hair glistened with tones of greens and yellows.

The Green Fairy flew over and sat down on a small rock near the water's edge. She picked a little mushroom and began to take tiny bites of it.

George pulled out the journal and looked up what kind of magic the Green Fairy had to offer.

"The Green Fairy's magic is to give one the ability to extract powerful healing potion ingredients from plants," read George.

"I need a gift," George said to himself.

From his pocket, he pulled out a glass marble and rolled it between his fingers.

"Hem, this might due. Now to approach her without scaring her away," said George.

George lay on his stomach and wiggled slowly toward the Green Fairy. He got close enough to push the marble with a stick over next to the Green Fairy.

The Green Fairy turned her head to see what was coming up next to her. Her reflection caught the Green Fairy's eye in the convex curve of the glass. She turned her head one way then another smiling at her image.

The Green Fairy stood up and got closer to the marble. She rubbed the smooth glass surface with her hands while still moving her head one way then another.

George stayed very still as he watched the Green Fairy closely. That was when the Green Fairy looked through the glass marble to the other side.

There was George's concave face in the glass. The Green Fairy moved her head from side to side looking at George. Then she peered around the marble to see George lying there on the grass.

She tapped the glass marble with her hand and then tapped her chest with a question type expression on her face. George smiled and nodded yes. The Green Fairy giggled and clapped her hands in joy.

From the water, the Green Fairy produced a tiny clear rock with a single green dot in the middle and waved it at George while holding out her other hand.

George put his hand out on the ground palm up. The Green Fairy flew over and sat the clear rock with a single green dot in the middle into the palm of his hand.

After that the Green Fairy and the glass marble disappeared from sight.

George stood up and put the clear rock with a single green dot in his pocket for safe keeping.

"Hey what'cha doing?" called out Eric.

George dared not tell him what had just happened. "Just playing in the water," said George.

Eric leaned down to George and said, "If you look hard enough some say you just might see fairies bathing in the water."

George peered at the water and then back to Eric. "Have you seen the fairies?"

"No not yet, things around here are still pretty much just a fairytale story for me," said Eric.

As they walked back to where Gracie was, Eric put his arm on George's shoulder.

"I need some help in understanding something. Has your sister always dressed like a grandmother or is she purposefully trying to ward off suitors?" asked Eric.

"I don't know. I guess she always dressed like that. Gracie didn't care for any of the fashions our parents designed. She was creating a line of clothing before our..." George's sentence trailed off.

Eric knelt down to George. "Listen, it's okay, we can talk about something else. I didn't mean to bring up bad memories..." Eric was interrupted by Gracie coming over to see what was wrong.

"Are you alright George?" asked Gracie.

"I'm alright Gracie," said George.

"I'm sorry. It was my fault. I hit on a sensitive subject. Listen it is getting late maybe we should pack up our picnic," said Eric.

Chapter Seven
Truth or Dare

Very early Monday morning a couple of days after the summer solstice Mindy, Searat, and Eric were sitting in the study of the McDermit's house where Mindy grew up. They were secretly discussing a plan that would change the town of Broomstick forever.

On a piece of paper with monetary figures in the billions of wizens converted to dollars was sitting on the table.

Eric said, "Are we going to upgrade the vacuum production?"

Mindy clamored, "I'm going to do better than that. I am planning to buy that outdated vacuum cleaner company and kick it to the curb!"

Eric sat at a computer keyboard and typed every word Mindy dictated. Some things that Mindy said didn't make sense as it had to do with the magical world of business.

Later that morning, after the stock market opened, Mindy, Eric, and Searat were the owners of almost all the stock of the declining vacuum company.

"It is up to you to convince your father to sell us the magic broom factory," said Eric to Mindy.

"I'll do that at morning's breakfast," said Mindy.

Cyndi and Wendy were sitting at the breakfast table with their parents, Agnes and Franklin. Mindy, Searat, and Eric came in from the study to join them.

Mindy started a conversation with, "Today is the day the board is meeting to vote on downsizing the vacuum company. I was wondering what your thoughts are, Father?"

"I haven't heard any of the suggestions. I'll hear them for the first time today," answered Franklin.

Then Mindy came out bluntly, "Father I want to buy you out of the magic broom factory, today, right now in fact."

Mindy pushed a slip of paper over to her father. Franklin picked it up and read it. "Five billion wizens?" Franklin looked at everyone around the table. "You three are in this together?"

"It is all in pure gold and it is waiting at the bank ready to be transferred to your personal account," stated Mindy.

"Where in the world did you get five billion wizens in gold?" asked Cyndi.

"From the bottom of the ocean in the Caribbean," answered Mindy. "Father I need the broom factory for the biggest project Broomstick will ever see. Please Father. I need your answer before the meeting."

Agnes leaned over to Franklin. "Give the broom factory to her."

"Mom, it has to be a financial deal. I have to buy it," said Mindy.

"One Billion and not a wizen more," said Franklin.

"Okay then, one billion wizens," answered Mindy.

The deal was signed with the whole family witnessing the transaction. The magical document glowed with three dimensional images rising up from it.

There was a bank teller's face within the glow. "Good morning. I am Miss Patty Whack. I will be conducting your business transaction today."

Everyone at the breakfast table said in unison, "Good morning."

"Let's see, Mindy McDermit, Eric Braun, and…" There was a long pause. "Is Searat you legal name?"

"Stearates Herzog," answered Searat.

"Your records show you were lost at sea over a thousand years ago…"

Mindy interrupted, "I can vouch for him that he is the real Stearates Herzog."

"Very well, you are purchasing the McDermit Magical Broom Company for one billion wizens from Franklin McDermit. Is that correct?" asked Miss Patty Whack.

"Yes," said Mindy.

"Hem, do you have consent from the parent company for this transaction?"

Franklin looked at Mindy and said, "That was part of the original deal that it belonged to Whitewing Brooms. I just controlled the operations."

Mindy looked at Miss Patty Whack and said, "I have the controlling interest of Whitewing Brooms here."

Through the magical image, Miss Patty Whack read the stock transaction from earlier that morning.

"I see, yes, you do have the authority to do this transaction," agreed Miss Patty Whack.

The family's jaws dropped as they sat there staring at Mindy.

"I'm sorry Father. This is a hostile takeover of that knotem's dull vacuum cleaner factory. That old guy that swindled you into that agreement has taken his last wizen from Broomstick," said Mindy with conviction.

"The transaction is complete. Is there anything else I can help you with this morning?" asked Miss Patty Whack.

"No. Thank you very much for you service," said Mindy.

The image faded away and Mindy picked up the completed document. Mindy put it in a brief case filled with the other documents that she will need for the meeting later that morning.

Mindy, Eric and Searat were sitting there on one side of the table. On the other side of the table sat Robert Brown. He was a holdout on selling his stock. They were arguing.

"Your shares are worthless as of this morning. You do not have any voting rights. Whitewing Brooms no longer exist as this morning. We are now 'Spell Caster Enterprises'. I am the CEO, Searat is the CFO, and Eric is the design engineer. Here are the documents."

Robert Brown scanned through the documents. He mumbled as he turned the pages. The emotions on his face turned from anger to frustration.

"What? Is that legal?" asked Robert Brown.

"It is legal right down to the very last period in this document," said Eric.

What about my stock?"

"Mr. Brown, it isn't worth the paper they are printed on," said Mindy.

Robert cried, "What about the vacuum cleaner orders? What about the job force? What about MY JOB?"

"Well Robert, we will sell you a single vacuum cleaner manufacturing line. We'll even move everything for you for two hundred million dollars in gold certificates. Just say the word and we'll tell you where your new business is located," said Eric.

"I...I...don't have that kind of money," insisted Robert.

"Sure, you do Mr. Brown. It's in that off shore account you've been funneling money to from for Edna's Antiquities down in the preter-normal business district," stated Mindy with a bewitching smirk.

Robert stumbled, "Ah, um, well I could at least put ten percent down until all the arrangements have been completed."

"All of it or none of it. Which will it be?" stated Eric.

Robert tightened his fists and stretched his fingers out several times due to the stress of the decision. Finally, knowing magic was involved, Robert narrowed his eyes and said, "Okay let's do it."

"Done and done. Sign here and your new vacuum manufacturing company will be on the east side of Broomstick ready to start production tomorrow," stated Mindy.

Robert picked up the pen and signed down at the bottom of a single piece of paper and added one line. "I want it renamed to RB's Vacuum Manufacturing."

After Robert left the board room, Searat asked, "The east side of Broomstick? Isn't that the Troll district?"

"Just on the edge, where the sidewalk drops off into the gutter," smiled Mindy.

That same Monday morning came very quickly for Gracie. It seemed like she didn't sleep a wink that night. Something in her sub-conscious brain was trying to come out through her dreams.

Gracie got up and ran water over her head in the shower trying to get going. She barely got to work on time. Gracie gulped down the first cup of coffee.

One of the girls that worked at the Ex-Pressed coffee shop said with a smirk, "We heard you had a great weekend. Two dates with Mr. Einstein. How did you manage to get the most eligible bachelor in Broomstick to even notice you?"

"They weren't dates. We just happen to run into each other on Saturday when I was taking my brother to the movies," said Gracie.

"And you just happen to run into him at the park with a picnic basket?" laughed another girl.

"We're just friends, and what do you mean by Mr. Einstein?" answered Gracie.

"Wow you don't know?" said the first girl.

"He worked in research and development, so what?" stated Gracie.

"He is almost finished with his PhD on Nano-gyro guidance systems for stellar space travel," answered the girl.

Gracie made another coffee with extra sugar.

"You're late," said Kizee.

"According to the magical book, a wizard is never late. He arrives just in time to save the day," said George.

"I believe that is a knight in shining armor that saves the day," laughed Kizee.

"You won't believe what happened Saturday. I was at the park where the waterfall fountains are and saw near the water the Green Fairy. She gave me this," stated George.

George held out his hand with the clear rock with a single green dot in the middle in his palm. "I don't know what it is supposed to do."

"That is a vision stone. It gives you the magical power to see things close up," explained Kizee.

"Now that I have these two fairy powers, what do I do with them?" asked George.

"Not here, I'll talk to you later at your house," said Kizee.

"Um okay, what do you want to do today?" asked George.

"Would you help me here in the booth?" asked Kizee.

"Sure, what are we going to do?" queried George.

George followed Kizee to the back of the booth where a table and boxes of small bottles were stored underneath. On top of the table was a large drum with a small petcock valve.

"We are going to fill these small bottles with liquid green Sunset Flash. I'll fill them, you cork them," explained Kizee.

"What is liquid green Sunset Flash?" asked George.

"It's a good thing you moved here to Broomstick. You weren't learning anything about magic in San Francisco. Liquid green Sunset Flash is the residue left behind on tree leaves after a Sunset green flash. Here, stick out your tongue," said Kizee.

George hesitantly stuck out his tongue as Kizee dropped a single drop of Sunset Flash onto it. His tongue suddenly went numb followed by intense tingling.

George had a sudden surge of emotions. George stood back from Kizee with horror.

"Listen, I got to go." said George without giving any reason.

"Wait, you said you would help me fill these bottles," cried Kizee. Not thinking that she already had with the drop of sunset flash, Kizee wanted to put a spell on him to make him stay.

George spent the morning in the garage feverishly going through the moving boxes. Things were randomly taken out and set on the floor as George went from one box to another.

George didn't stop until he came across the one box he was searching for. In it were all the family pictures that had hung on the wall around the house when his parents were alive.

Gracie had thought it was best not have sad reminders here in their new house.

George pulled out the last family portrait and sat it upright on top of a box. He sat down on the floor and stared at it.

"George, are you in here?" called a voice.

George didn't answer as he was oblivious to his surroundings. Harriet with Kizee behind her walked up to George.

"George, are you alright?" asked Harriet.

"They're dead you know," said George.

"Yes, I know George. What about you, do you really know their dead?" asked Harriet.

"I only saw the urns. Anything could have been in them," said George.

"Sometimes it is better not to see, but to keep a beautiful memory in your mind," answered Harriet.

Harriet held out her hands to George. He held Harriet's hands as she helped him up off the floor. George hugged Harriet and started to cry. Harriet rubbed George's head to comfort him. Harriet's touch felt soothing to George. The pain of losing his parents quieted down in his mind.

"I'm sorry George, I shouldn't have given you that drop of Sunset Flash," said Kizee.

Harriet said, "It's alright Kizee, I think maybe you did George a big favor."

Just at that moment, Gracie was standing at the garage door with Winston behind her. She was slightly ill from the magical transport to the garage.

"Is George alright? Is he hurt? Does he need a doctor?" blurted out Gracie.

"No, everything is alright. I sense something isn't quite right between the two of you though," said Harriet.

"What exactly do you mean something isn't quite right between us?" asked Gracie.

"You're hiding something about your parent's death and George feels it because the ghosts of your parents are here with these boxes waiting to move on," said Kizee.

Gracie rubbed the back of her neck feeling the hair stand up on end. Then the guilt she had been holding in for so long flooded her emotions. "George, the coroner is holding our parent's remains until the investigations are complete."

"Who were in the urns we buried?" asked George with tear stains on his face.

"I'm sorry George I did it for you. The urns were empty. I was going to have our parent's remains put into them later after all this was done," explained Gracie.

Gracie and George were left alone for the rest of the day to talk. The family portrait was hung up in their living room over the fireplace.

"No more hiding the hurt in cardboard boxes," said Gracie to George as they looked together at the family portrait.

Slowly and methodically together they unpacked the boxes and started putting their home together.

Gracie didn't see Eric for over two weeks. She pretty well had written him off as not interested and left it at that.

This gave Gracie time to get used to the idea of Broomstick being a magical town. "I'm living in a town full of witches and wizards doing magic spells and whatever else they do."

It was about that time when Gracie received a letter through the normal mail service. It was from the Mayor's Office of Broomstick.

Gracie opened and read, "Miss Düben, please come to my office at City Hall Tuesday at ten o'clock to discuss a business matter."

Gracie wore her best outfit with her hair pulled up into a bun. This look made her look like a spinster of the nineteen thirties.

A scenario played in her head, "We are sorry but we have to stop your scholarship. Conflict of interest you know."

Winston was sitting at his desk sipping coffee and reading a report. "Come on in Gracie," said Winston with a smile.

Gracie was always nervous around Winston, knowing what she knew. "I...I, took off work to make sure I was here on time. Is something wrong between George and Kizee?"

"No, they are getting along just fine. Kizee isn't interfering with your personal life is she?"

Gracie stood there and looked at Winston. "Well, no." Gracie bit her lip thinking she should have just said everything was alright.

Winston buzzed the outer office. A man came in and sat down in a chair up against the wall.

"Mr. Davenport, what are you doing here?" said Gracie.

"Mr. Davenport came all the way here from San Francisco at my request," said Winston.

Gracie looked at Winston. "Eric told you about my refrigerator, didn't he?"

"I assure you Eric Braun hadn't told me anything. I received this letter from the San Francisco bank asking about your scholarship status. This led me to making a few calls. One was to your lawyer Mr. Davenport," answered Winston.

"Miss Düben, I'm here because Mr. Wisestone has learned of your legal matter through improper channels. As your lawyer, I am here to explain the difficulty of getting it resolved," said Mr. Davenport.

"I fired you. You didn't represent my interest against the bank that is holding my inheritances except to collect your fee. Mr. Wisestone he is not my lawyer," shouted Gracie.

"Now calm down Miss Düben," said Mr. Davenport.

"No I will not calm down. What are you charging for your services this time that no good will come out of?" shouted Gracie.

"Miss Düben, Gracie. Please calm down and take a seat," said Winston.

Gracie sat down but did not calm down. She stared hard at Mr. Davenport.

"I have a solution that will end your problem," said Winston.

Gracie sat back in her chair with suspicious eyes looking at both Mr. Wisestone and Mr. Davenport.

Gracie asked, "What kind of solution?"

"Your problem with the bank is a simple fix..." started Winston before he was interrupted by Mr. Davenport.

"I assure you it is not a simple fix, Mr. Wisestone. If it were, I would have had this matter closed a long time ago," said Mr. Davenport.

Gracie looked up at the ceiling and rubbed the back of her neck. "The bank investigators think the crash wasn't an accident. The coroner is holding our parents remains until the investigation is complete. They think our parents were laundering money overseas through some little company I never even heard of. There isn't any proof of it."

"That is exactly what I had been discussing with Mr. Wisestone. Let me handle this. You need to stay focus on your college studies and not take on such a heavy burden," said Mr. Davenport.

"Let me finish Mr. Davenport. Gracie, it is an easy fix because Mr. Davenport hasn't given the investigators the documents that will clear your parents of money laundering. Isn't that correct Mr. Davenport?" said Winston.

"Uht, uht, uht, I uh don't know what you're referring to. There isn't, aren't... any documents. I-I don't have any documents," stuttered Mr. Davenport.

"Tell me it isn't true that you don't own controlling interest in an Indian fabric weaving company that supplied the Düben Fashions with their raw materials. And you didn't personally oversee the money transactions between the San Francisco bank and the bank in India? Those are the documents the investigators want and you are holding them because they would clear Düben Fashions and implicate you directly of money laundering," stated Winston.

"Is this the simple fix you are referring to, Mr. Wisestone?" asked Gracie.

"The simple fix is that I invest into Düben Fashions and we will have our company up and running in the black by winter solstice. Between the two of us you know my lawyers will prove what I have just stated," said Winston.

"That's ridicules and absurd. There is no way you can prove those outrageous allegations. You can't pin any of what you said on me. I'll bring suet against you for deformation of character," exclaimed Mr. Davenport.

Winston walked over to a box and pick out a very thick folder. He walked backed over to his desk and dropped the folder in front of Mr. Davenport.

"I can and I will because this morning I bought that little Indian fabric weaving company," said Winston.

"You, you're the one that implemented the hostile takeover?" exclaimed Mr. Davenport.

"Right down to the last piece of paper with your name on it," said Winston with a smile.

"What is it you want?" said Mr. Davenport.

"I want you to go to prison," blurted out Gracie.

"Wait, I can fix the reports to make it look like an accounting error. No one has to go to prison," said Mr. Davenport.

Winston laughed. "You are going to prison for a very long time."

"You're going to let him walk out of this office and trust the authorities to do the investigation?" asked Gracie.

"I didn't say who was going to do the investigation. Mr. Davenport will be escorted by a special security company to his destination," said Winston with a smile.

Gracie sat there glaring at Mr. Davenport. "You were waiting for me to lose the company and you would have bought it pennies on the dollar leaving my brother and me out in the cold."

"It not what you think, Mr. Wisestone has fabricated all this to gain control of your company, not me. You can't listen to him. I've been your family lawyer for over two decades," declared Mr. Davenport.

Gracie sat there thinking of questions that needed to be asked. "Which brings up two very interesting questions, how much did you steal from my parents and for how long?" asked Gracie.

"All that will come out in his confession, I assure you," said Winston.

"I'm not going to confess to any of this. You're crazy if you believe him Gracie," exclaimed Mr. Davenport.

"I'm through talking to you. How much will I receive for a piece of Düben Fashions?" asked Gracie.

"One hundred and fifty million for twenty five percent ownership of your company," said Winston.

"Honestly Mr. Wisestone, it isn't worth that much," said Gracie.

"Not by a long shot. It is estimated at barely two million dollars," said Mr. Davenport.

"Shut up you," said Gracie angrily. "Why so much money?" asked Gracie.

"Between you and me, Gracie, I have a global market waiting for your new designs and we can make ten times that amount," explained Winston.

"My designs, you want me to design clothing? For who? Then it hit her. For…Witches?" asked Gracie.

"Yes," said Winston straight to the point.

"Can't you just hire special talented people to get the same results?" questioned Gracie.

"It isn't that easy Gracie. We need a new perspective that can think outside the box. We'll talk in private about our new venture," said Winston.

"As your lawyer, I am against all this. You will be prosecuted for your parent's crimes," said Mr. Davenport.

"You're not my lawyer," said Gracie.

"Gracie, are you in?" asked Winston.

Gracie took a moment to think to herself. "I'm playing a real life game of truth or dare."

"Yes, Mr. Wisestone, I'm in," said Gracie on the premises she was doing it on a dare in accepting there is a magical world surrounding us.

When Gracie got back to the coffee shop, she found a note waiting for her. The note came with flowers.

Gracie opened the note. She read the note to herself as there were others trying to peer over her shoulder.

"I'm sorry I couldn't say anything about my work related trip. Is our friendship agreement still in effect?" signed Eric, City Hall ext. 2225.

Gracie smelled the flowers. "What a liar." She called the number on her next break.

Eric said, "I saw you coming out of Mr. Wisestone's office. I tried to catch you,"

"I had a meeting with him and my ex lawyer," said Gracie.

"Your ex lawyer, what was he doing here?" asked Eric.

"Mr. Wisestone cleared up a legal matter for me," said Gracie.

"Can you talk about it?" asked Eric.

"Mr. Wisestone and I are going into the clothing business together," said Gracie.

Eric asked, "That sounds great, how about a celebration dinner tonight?"

"After receiving flowers from a liar, this sounds like, a forgive me, date you're asking me out on," said Gracie.

"No, no date. I'll come over and cook you and George a fabulous high end restaurant dinner right in your own kitchen including my special dessert. I'll explain where I have been," said Eric.

"Including your special dessert, wow I can't turned down that offer. Under one condition though, you tell me why you are paying so much attention to me when there are so many other better qualified date hungry girls drooling to go out with you," questioned Gracie.

"Because I'm not drooling to go out with them," stated Eric.

"Is it true that you are almost finished with your PhD?" asked Gracie.

"Oh, you heard about that. I'm not the Brainiac everyone thinks I am. My thesis is a work of science fiction from my childhood imagination. I wrote this story of riding an atom size spaceship with a neutrino gyroscope control system to speed me through space at the speed of light," explained Eric.

"The question is will it work?" asked Gracie.

"That is my stumbling block. I can't get my simulation program to work. If I were a real genius my silly program would have me sitting in the cockpit whizzing through intergalactic space firing photon torpedoes at the alien lizard's spacecraft," stated Eric.

Gracie laughed with a smile. For a moment, she had forgotten the sorrows life had put her through.

When Gracie got home, the phone rang. She could see on the display it said Winston Wisestone. Gracie picked up the receiver.

"Hello Mr. Wisestone, something I could do for you?"

"I was thinking perhaps tonight would be a good time to sit down together and talk about the future. A celebration dinner will be on us," said Winston.

"Eh, Eric was supposed to come over and cook us dinner. I really don't feel like celebrating anything just yet," said Gracie.

"I'll call him and send your regrets," said Winston.

Gracie knew that meant she couldn't talk her way out of this. "No, I'll do it," said Gracie.

"I'll take care of it. I will be seeing him shortly about his trip," said Winston.

"I'll talk to Eric myself," said Gracie.

"Dinner at the Poison Apple Tavern about seven?" said Winston.

"I don't know where that is," said Gracie.

"I'll send a car around six thirty to pick you up," said Winston.

"Sure, sure that will be fine," said Gracie.

Gracie hung up the phone and then dialed the City Hall extension 2225. No answer. Five minutes later she tried again, still no answer. Gracie tried all afternoon. Finally, she gave up.

In the evening, Eric knocked on the door. When Gracie answer the door, Eric said, "I heard you were invited out to dinner with the Mayor."

"Yeah, I tried to call you. Come on in," said Gracie.

Eric could see the house looked completely different from when he was there two weeks ago. Pictures were hung on the wall. Vases on tables with flowers in them and other little things that said this is home.

"You've been busy I see. Looks very nice and feels warm," said Eric.

"Listen about tonight. I tried to reschedule the dinner celebration some other time. Mr. Wisestone didn't take no for an answer. He is sending a car to pick George and I up," explained Gracie.

"So, I've been told. Hey, can I see George I got something for him," said Eric.

"I think it is too early to start trying to win his affection with presents," said Gracie.

"This isn't a present to win anyone's affection," said Eric.

"What is it then?" asked Gracie.

"Something every young American male should have," said Eric.

"You're not going to tell me are you," queried Gracie.

"Nope," said Eric. Then Eric called out, "Hey George."

George heard Eric call his name. He came out of the family room where he had been unpacking a box of old vinyl record albums his father had collected.

"Hey George I was wondering if you own a baseball glove?" asked Eric.

"No," said George.

"Well you do now," said Eric tossing George a baseball glove.

"Something every young American male should have is a baseball glove?" said Gracie.

"Not just a baseball glove. This is the glove used by the best triple A baseball pitcher of all time to throw a no hitter in his last game ever. And I have the catcher's mitt to match," stated Eric.

"And you're going to what, play catch?" asked Gracie.

"Play catch, come on I can do better than that. George, here is a book on how to pitch I read when I was your age, which wasn't that long ago," said Eric.

"Who was this great triple A pitcher of all time?" queried Gracie.

"He was known as Eric the Dread."

"You," said Gracie.

"Me," said Eric.

"Hey Gracie there are four tickets in the book for the baseball game on my birthday," said George.

"Four tickets, who is the fourth ticket for?" asked Gracie.

"I thought maybe I would bring a date along with George, Kizee and I," said Eric.

"Do you have someone in mind?" asked Gracie.

"Yeah maybe a drooling to go out with me bleach blonde," answered Eric.

"Nope, try again," said Gracie.

"A drooling to go out with me brunette?" said Eric.

"Not even," said Gracie.

"Hem, what about a redhead that doesn't want to call it a date?" suggested Eric.

"That is much better, however this time you can call it a date," said Gracie.

"Oh hey, it's almost six. You should be getting ready," said Eric.

"A half hour to get ready, I haven't even thought of what to wear," exclaimed Gracie.

"May I suggest the wildest collection of colors you could imagine," said Eric.

"Oh really, now I should be taking fashion tips from you?" said Gracie.

"By no means is this a fashion tip. I've been to the Poison Apple Tavern and fashion is not the word I would use to describe what they wear," said Eric.

"I wonder where the chauffer is. He should have shown up by now," asked Gracie.

"That is why I'm here. I was asked to be your chauffer for tonight," stated Eric.

Eric opened the door of the car to let Gracie and George out in front of the Poison Apple Tavern. They stood there staring at the flaming sign above the double wood doors.

Gracie felt a little stiffness in her shoulders and neck from typing college reports or was it the uneasy feeling she was getting from this odd part of town.

"Where exactly did you say, we were?" asked Gracie.

"The preter-normal business district," said Eric.

"Preter... meaning what exactly?" asked Gracie.

"It is best to observe for yourself," said Eric as he opened the door to the tavern.

Gracie walked in with George right behind her. The uneasy feeling now ran all the way down to her little toes. She turned to look for Eric. The door was closed and Eric wasn't there.

"Eric?" whimpered Gracie.

"Gracie," Winston called out.

"Welcome Gracie, George," said Harriet.

One would think Winston would have had this important dinner meeting in the back room of the Poison Apple Tavern where private conversation could be, well almost private.

Winston offered Gracie a seat at a round table in the center of the tavern. George took the chair next to Gracie. Kizee pulled her chair ever so close to George.

"Kizee, pull your chair back over here," said Harriet.

Kizee made a sad face as she scooted her chair away from George making sure it screeched to enhance her disappointing action.

Gracie looked around the tavern to observe the other patrons. Gracie's hair was curling on her neck with goose bumps running across her shoulders.

"Eric was right about this not being a place to find a fashion statement. However, the fashion world would have a field day in naming this way of assembling thrift store rejects," thought Gracie.

Gracie did notice Harriet was dressed different from everyone else. "Like a twenty first century…woman of Halloween's dark realm," Gracie didn't want to think the word, "Witch."

Bee walked around the table setting down glasses. "Here you go. I remembered this was what you liked from the party," Bee said to Gracie.

George took a sip of his drink. This was his first taste of rich foamy carbonated witch hazelnut soda.

"Why is everyone staring at me?" asked Gracie.

"They all want to be your first customer," said Winston cheerfully.

Bee brought out a couple trays of appetizers and sat them in the middle of the table. Gracie had no idea what they were. She picked a couple that looked safe and placed them on her plate.

Gracie thought about all those times with her parents eating at expensive restaurants when someone else was paying the bill. "Smile and eat it," her mother would whisper.

"In six months, your parent's personal bank accounts will be released and by then Düben fashions will be ready to start up again. We'll need to put together a board of directors with you as the main designer," said Winston starting the conversation.

"I'm not ready to move back to San Francisco to oversee the day to day operations. This whole idea needs to start slowly. I mean the sewing shops are sitting idle with all the workers locked out. Who knows how many of the workforce we'll get back. I can't quit school to run this," said Gracie.

"Who said anything about moving back to San Francisco? We'll base our new company right here in Broomstick. I can have the entire operation moved here at a moment's notice.

"No doubt," thought Gracie.

"Not too far from here are old warehouses we can rebuild to be our manufacturing facility with offices," suggested Winston.

As Bee put down the entre in front of Gracie Bee said, "I know someone that could help you get things going. She has an antique store down the street. She was in the fashion industry many years ago, maybe you heard of her."

Gracie looked up at Bee who was now on the other side of the table serving Harriet.

"You're not talking about queen of gossip, are you?" asked Kizee.

"Kizee, take George for a walk through the cemetery and introduce him to your friend while we continue with our business," said Harriet.

"Oh, that won't be necessary. I have to get up early tomorrow. We can discuss everything at your office, Mr. Wisestone," said Gracie.

Harriet looked at Kizee and motioned with her head to go ahead and take George away.

"No really, we must be going," insisted Gracie. "George, stay here."

Kizee grabbed George by his arm and pulled, "Come on, the cemetery is loads of fun at night."

"Do you know Edna Brown?" said Winston.

"Edna Brown the teen fashion model?" questioned Gracie.

"You know her?" asked Harriet.

"Not personally, I have heard of her though. She lives here in Broomstick? How in the world did she wind up…" Gracie stopped herself before she said something stupid.

George followed Kizee out of the Poison Apple Tavern and down the street. George was reading the store signs.

"Most of these stores had booths at the renaissance faire," noticed George.

"My mom's potion shop is down there," pointed out Kizee.

They walked up the street and crossed over toward Broomstick's cemetery.

"Don't you think it is creepy to go walking through a cemetery at night?" asked George.

"Are you kidding? That is the best time except on cold rainy and foggy days. In an hour, the full moon will be coming up. Maybe we'll see the Ultra Violet Fairy. She is the protector of the dark magic forces," said Kizee.

"She hangs around the cemetery?" asked George.

"Sometimes, depends on her mood," answered Kizee.

"A cemetery is not my first choice to go to get cheered up" said George.

Kizee made a detour over to the corner mall where the bakery was.

"If the Ultra Violet Fairy shows up you'll need a dark chocolate treat for her, said Kizee.

George followed Kizee into the bakery where Mr. Olsen was cleaning up getting ready to close. "Hello Kizee and you are George I believe?"

"Good evening Mr. Olsen, yes this is George and he needs a dark chocolate treat for the Ultra Violet Fairy if we happen to see her," said Kizee.

"Well let me see what I have left. Hem, how about a Royal Dutch black chocolate truffle?" asked Mr. Olsen.

"Perfect," said Kizee.

"Since I'm closing up, how about I give you the last three truffles," said Mr. Olsen.

Thanks Mr. Olsen," said Kizee with a big smile.

"Uh, yes thank you Mr. Olsen," reiterated George.

George stood at the old iron gate staring in at the somber scene. The air was warm with a slight breeze. Not a single cloud in the night sky. It was dark with only the starlight to see by.

"I need to ask you something. I think I already know the answer, but I want to be sure," said George.

"Ask me anything, Georgy Weorgy."

George let that idiom slide. "Are you a witch? I mean a real witch that does magic spells and grant wishes?"

Kizee stared at George strangely. "Well of course I'm a real witch silly. You already knew that, and you should also know witches can't grant wishes."

"Um yeah I was just checking. We should have brought a flashlight," stated George

"Come on, I'll introduce you to our guide. He is an old friend of mine," said Kizee.

George followed Kizee into the cemetery. Soon after they passed through the gate George saw an oil lantern coming toward them. At first, George could have sworn it was floating by itself through the air.

A shadowy figure appeared behind the lantern wearing colonial clothing with a triangle style hat.

"Good evening Clancy," said Kizee.

The ghostly figure stood about five and a half feet tall. "Good evening Kizee, who's your friend?" asked Clancy.

George was standing there frozen at the sight of an eighteenth-century ghost.

"This is my best friend George," said Kizee not showing any hysterical emotions like George was feeling.

"Hello George how goes the war?" asked Clancy.

"The war, what war?" asked George still quivering in his shoes.

"The war against the Crown," answer Clancy.

Kizee answered for George, "Cornwallis surrendered at Yorktown."

"Hail General Washington, hail the colonies," said Clancy.

Kizee whispered to George, "He always asked that question and I give him the same answer each time. Come on this way."

Kizee lead the way with George close to her. Kizee took hold of his arm and squeezed it. Behind them was Clancy holding the lantern up high.

The full moon was just beginning to crest over the eastern horizon. George started to see long lunar shadows being cast by the grave stones.

Suddenly Kizee stopped. "Over there sitting on the wall in front of that crypt. Do you see her?"

George stared where Kizee was pointing at. Sure enough, sitting on the half wall was a luminance figure with butterfly type wings. Her head was bowed down as in prayer.

"What is she doing?" asked George quietly.

"She is collecting the day's dark magical forces from the world. With the polarized light from the moon she transforms it to pure clean magic for the next day. At full moon is when the pure magic is the strongest. That is when it is best to do purification and healing spells," explained Kizee.

"I guess we shouldn't disturb her then," said George.

"It's alright. Just slowly walk up to her with the truffle. Don't say anything just stand there," instructed Kizee.

George pulled out a truffle and handed it to Kizee. "Thank you for, well, for being my friend. What I'm saying is um, I'm beginning to like you. Not that I didn't like you when we first met. Just well you know, I like you more, different sort of. I mean like real friends should."

This time Kizee kissed George and put her forehead against his. "Friends forever like we promised, right?"

To George, this kiss was a far more powerful promise than their pinky finger promise. George knew he could never tell Gracie that Kizee was a witch. She wouldn't understand.

George kissed Kizee back. "Friends forever, like we promised," answered George.

George took another truffle out of the bag and quietly walked toward the Ultra Violet Fairy. When he was about two feet away from her, George held out his hand with the Royal Dutch black chocolate truffle on his palm.

The Ultra Violet Fairy raised her head. George stood as still as he could although he was trembling all over.

The Ultra Violet Fairy moved toward George and picked up the truffle from George's hand. She gently took a bite. Poetically she ate the truffle like art in motion.

After the Ultra Violet Fairy finished the truffle she smiled at George. She raised her hands toward George's face and gently placed her fingers over his eyes. After a long moment, George opened his eyes. The Ultra Violet Fairy was flying away toward the full moon that was now hanging above the eastern horizon.

Amazingly George could make out every detail of the cemetery. The colors were different with a fluoresce glow to everything.

Kizee stood out with a blue aura surrounding her. Close to Kizee were two ghostly figures. George walked over to Kizee.

"Kizee, my parents are standing next to you," stated George.

"Yes, I know. I saw them in your garage among the boxes. When you unpacked the boxes, you released their spirits. Now they are free to go toward the light. They're here to say goodbye," explained Kizee.

George tried to smile at the ghosts of his parents as they were smiling at him. It was hard seeing them this way, but they're expressions looked so peaceful.

"I told them this would be the best place for you to see them," said Kizee.

The ghostly images of George's parents faded away. George felt in his heart a sense of tranquility as if they really never left.

"Here, eat your truffle. The chocolate will make you feel better," said Kizee.

"You certainly see the world in a different way. Have you always talked to dead people?" asked George.

"I don't talk to dead people. Moxee the undertaker does that. She talks to the cadavers. I see and talk to ghosts. I try to help them move on to the afterlife. That is my special talent," stated Kizee.

"Now I understand why you like the cemetery at night," joked George.

Waiting for Kizee and George at the cemetery gate was Maranda the White Fairy.

"This is the third picnic you didn't invite me to George," said Maranda.

"What is it you want Maranda?" asked George.

"I told you before Georgie, I want to help you find the lost magic wand. Here, I'll spell it out to you George. I want you to finish collecting fairy magic and put them in the magic wand," answered Maranda.

Kizee stepped between Maranda and George. "This isn't about a lost magic wand. Your fight is with me."

"You are so right my little witch. You will agree that George here is the prize that goes to the winner," said Maranda.

"What is this about?" questioned George.

"Remember the wish I told you about?" said Kizee.

"About wishing for a friend, yeah, I remember," said George.

"Is that what she told you George? Her wish was for a friend?" Maranda broke into uncontrollable laughter.

"You can stop laughing, I won. I got him to promise to be my best friend forever," shouted Kizee over Maranda's laughter.

Suddenly Maranda stopped laughing. "You used a green magic drop spell on him. That nullified any promise you two made. Oh, and that kissing stuff earlier doesn't count either. So, I won the prize, he is mine," as she reached out to pull George to her.

Kizee grabbed George's arm and pulled him away from Maranda. They went running out the cemetery gate toward the bakery.

"She can't follow us once we're passed the bakery," shouted Kizee with shortness of breath from running.

Once they were on the main street of the preter-normal business district, Kizee and George stopped running.

"Tell me about the wish," asked George.

"It's not your concern," said Kizee.

"It sure sounded like it is my concern back there. Why did she make it sound like I am a prize to win then?" asked George.

"Alright if you must know, every story I read ended in true love. One day I was sitting under a tree that happened to belong to Maranda. I made a wish to someday find true love. Maranda heard my wish…" explained Kizee but did not finish her story because George jumped in.

"And Maranda granted your wish and chose me to be your true love if I kissed you," finished George.

"No, it's not at all like that. Maranda said she would take anyone away from me that could remotely be my true love. When we ran into her that day of the picnic with the Yellow Fairy I decided to end this war with her," said Kizee.

"You gave me the drop of Sunset flash to ensure I will be your friend forever?" asked George.

"Yeah…I'm not too proud of myself considering the consequences it caused," stated Kizee.

"Ho boy what a mess. What are we going to do now?" said George.

"Keep our guard up, which means we must find that magic wand. She wants you and it for some reason. I need to do research to find out why a magical fairy wants you and that magic wand together," said Kizee.

Just up the street Eric had just pull up in front of the Poison Apple Tavern.

"George, do me a favor and tell your sister I'm out here whenever she is ready to leave," asked Eric.

"Okay Eric," said George as Kizee and him went into the Poison Apple Tavern.

George found Gracie standing at the round table with a large sketch pad and charcoal drawings spread out with possible ideas of outfits and dresses as witches and wizards were talking and giving ideas to her.

"Gracie, Eric is waiting outside for you whenever you are ready to leave," said George.

"Oh, what time is it? I have to get going. I got to get up early tomorrow for work at the coffee shop," exclaimed Gracie.

Peter Candlewick, who was standing close by got closer to Gracie. "I already arranged for you to be off tomorrow."

"And who are you?" asked Gracie.

"I'm the owner of Ex-Pressed Coffee Shop," said Peter.

Gracie thought to herself, "Is there anyone that isn't a witch or wizard in this town besides me, oh Eric."

Chapter Eight
Spooky Girl Spells

Gracie hadn't slept well in weeks since that dinner at the Poison Apple Tavern. She had dreams about styles of clothes that were so unconventional it bordered on frenzied hysteria. Every morning when Gracie woke up she went to her drawing easel and started scribbling. With artist chalk she colored in her designs.

There were black with multi stripes pullovers, hooded cloaks with star constellations across the front and patchwork skirts with no repeating patterns to name a few from her dreams.

"Bazar, just totally bazar," Gracie would say at each drawing.

One sketch stood out from all the rest. It was a silk aqua blue robe that hung straight down from the shoulders. The cape wrapped around the front and hung down on one side covering the right arm.

"This one, this one for sure," said Gracie on this one particular morning.

Gracie rolled the drawings up and stuffed it into a cardboard tube. She sat the tube in the corner of the room with the others waiting for the day Düben Fashions would start up.

George was still asleep when Gracie left for work. It wasn't long after that Kizee was standing at the foot of his bed. She stood there watching George sleep.

Unintentionally, Kizee's magic affected George's dream. Voices were calling to George from in and out of magical realms. Kizee's image was all through his dreams with warnings he couldn't understand.

Kizee couldn't help herself. She reached out and gently rubbed George's feet that were sticking out from the blanket.

George slipped out of his dreams. He opened his eyes to see Kizee standing there at the foot of his bed rubbing his feet.

"What are doing in my bedroom?" asked George as he pulled his feet under the blanket.

"I couldn't sleep last night thinking about the blank page and the magic wand. I found this book in Mom's library," said Kizee holding up a large leather book.

"Did Gracie let you in?" mumbled George.

"Of course not, silly. I waited until she left. Come on get up. I have magic to do to make the blank page visible to us," said Kizee.

"I'll be out in a few minutes after I, you know take care of personal business," said George.

"I'll wait here until you get dressed," said Kizee.

"I can tell you don't have any brothers. Wait for me in the kitchen, please," said George.

"Well okay, but I could be telling you what I found in this book while you get dressed," said Kizee.

George turned over and buried his face in his pillow for just a second before he got up. He looked at the foot of his bed to see if Kizee had left.

George stared at his door. "Maybe Gracie oiled the hinges."

When George opened his bedroom door it squeaked as usual. George stared at the door hinge.

When George walked into the kitchen, Kizee was sitting at the kitchen table with breakfast ready. In a bowl was, scrambled dragon eggs. On a plate was sizzling slices puja. Kizee tried to make her mom's coffee cake.

"Just to let you know, I can cook," said Kizee with her cheek stuck out waiting for some sort of appreciation gesture.

George stared at the coffee cake. "Exactly what is that?"

On the plate was a glob of half-baked dough with red jelly running down the sides like lava from a volcano.

"Well the coffee cake didn't quite turn out like the way mom makes it. But it should still taste good," said Kizee.

George looked around the kitchen. Nothing was out of place. There weren't any dirty pans on the stove or in the sink.

"I'm going to have to ask Gracie if all girls are this strange," George thought.

While eating the strange tasting eggs and what George thought was bacon, he looked at the book Kizee had brought over. On the front stamped into the leather was the words 'Archaic Gramarye Theurgy Spells'.

"What does that say?" asked George.

"It translates to 'an old book about magic spells'," said Kizee.

"That's too simple. What does it really say?" questioned George.

Kizee pointed at each word, "Archaic, meaning very old or prehistoric. Gramarye means written words within a book, and Theurgy is concerned with the power or spirit of spells."

"Hem, it's an old book about magic spells. Now I get it," said George.

George was sitting next to Kizee as she turned the pages of this very old book. It was made pretty much the same way as the magic journal. It had an index that George couldn't read.

Kizee ran her index finger down the list with a stern mesmerized stare. At each point, she shook her head.

"The clue may be centuries old, you know. Still, the clue should tell us where to look for the magic wand," said Kizee.

George said, "Maybe it's a map showing how to get to where the wand is hidden?"

"That is why I am here. We are going to do a magic spell together to make the clue show itself," stated Kizee.

George pulled out the journal from his bag and set it on the table.

Now let's get going on making this clue appear," said Kizee with new inspiration.

Kizee went to another part of the book. She ran her finger down the page reading spells.

"We are going to need some items. Do you have an iron spiral spirit conduit coil?" asked Kizee.

"No," said George looking at Kizee oddly.

Kizee queried, "How about dragon's blood incense?"

"Sorry all out," said George.

"You do have a glow-stone and a black rock, don't you?" questioned Kizee.

"I haven't got a clue what a glow-stone or a black rock is," answered George.

"A glow-stone protects your home from curses and the black rock is to trap evil spirits. Perhaps we can improvise. Let's see…" said Kizee.

Kizee walked around the house picking up knick knacks. She rubbed some with her hands. George thought she was expecting something should appear from them like a fabled genie, perhaps.

On the fireplace mantle were two seventeenth century iron spiral candle holders. Kizee picked one up and removed the candle. "We can use this for the spirit conduit coil."

"Can any incense work? Gracie has some vanilla stick incense in the bathroom," asked George.

"We can try it. Perhaps the spell might work better with a nice smell. Now for a glow-stone and a black rock," said Kizee.

Kizee walked from room to room followed by George until she entered the entertainment room. Inside a display cabinet was a large segment of petrified wood and a big piece of coal.

"You're just playing with me, aren't you?" smiled Kizee as she lifted the heavy rocks off the shelf.

Kizee carried the petrified rock and coal into the kitchen with a big grin. "I don't know why you fool with me about not knowing much about magic. Here's your glow-stone that protects your home along with the black rock to trap evil spirits."

George just stared at Kizee. He had relented anything she does for now on isn't strange anymore.

Kizee arranged the items on the kitchen table. She put the iron spiral candle holder at the top of the map. Kizee set the petrified rock which she called a glow-stone on one side with the black coal rock on the other side.

"Put your vanilla stick incense in the candle holder pointing up. Now light the incense," instructed Kizee.

George picked up the vanilla stick incense from the kitchen table and slid it down into the candle holder. George lit the incense stick and stood back.

Kizee waved her hands around to move the smoke of the incense around. From the old book Kizee began to recite the magic spell she picked.

"Old spell, new spell. Ring the bell to call the spell. Drop it down the well to drown the old spell."

Kizee pointed at George, "On the table, rap and tap to close the gap."

George gave a quizzical look at Kizee. Coming in from the kitchen window the sunlight reflected off her hair giving her an aura of golden purity. Kizee's gentle words echoed within his head as the vanilla incense and her natural fragrance filled the air. Then he started the rap and tap with his knuckles.

"With my magic blue and new, release the hidden clue," chanted Kizee.

The petrified rock began to glow in the center. "What is it doing?" asked George.

"The glow-stone is purifying your home. And the black rock is removing the bad karma that exists here. Gauging by the luminosity, the glow-stone is emitting good vibrations," explained Kizee.

"Okay now, it's time to find out what this clue has to show us. Swallow the tiny clear rock with a single green dot in the middle."

"What?" queried George.

"We are going to use your three fairy magic's. You already have the aura sight from the Ultraviolet Fairy inside you. Now swallow the clear rock," insisted Kizee.

George swallowed the clear rock.

"Now sprinkle some yellow fairy dust over the page" said Kizee.

George opened the bottle he received from the Yellow Fairy and sprinkled some yellow dust on the page.

They both looked at the page. "Can you see anything?"

"No, it is still blank," said George.

"Hem, I need to know, did the book seller hand you the magic journal with his bare hands?" queried Kizee.

"I don't think he was wearing gloves. Is that another clue?" asked George.

"Worse," said Kizee.

"That doesn't sound like I want to hear what is next," said George.

"It matters who really gave you the journal." Kizee looked up at George.

"What do you mean who really gave me the journal?" questioned George while grimacing.

For the first time Kizee truly lost her smile when she said, "You've been put under a magical spell that holds you to the promise of finding the magic wand."

George asked, "How can you tell I have a magical spell on me?"

"The glow stone has put an aura around you. According to this book, the color pattern you have around you indicates…Hem…" Kizee stopped to turn a couple of pages. "It's a…this doesn't make sense."

"What doesn't make sense?"

"By having you take it out of the book seller's bare hands you were chosen to be the successor of the magic wand. Oh no! I'm thinking Maranda may have gotten to you before we pinky swore our friendship," explained Kizee.

"I'm thinking it was Maranda in disguise that gave me the magical journal," stated George.

Kizee said in agreement, "Exactly!"

"So you're saying I became her pawn when I received this magic journal?" exclaimed George.

"Not yet. Maranda wants the magic wand. She is waiting for you to find it to make her next move.

The only way to fight back is to retrieve the magic wand and use its power against her," explained Kizee.

"We still can't do that without this clue," said George.

"George, put both your hands on the pages," ordered Kizee.

George placed both his hands on each side of the pages. Kizee could see his whole aura glowed around the page. Words and symbols began to illuminate showing a map.

"You did it George! You opened the clue!" yelled Kizee.

With a magnifying glass, Kizee studied the map carefully. At the top of the map were two rings. With the aid of the magnifying glass, George looking over Kizee's shoulder saw symbols inscribed in the two rings.

"These symbols are nothing I've ever seen before," said George.

Kizee held the magnifying glass where they both could examine the symbols. She opened the old book to new pages with symbols on it.

"The lettering is old alphabet," said Kizee.

Kizee ran her finger across a page of words as she compared them to the translations to modern English.

"Write this down. Exsedia diplorteum centuraztix tyaxcuzphivb" said Kizee.

"Hold on there. How am I supposed to write down something I don't know how to spell?" quickly questioned George.

"No not that. Wait for the translation. Within my magic wand lays dormant my amuletlated power," stated Kizee.

George asked, "Whose amuletlated power?"

"Here," pointed Kizee. "The name of the wizard is… Zweig." Kizee paused.

"Hold on, you're weirding me out," said George. Then he thought to himself. "Everything Kizee had done up to this point has weirded me out."

Then it struck Kizee bluntly, "Of course, oh George I love you! Don't you see? The spell you are under was put on you by Zweig the Wizard through his journal. Maranda wants Zweig's magical wand for her own selfish schemes of…of… terrible things even I can't imagine," explained Kizee.

"Why me out of everyone else in the world?" asked George.

"Silly, I told you. Maranda is using both of us because of my wish for a best friend."

Kizee again ran her finger down the page of spells and stopped on one close to the bottom of the page.

Kizee again swirled her hands around the vanilla incense smoke. She read the spell slowly and carefully as not to make any mistakes.

"Let the incense spin faster. Candle waxer, muster plaster. Obey this spell castor. Show us the Wizard Master," exclaimed Kizee with a fiery voice.

The vanilla incense smoke rose up into an image of an elderly man standing there in a very old rough weaved hand stitched style wizard's robe and woven reed hat.

"My name is Zweig. I am at the end of my days without an heir to my magic. Within this magic wand, I have placed my amulet and powers. I placed a spell upon this map to hold fast. Only a person true of heart will retrieve my wand and inherit the power within."

"How can someone find out this information if no one can open the map in the first place?" asked George.

"I bet Maranda knew that the only way was to give you his journal," said Kizee.

"You need to ask Maranda a few questions," suggested Kizee.

"Me? You want me to talk to Maranda?" questioned George.

"Yes," stated Kizee.

"Alright um, where should I look for Maranda?" asked George.

"You don't find her, she'll find you. We just have to give her a reason to find you," said Kizee.

Kizee held her hands out to her side closed her eyes and chanted, "Close my spell before the twilight of dawn."

The incense was burned out and the petrified rock wasn't glowing anymore. George sat there with cold chills and eerie feelings wiggling up and down his body like he was dunked into a vat of ice cold water with leaches squiggling around his skin.

After George recovered he said, "You know sometimes I'm glad you're on my side."

Kizee laughed thinking George was just making a sarcastic comment.

June soon turned to July and George's birthday was right there at the beginning. Eric had taken George and Gracie with Kizee to the ballpark for what was recorded as an official date between Gracie and Eric.

The last place one would expect a confrontation with a fairy would be at a stadium full of knotems. George was standing in line to get a hotdog when someone gently grabbed his arm and started to squeeze it.

"Don't call out unless you want your arm broken," said Maranda the fairy.

She led George out of line into an empty corner away from nosy people.

"I'm growing weary waiting for you to find that magic wand," griped Maranda. "I don't have much time left. I want that wand. So stop wasting my time,"

"I've been working on it. I'm sure you being a fairy, you could do the job better than me," said George.

Maranda changed her attitude. "Listen George, I'm doing this for you because if you haven't noticed, that little wicked witch is using you for her own selfish gain. She doesn't want you to become a wizard, whereas I do."

At that moment Kizee called out, "George?"

Maranda took that moment to evacuate the scene leaving George standing there alone.

"Was that Maranda?" asked Kizee.

"Yeah, she was asking for a progress report," said George.

"Eric and Gracie were getting worried. You hadn't returned," said Kizee.

"I think we should plan a picnic," said Kizee.

"I think your right. It is a good time to have a picnic. Who knows maybe a certain fairy may give us a clue or two," agreed George.

That next Saturday Kizee and George set out with his wagon and some simple food to where Kizee first met Maranda.

They sat under the tree and ate a sandwich and potato salad while drinking lemonade.

"Well, well, look who is having a picnic and once again I wasn't invited," said Maranda.

"Oh, but you are invited. You're the guest of honor," replied Kizee.

"Do I get to sit next to Georgie and play with his hair?" asked Maranda.

"Only if you will behave yourself," said Kizee.

Maranda flew down from the tree branch she was sitting on and landed right next to George. George offered her a plate with a sandwich and potato salad with a glass of lemonade.

As Maranda sat there nibbling at her sandwich she said, "You two are being too nice to me. I sense you want something."

"We opened the clue in the journal. We know about Zweig the wizard. We also think you know something about the magic amulet he left behind," said Kizee.

"Will you tell us about Zweig the wizard?" asked George.

"Anything for you sweet pie," said Maranda as she curled George's hair around her finger.

Maranda started to explain, "I have been searching for an heir to Zweig's magic for the past thousand years waiting for the right person to retrieve it."

Kizee whispered into George's ear, "She is lying or hiding something evil."

"Now I wonder, why a fairy would want to help an heir to some old wizard's magic?" questioned Kizee.

"I think I know," said George. "Zweig broke the rule about fairies."

"Which rule was that, George?" asked Kizee.

"Rule number three, never have a love affair with a fairy. You will lose your heart and possibly your magical powers. Maranda, you were trying to obtain Zweig's magical powers, but he hid it from you," said George.

"We were partners in a magical endeavor to collect fairy powers into an all-powerful magic wand." said Maranda.

"We know the wand has Zweig's magical amulet inside it. That is what you really want," said Kizee distrustfully.

Maranda shifted her eyes. She knew that Kizee and George hadn't discovered where the wand was hidden yet.

George exclaimed, "So, this game you've been playing is about Kizee's wish. You want me because I have the power to fulfil her wish and you don't want that to happen"

"And George has proven he is true of heart by opening the map. Zweig's magical journal chose George as the rightful heir," Kizee pointed out.

"Yeah, about Zweig choosing George as an heir, I've been looking at true of heart the wrong way for a thousand years until you made your silly wish for true love," said Maranda.

"Am I Kizee's true love?" queried George.

"I haven't got a clue. You're cute enough to be. However, I, me, and no one else selected you to find Zweig's magic wand. That is why I want you." Maranda snickered while rubbing George's face with the back of her hand.

"You guided George to Broomstick?" asked Kizee.

"I had to do something about Zweig's magic. And there was you, Kizee," explained Maranda.

"Me?"

Maranda laughed out loud. She looked at George. "She was following you around the renaissance faire all morning waiting for a chance to meet you."

Kizee's face turned red with that bit of information coming out.

George turned to Kizee. "You were following me around the faire?"

"Stay focus on the present George," said Kizee as she half rolled her eyes and smooched her mouth.

"You need one more fairy magic to complete the power of the wand. And I am the only one that knows which fairy magic you need," instructed Maranda.

"Does this mean you are on our side?" asked Kizee.

"I was always on your side my cute little freckled face witch. I just like causing mischief. Look, I found you a friend, and who knows, maybe your wish for true love might come true in fifteen years… or not," Maranda quipped shrugging her shoulders.

"George, think about a special relationship with me as my wizard apprentice," said Maranda getting her face close to George's.

George was ever so frozen as Maranda was just about to fly away with him. Kizee jumped up and jabbed her arm between George and Maranda.

"I told you George, Maranda is a bad fairy. We cannot trust her," exclaimed Kizee.

Maranda fluttered away waving at George with a crinkly nose and girlish smile. "Next time George, next time."

George and Kizee had been studying the map closely to discover all the clues they could. The magic wand was hidden in a deep cavern. The map was very descriptive in details on how to transverse the cavern. Kizee was translating the old witch language as best she could to modern English.

"Is this cavern close by?" asked George.

"No, it is very far away in a magical realm," answered Kizee.

"I read the rules of realm travel. Which realm are we going to?" queried George with some excitement.

"The Smether Realm," said Kizee.

George asked, "What is the Smether Realm?"

"It is the realm of the Smether dark elves," shuttered Kizee. "They kidnap children while they sleep to work their mines. Their magic is very evil. I don't know why Zweig would hide his magic in their realm, but if the dark elves are connected to this wizard's magic, there is certainly something horrific waiting for us," concluded Kizee.

"How do we get there?" asked George.

"We must travel by balloon through the double rainbows after a terrible storm. We will need the help of the lightning fairy to achieve the power to do it," stated Kizee.

Again George had to ask the obvious question to get an answer from Kizee. "How do we find the lightning fairy and how do we get her help us?"

"We need a summer thunder storm. I'll do the magic needed to get us there," said Kizee.

George had been watching the weather reports for any summer storms to pass through Broomstick. It was midsummer according to the weather forecasters when a server thunder storm was predicted to pass through Shadow Creek Valley.

George read from the old magic journal on how to collect magic from the lightning Fairy.

George exclaimed, "It says to gain this incredible power of nature one must experience its force first hand. During the storm use your magic wand as a lightning rod by directly pointing it at the lightning fairy."

"We need to stand out in a lightning and thunder storm and have the lightning fairy hit your magic wand with a lightning bolt? This sounds very dangerous. We could get killed doing this. I think I'll pass on this." said George to Kizee.

"I'm sure my sister won't allow me to go out in the storm, unless…" said George thinking out loud.

"Unless what George?" questioned Kizee.

"Unless I make it a science experiment, I could get Eric to help me. Do you know of the experiment that Ben Franklin did with a kite?" said George.

"Do I? That is the first time anyone ever collected this magical flux from a Lightning Fairy. And do you know what he did with that magical power?" said Kizee.

"Um, invent the static electric generator?" said George.

"No silly, he used lightning flux to influence opinions in favor of the revolution, especially the French. Without it the British would have won the war. That is how powerful this magical force is," said Kizee.

"I don't remember reading that in the history book," said George.

"It was the first Saturday in August. Gracie Eric and George were out in the backyard barbequing for their family night together.

Eric had been instructing George on pitching a baseball. Eric was crouched down and gave George the two finger sign for a curve ball.

"Strike three called the umpire for the final out of the game. Fireball George Düben has pitched a no hitter game," described Eric.

"That's pretty easy since there weren't any batters," joked Gracie.

"It will happen, you'll see. George is a natural born pitcher," said Eric.

"Eric… I was wondering if you could help me with an experiment I would like to do. You know how the teachers always want you to write about what you did last summer. Well I want to write I reenacted Ben Franklin's kite experiment. According to the weather report in a couple of days a thunder storm is supposed to roll through here," asked George.

"That sounds too dangerous. Absolutely not, find a safer science project like growing plants," said Gracie.

George looked over at Eric with sad eyes hoping for some support.

"Where the sense of adventure in growing plants? I'll help him and ensure everything will be safe. George will surely get a top grade for it," said Eric also with puppy dog eyes staring at Gracie.

"Safe, you promise it will be safe. No coming back and saying it was just a small burn over eighty percent of George's body," said Gracie with reservations.

"Safe, absolutely, one hundred percent," said Eric.

"Alright I'll allow you two nerds to do this shocking experiment," said Gracie.

George and Eric did a high five with their baseball mitts.

George studied Ben Franklin's kite experiment and collected the necessary equipment to build a Leyden jar. The kite was easy to make with balsa wood, string and plastic sheeting.

George wrote in his computer diary what he was about to do with Kizee. He had kept a good journal of all the events that had happen this summer so far.

George paused before he finished his last entry. Next to George was Zweig's journal. It was opened to realm magic.

"Kizee said I need to trust her magic. George downloaded the entire diary onto a flash drive and wrote a note. "In case something goes wrong."

The wind that morning was picking up. Dark cumulonimbus clouds were rolling in quickly with the echoing sounds of thunder.

Eric, George and Gracie accompanied by Kizee headed out to a wide open field not far out of town. Eric and George launched the kite from a portable grounded shed.

The kite climbed high and far as George let out the control string. The rain started light with tiny taps on the roof of the shed. As the hour ticked by the rain grew louder as the drops the size of a quarter hit the ground.

In the distant, lightning could be seen weaving through the clouds. On occasion, a bolt of lightning would hit the ground.

The storm rolled their way with intense thunderous claps and flashes of bright hot light.

"Are you ready George?" asked Eric with excitement.

"As ever as I ever will be," said George.

Lightning sheared through the air around the kite. The storm around them slammed the area with heavy amounts of precipitation. Water was accumulating in deep puddles around the portable shed.

Lightning bolts were numerous with an increase of lightning strikes hitting the ground. George knew this was now or never.

Without any warning, Kizee with George ran out of the shed straight into the rain soaked field. Kizee pulled out her magic wand from inside her raincoat. George was holding onto Kizee's left hand with his right hand. In George's left hand was Kizee's magic broom.

Kizee pointed her magic wand high up into the air.

"Kizee, George, what are you doing? Come back here!" yelled Gracie.

Eric scrambled out the door of the shed toward Kizee and George. It was too late. A bolt of lightning struck the magic wand.

In the sky Kizee could see the image of the lightning fairy glowing as she shot out her bolt of plasma at her wand.

The lightning fairy's bolt hit straight on the tip of the magic wand. At that moment, Kizee's magic broom turned into a hot air balloon. Kizee and George were inside the basket. The balloon flew straight up into the storm and disappeared from the field.

"Noooooooooooooooooo!" cried Eric as he fell to his knees into a muddy puddle.

Gracie stood there in the pouring rain staring where Kizee and George had been standing. She was in complete shock. She fell to the ground and could not move.

Gracie began to cry like a little girl.

Chapter Nine
Get the Lead out

No one knew of the map or the plan to find Zweig's magic wand except Maranda the tree fairy. Strangely enough, this had been the best kept secret in Broomstick.

Agnes and Harriet were helping customers when the storm passed through Broomstick. Harriet knew of the Ben Franklin kite experiment Eric and George were doing. She didn't have any idea what Kizee and George were really up to.

Suddenly, Harriet fell to her knees. "Kizee, No!"

Agnes felt the high power of magic vibrate through her. She saw her sister fall to her knees.

"I felt it too. You know what just happened," said Agnes as she helped Harriet up.

"Kizee...she...used the lightning fairy's power... for a spell," stated Harriet as she caught her breath.

"What spell could she be doing that needed that much power?" queried Agnes.

"I don't know."

"Call her to you and let's find out before this gets out of hand," stated Agnes.

"One two, ebelie doo. Kizee's playtime is through. Magical spell bring Kizee home," chanted Harriet.

Winston appeared in the potion shop with apprehension in his face. "I just came from the field where Kizee was. Kizee disappeared into that storm and at first glance it looked like she pulled everyone with her! Do you know what spell she was doing?"

"No, I did my calling spell to find out. It didn't bring Kizee to me," stated Harriet.

Winston stood straight with his hands out and up. "Wach match burn well. Heed this spell. Kizee appear before me at the strike of the twilight bell."

Winston had the look of anger when his spell didn't work either. "Your daughter has undoubtedly figured out how to do black magic spells. I knew this day would come when her black side would emerge."

"Hey don't blame that black magic streak on my side of the family," said Harriet.

"This is not the time to discuss our blood line. We need to figure what Kizee and George had been up to," insisted Agnes.

"This will be difficult. Gracie and Eric are gone as well," said Winston.

"There should be remnants of Kizee's spell in the field where they were earlier," suggested Agnes.

Franklin joined them at the field just outside of Broomstick where the kite experiment was. The shed was there lying on its side mangled.

"You can see in the trampled grass where each one was standing last," said Winston.

Harriet was standing where Kizee had been last. "Next to Kizee's footprints are George's footprints."

Harriet knelt down and picked up a broom straw. "Now why would George, be holding Kizee's broom?" asked Harriet.

"Going by where the kite had fallen, George let go of the kite way back at the shed before running out to where he was standing last," stated Franklin.

Winston was examining the grass impressions between where Kizee and George were standing and where Eric and Gracie had fallen.

"Kizee and George flew straight up from here into the storm. Eric, here by his weight compared to Gracie over here didn't fly up. They were taken away from here by another spell," insisted Winston.

Agnes was making circles with her wand and mumbled to herself. "I need all of you to move away for a minute."

Agnes then flung around ground up caterpillar fuzz. The fuzz stuck to the last image of the four just before they disappeared from the field.

"Look, Kizee's broom is starting to turn into a hot air balloon," said Franklin.

"Where are they heading to?" said Winston.

"My little witch, what are you up to?" asked Harriet not expecting a response.

"If she is heading to a realm, we may need Mindy to help track where they went," stated Agnes.

"What happened to Eric and Gracie?" asked Harriet.

"They were swooped off in different direction by the way the fuzz is stretched out," said Agnes.

"Never mind those knotems. We have to go after Kizee! My little witch is in real trouble," exclaimed Harriet

"We don't have the knowhow to follow them. Mindy would be the only one that could pick up their trail and follow them in a storm. I'll send an emergency message to the Wanted Pirate for Mindy to come home," said Agnes.

"Please tell me you're not going to send that SNARF mail. I wouldn't trust any of those lollygag fairies," said Harriet.

"I'm not using SNARF mail. I will send a soldier of the wizard guard," answered Agnes.

The Wanted Pirate was on the high seas crossing the equator with Captain Davy Jones on board participating in Shellback day for the paid customers of the adventure cruise line.

Mindy was in the chartroom ensuring the ship is on course and the arrival back to homeport will be on schedule when the candlelight flicker caught her attention. It wasn't any normal flicker with the air moving in the chartroom. It was a spell notice. Colors appeared and changed in a sequence only Mindy knew, "A message from home!"

Mindy completely forgot what she was doing with the ship's charts. Instead she was wondering if something happened at Spell Caster Enterprises.

Mindy and her sailor friend were still quietly pirating treasure right under the nose of Davy Jones from the bottom of the ocean in the Caribbean and putting it in the Wizard's Bank to fund their research and development of something that would change the town of Broomstick forever.

It was a couple of minutes later after Mindy's warning when the soldier flew down from the clouds and landed in front of Captain Ann Bonny.

While saluting, the soldier said, "Sorry for the sudden drop in Captain, but I have an urgent message for one of your crewmembers."

Captain Bonny returned the salute and said, "Which member of my crew is the message for?"

"Mindy McDermit, Captain."

"Watch, notify Navigator McDermit her presences is required," ordered Captain Bonny.

The chartroom door opened. "Yer wanted by the Skipper," said the deck watch.

Mindy promptly went to Captain Bonny. As she approached, Mindy flipped a salute. "You called for me, Captain?"

"The soldier here has an urgent message for you."

Mindy looked over at the soldier of the wizard guard. Suddenly Mindy became worried it was worse than she had thought. The soldier handed Mindy the letter. Mindy ripped the letter open and began to read it.

> **Mindy,**
>
> **Something is magically wrong in Broomstick and we need your help. Kizee is gone to an unknown realm in a balloon.**
>
> > **Mother.**

"Captain, I'm needed back home. There is magical trouble in Broomstick. My cousin went missing into another realm."

"Fourteen days' emergency shore leave is granted, Lieutenant McDermit," said Captain Bonny.

It was right after that Mindy went to Captain Davy Jones for a most unusual request. "Captain, I need Searat to help me track what realm my cousin went to. I assure his return as I have in the past."

"The same agreement will stand as before," said Captain Davy Jones.

"Aye, aye, Captain," said Mindy.

Mindy knew she and her sailor friend were on a tight schedule. It was already full moon that night.

"Be him back before the next new moon or you will serve me for a century," stated Davy Jones many a time Mindy had taken her sailor friend.

Mindy arrived in Broomstick in a wind funnel of salt water. Dripping wet both Mindy and her sailor friend stood on the porch of Mindy's home.

"Mom, I'm here," yelled Mindy through the door as she dripped salt water on the porch.

Agnes opened the door to see Mindy and her friend standing there in a large puddle of seawater smelling like a sardine canning factory. "Come around to the mud room and we'll get you two out of those clothes."

Later, sitting in the kitchen eating hot soup and drinking hot coffee, Mindy was listening as Agnes told the bazar tale of events.

"We'll never catch them if we follow them in a balloon," said Agnes.

"I can," said Mindy.

"You can...what?" questioned Agnes.

"Catch them," said Mindy.

"You're saying you can catch them in a hot air balloon. You don't even know where they went," stated Agnes.

"Once I know where they've gone, Searat and I can catch up to them in a zeppelin we are building at Spell Caster Enterprises."

"Who are you?" asked Agnes.

"Captain Herzog. At your service madam," said Searat as he drunkardly stood up and bowed almost falling down.

Mindy caught Searat and helped him sit back down.

"That was before I began to serve Davy Jones. Now I'm known as Seaman Searat" said Searat.

Harriet spoke up, "You're in no condition to fly a paper airplane."

"Madam, try being at sea for thousand years on Davy Jones ship and see how well you can walk on land," stated Searat.

"Seriously Aunt Harriet, Searat hasn't had anything to drink since...since I have known him," said Mindy.

"Madam, the magical workforce has been building a zeppelin in the last few months I designed," said Searat.

"I have all kinds of charts and maps of realms and dominions. I will figure out where they went and why," stated Mindy.

"How will you do that?" asked Harriet.

"There aren't too many realms that are on the other side of a storm," said Mindy.

How do you know you'll catch up to them in time?" queried Agnes.

"We can get there much quicker through a storm under engine power. I can assure you we will be there just as they are landing a balloon," said Searat.

"That is a large order to fill. Alright Mr. Herzog get started on your plan," said Agnes.

Back in the early part of summer, Eric Braun and Searat Herzog drew detail drawings of a zeppelin for the magical broomstick workers to build. All rope was spun by the Stiltskins. The elves built the gondola in the shape of an old sailing ship with highly polished wood. The nymphs hand sewed the gas bag and the outer covering for the rigid structure. Running along on each side of the gondola ship were two huge broomsticks to power the zeppelin.

Wizards and witches installed all the technical equipment needed to control the ship. Some were experimental like the propulsion system to increase the power of the two brooms as needed for flight. And then there was the Nano guidance system that Eric was designing for space flight.

Young wizards and witches from the broom flight testing team signed up as the zeppelin's crew.

Mindy made uniforms for the wizard and witch sailors. As for Searat, Mindy designed a special Captain's uniform.

"I'm proud of you that you are willing to take this dangerous assignment," said Mindy.

Mindy hugged Searat and gave him a hard kiss. She whispered a question in Searat ear.

"Why did you change your first name?" asked Mindy.

"Stearates, it's not a very salty name when you're on board a ship of the doomed souls," said Searat.

Mindy was saddened to think of Searat being a doomed soul of Davy Jones crew. She hugged him once again tightly before she stood back to admire his new uniform.

Searat smiled at Mindy as he stood there in his new uniform. "I could use a good first mate. That is, if you want me."

Mindy stood there for a minute wondering exactly what this salty old sailor was really asking her. He may be a thousand years old, but Searat didn't look any older than twenty nine.

Mindy knew after all this was over, he must return to Davy Jones ship and she would never see him again as his tour on board Davy's ship will soon be over. It was time for Searat to go deep under to his final rapture.

Searat picked up on Mindy's hesitation. "Um, I was meaning in a purely professional way," said Searat with a slight disappointment in his voice.

Mindy smiled knowing the true meaning. "Oh, of course you meant in a pure professional way. I didn't take it any other way. I would be proud to be your First Mate on this last voyage we'll have together."

As the zeppelin was taking shape, Searat was standing in the field with Mindy and the zeppelin crew. "She should have a name that inspires courage," said Searat.

A wizard asked, "What about a name being fearful?"

"I think the name should be majestic or poetic," said a witch.

Mindy spoke up and said, "It should all those things."

"Hem," said Searat, "How about the Raging Queen?"

"Odd you would think of a crazy name like that," said Mindy.

"I was thinking without you, this idea would have never got off the ground," said Searat.

Before Mindy could object, the crew had already started calling the zeppelin by the crazy name Raging Queen. Mindy reluctantly smiled.

Chapter Ten
One chance to escape
and only one shot

Something awful happened to Broomstick that day. In the instant when George and Kizee flew away in a hot air balloon during the storm, a spell of great magnitude hit like a lightning strike. Gracie and Eric were transported far away from Broomstick.

Maranda the White Fairy who was manipulating the events of the day used magic to banish Gracie and Eric from Broomstick. Maranda was ensuring Gracie would be completely out of her way if Kizee and George return with Zweig's magic wand.

Very early the next morning, Gracie Düben found herself standing in the middle of Golden Gate Park in San Francisco. She was soaking wet and completely delusional. "Curse you Eric Braun!" Gracie yelled out for no apparent reason.

Not too far from Gracie was a man sleeping in a cardboard shelter hidden in the overgrown bushes. He was awoken by a loud thunderclap.

Looking out from his shelter he saw Gracie standing there. He stumbled out from the bushes toward Gracie.

"I've seen that look before," he called out to Gracie.

Gracie was rubbing her face with her hands trying to clear the cobwebs from her brain. She turned and stared at the homeless man.

"What did you say?"

The man repeated himself, "I said, I have seen that look before."

"What look?"

"The look of bewilderment after you have been banished from the magical world," said the homeless man.

"I…I haven't…No! Wait, where am I?"

"Aha, I'm right. You don't where you are."

Gracie squeezed some water out of her hair. "Would you tell me where I am?"

"Why don't you tell me where you were?" asked the man.

"Where I was, was in a field just outside of Broomstick."

"This is Golden Gate Park in…"

"SAN FRANCISCO!" yelled Gracie. "No, no, no…this isn't happening. My brother was taken by a young witch up into the sky. Eric is missing. And…and I'm soaking wet from the rain storm. I am NOT in San Francisco!"

"Oh, but you are. My name is Randle. I didn't catch your name," said the homeless man.

"I didn't tell it."

Randle was well over six feet tall and strong as an ox with a gentle mannerism. "Well…"

Gracie looked up at this homeless man. "Gracie, Gracie Düben."

The homeless man stared at Gracie. "Wait right here."

He shuffled back into his cardboard shelter. A minute later he came out waving a section of newspaper.

"You're Gracie Düben of Düben fashions!"

"Well yes." This gave Gracie an idea. "If you help me, I will help you. You said I was banished from the magical world. What do you know about the magical world?"

"Wait here."

Randle again shuffled into his cardboard shack. When he came out, Randle was holding dry clothes and a book.

"Let start by getting you out of those wet clothes. Public restrooms are over there," said Randle.

Gracie took the clothes and went to the women's restroom. She pulled the oversized shirt over her head and tied up the excess material. The pants were snug but at least they were dry. The shoes were worn, but they fit.

Gracie noticed she didn't have anything in her pockets. "That figures, no keys. No money. No credit cards. And no driver's license"

Gracie walked back to Randle. "I can't pay you for these clothes or even buy you breakfast."

"Stick with me. I'll get us some breakfast and you can tell me what happen to your brother," said Randle.

That morning at breakfast in a skid row soup kitchen, Gracie told Randle her story of moving to Broomstick.

"...So, we were in this field on the outskirts of Broomstick. Eric was helping George with the reenactment of Ben Franklin's kite experiment, when all of a sudden Kizee grabs George and pulls him out into the middle of the thunder storm. She points her wand at the sky. A bolt of lightning struck the wand. Instantly they were flying straight up into the storm in a hot air balloon."

"And now you're here the next morning in San Francisco. Hem, someone doesn't want you in Broomstick anymore," said Randle as he shuffled through a burlap bag.

After he had pulled something from the bag, Randle said, "I have something for you. It's a book about the magical world."

Gracie read the book cover aloud, "Knotems guide to the magical world. What is a knotem?"

"You are a knotem. We are the not magical people, hence the name knotem. Don't just read it, study it. Learn the secrets to survive in their world."

"Where did you get this book?" asked Gracie.

"It was given to me by a stranger after I was banished," said Randle with his head hung low. "I've had nothing but bad luck since then. The book didn't help me, but I'm sure it will help you."

"Well it is time your luck to change," started Gracie.

"I figured it might be time, you, Gracie Düben of Düben Fashions showing up here at this moment."

"You believe it wasn't a coincident that I showed up in Golden Gate Park as to anywhere else in San Francisco?" queried Gracie.

"I've been in the magical world. This was done on purpose. Let me show you why."

Randle pulled out and showed Gracie a worn water spotted sketch pad. It was filled with clothing designs. Gracie understood what Randle meant.

Gracie whispered, "Listen, if you let me handle this, I will make you rich."

"What do I have to do?" questioned Randle.

"Help me get a hold of the fashion mogul Stephan Chambers. I need to use your sketches to get his attention. When the time is right, Düben fashions will manufacture you line of clothing. What would you say to seventy-five twenty-five split?" said Gracie.

Over an intercom phone, the receptionist whispered, "There are two homeless looking people to see you. The woman says she is Gracie Düben. Should I call security?"

Stephen Chambers hung up the phone and came right out. "That is by far the worst fashion statement I've have ever seen from Düben Fashions."

Gracie smirked, "And hello to you."

"Come on in and introduce me to your husky bodyguard."

Inside Stephen's office, Gracie tried to explain her predicament without saying 'magical world'. It was very difficult.

"I need an advance to get back to Broomstick to start production. Here is my collateral."

Gracie showed Randle's sketches to Stephen.

"Well, these are good. You said Randle here designed these? You are truly a starving artist. And you're going to manufacture them in this little town of Broomstraw?"

"It's Broomstick, and yes."

"What if I made you an offer to buy your designs outright," said Stephen.

Gracie lied to Stephen, "Well, I estimate this line would gross sixteen million in the first year,"

"I don't think you have the staffing to keep up with the demand in Boomstuck, Seven million."

"It's Broomstick. I can have this line up and running and in stores by black Friday. Twelve million." bolstered Gracie.

"Hemp, I can do better, Labor Day weekend. Ten million and not a penny more," said Stephen.

"Ten million with Randle's name on the label also, and a job overseeing the production."

"You push a hard bargain, Gracie. Very well Ten million with Randle on the label and a job."

Gracie borrowed a car and driver from Stephen. Randle went shopping and found a townhouse for rent cash with no questions asked while Gracie did some digging on the town of Broomstick.

"I know a woman that clams to be a witch. She has done some very strange things I can't to this day explain how she did them," said Randle.

"Where I could find this witch?" asked Gracie.

"She lives over in North Berkley off of telegraph road. She has an herbal shop over there. You'll be able to find it easy enough," said Randle.

Gracie walked up the street of shops not exactly knowing what she was looking for. Squeaking in the breeze was a sign that read 'Witch's Brew Herbal Shop'.

Gracie tried to peer in through the old dirty window. It was too dark to make out anything inside. She grabbed the old brass doorknob turned and pushed the door open. The door stuck ever so slightly, but when it did give way an old fashion bell began to ring.

The air was musty with the smell of incense burning. Gracie scanned through the book section. The book shelves were full of books on magic from A to Z.

"Looking for a particular title?" asked the woman that appeared behind the counter.

"I'm not really looking for a book, just information," said Gracie feeling out of place.

"Perhaps a tarot card or a palm reading?" asked the woman.

"No, I need to find someone and I was told you might be able to help me. I'm looking for a witch by the name of Agnes," stated Gracie.

"Hee, hee," laughed the woman. "I need more information than that if I am to help you."

"She may live in a small town in the middle of the country just off the interstate. She has a sister by the name of Harriet. Does that help?" asked Gracie not wanting to give too much information out.

The woman nodded her head back and forth with her hand on her chin. "Hem, it almost sounds like you are referring to the town of Broomstick. It isn't really a small town, it just feels that way."

Gracie pulled out a map and with a magic marker. "Can you show me where this town is?"

The woman pointed at the map. "This is where you will find the exit to Shadow Creek Valley. Follow the road signs. Just stay on this road no matter what condition it is in. It passes through Witchaven and Shadow Creek. You will come to a fork in the road. To the left is back to the interstate. To the right is to Broomstick," explained the woman.

Gracie drew on the map with the magic marker. "How far does Broomstick extend, say this way?" said Gracie as she pointed at the map.

"Oh, you don't want to go there. The national forest in that area is inhibited by the worst of magical creatures you can imagen," said the old woman.

Gracie got what she wanted, another way in. She folded up the map and put it in his pocket. "Listen, I feel like I should pay you for your time. What does a card reading cost?"

"Let me see your hands," asked the woman.

She started to trace out Gracie life line, but quickly pulled her finger back. The tip of her finger was blistered.

"You can keep your money. Anything you touch will have your black magic curse upon it," said the woman sucking on the end of her blistered finger.

"What black magic curse are you talking about?" asked Gracie.

"Your life has been changed by a powerful black magic curse. Perhaps what you are seeking in Broomstick is not what you expect to find," said the woman.

Gracie felt really creped out by this woman. She backed out of the store.

At the townhouse, Gracie pulled out maps of where Gracie remembered where the town of Broomstick was located. One particular map was a U.S. Geological Survey map showing the national forest.

"Whoever it was that banished me from Broomstick, will be expecting me to take the off ramp from the interstate. There must be another way into that area," said Gracie as she studied the maps.

And there it was a hiking trail right into Broomstick through the national forest.

The day had come for Gracie to head out on her trek to Broomstick. "It's been a fast three days, but I think I am ready to meet the challenges the magical world can throw at me."

The last thing Gracie said to Randle was, "Good luck with your new-found wealth and identity. Don't let the magical world take this away from you," said Gracie.

Later that day Randle was checking in for his overseas flight.

"Your passport please. Traveling on business or pleasure, Mr. Connors?"

"Business, I'm in the fashion business, primarily exotic clothing designs," said Randle.

"Any luggage?"

"Just one carry-on," answered Randle.

The customs inspector for the Philippine Islands stamped the passport twice and initialed it. "Have a good trip, Mr. Connors."

"Thank you, I will," said Randle Connors.

Gracie got out of the semi-truck on a two lane highway south of Shadow Creek Valley. With a GPS compass and the U.S. geological survey map for the area, Gracie with a full backpack headed into the wilderness to hike to Broomstick.

"Thanks for the ride. I hope that is enough money for your son's operation," said Gracie.

"You're an angle from Heaven. I didn't catch your name, Miss…" said the truck driver.

"Remember our promise, you never gave me a ride or ever saw me," said Gracie.

"Right, you're traveling incognito," said the truck driver.

The trail head was clearly marked with a U.S. Forestry sign. Gracie read the small print just above the permit box.

"All backpackers must have a wilderness permit. Maximum stay is fifteen days."

Gracie filled out the permit, but made sure she didn't press hard to transfer her bogus information onto their copy. Then she crinkled up the permit and rubbed it against the wood sign.

"That's good. They can't say I don't have a permit. They just can't read it," laughed Gracie as she stuffed the permit in her pocket.

Gracie knew it was a hundred miles of rough terrain to get to the back road into Broomstick. No one would be looking for her here and whatever blocked that interstate exit most likely wouldn't think of someone coming in the hard way.

Gracie put on her headphones and turned on music to pass the time. She hiked for hours without stopping until the sun went down and the forest turned dark.

Gracie set up camp and heated up a freeze-dried meal. Sounds from outside her camp didn't exactly sound like normal nocturnal animals.

Snarls and growls with gruff human voices called out to Gracie all night.

"You'll never find him. He's erased from existence."

"Go back to where you came from, Gracie."

Shadows moved around the trees. Creatures swooped down flying past her grabbing at her hair. Small creepy crawly things moved up and down her sleeping bag.

Randle told nightmarish stories of what to expect from the magical world. Gracie attempted to prepare herself for what was to come.

From her backpack, Gracie pulled out a can of outdoor insect killer spray.

"Take that you vermin," yelled Gracie as she sprayed randomly around her.

Squeals and shrieks pieced through the air as magical creatures scrambled away from Gracie.

Gracie could hear little voices yelling at her, "Burn witch burn."

Gracie got up the next morning packed up and headed out. She knew from last night she was on the right trail to Broomstick.

As Gracie got closer to the back road, bigger creatures were abounding. Slithering on the trail was a Gorgon. This was the upper torso of a woman with her lower portion of a snake.

"Turn back," hissed the Gorgon with her forked tongue licking the air.

"I've come too far to let a creature like you dictate what I should do," said Gracie.

Gracie had pulled out a long sharp double edge sword. With the swiftness of a swordsman in a horizontal attack, Gracie swung the blade around her head. The Gorgon dodged the sword and snapped at Gracie with her fanged teeth.

From behind Gracie, she heard rustling of the ground cover. She peered over her shoulder to see a second Gorgon. Gracie swung her sword in a crisscross maneuver to keep both Gorgons at bay.

The second Gorgon pulled back then leaped forward. Down came Gracie's sword and severed the Gorgon's head. Gracie pivoted and again wheeled her sword in a crisscross pattern. Stepping forward quickly Gracie cut the first creature into several sections as the sword cut.

To ensure both magical creatures were dead, Gracie shoved the sword down into their hearts.

Gracie stood there holding the sword in front of her waiting. The forest quieted down. Gracie stepped over the first Gorgon and continued her trek.

Five days and very sore muscles later, Gracie came to the end of the trail and stood on the old forgotten back road that was on the map. An old rusty metal sign pointed the direction toward Broomstick.

"Five miles," said Gracie reading the sign.

At one point, Gracie came upon an old wooden bridge. Standing on the bridge were three short hairy ugly looking creatures.

"Stop, it is forbidden to cross this bridge," said one of them.

Gracie looked at the three. "I expect you three must be Trolls?"

"Yes, and this is our bridge," said another Troll.

"And you three think you can stop me from crossing?" stated Gracie.

"That's right. No one is allowed to cross," said the third Troll.

Gracie didn't mix words with these creatures. She pulled out from the side of her backpack a short-handled pump action sawed off twelve-gauge shotgun.

"Do you know what this is?" asked Gracie.

The three Trolls looked at each other, then one spoke up, "Nope haven't got a clue."

"Well, let me introduce you to my little friend," said Gracie.

Gracie pulled the trigger. The first Troll exploded into a cloud of flying hair.

"Now I'm going to cross this bridge. Anyone that tries to stop me will get the same treatment," snarled Gracie.

Gracie took a step toward the bridge.

"Stop, no one is allowed to cross this bridge," said the second Troll.

"Are you that stupid?" said Gracie. "I haven't got time for this."

Gracie pulled the trigger. The second Troll exploded into a cloud of flying hair. Not wasting any more time. Gracie shot the third Troll into oblivion.

Standing on the bridge, Gracie made a three sixty circle with her shotgun.

"Anyone else out there wants to try to stop me?" yelled Gracie.

Little voices rang out all around her. "Nooo."

"Good, let's keep it that way," said Gracie.

Gracie was walking by the iron fence that surrounded the town's cemetery. The scene was eerie with low clinging vapor at the ground. All the trees were naked of leaves with their limbs swaying back and forth in the breeze. Dark clouds painted the sky behind them.

Gracie could see ghosts lurking around headstones peering at her with devilish eyes. In ghostly voices Gracie could hear with high and low pitch changes, "Gooooooo baaaaaaaack. Neverrrrrrr reeeeetuuuuurrrrn."

Up the block from the cemetery Gracie stopped. There was a corner mall with a bakery, with a florist shop at the end.

Gracie walked into the bakery. She could smell the aroma of fresh baked bread. Gracie inhaled and for a moment she felt peacefully at home.

"Well, hello," said Mr. Olsen.

"Hello. Am I in Broomstick?" asked Gracie wanting to make sure.

"You sure are. Where did you hike in from?" asked Mr. Olsen feeling a little nervous with Gracie in his shop.

"Just south of here through a disquieting forest," answered Gracie. "Could you help me? I'm looking for Harriet Wisestone."

"Harriet Wisestone?" asked Mr. Olsen while thinking of that little black witch, which had turned all his truffles into fanged monsters.

"I don't know exactly where she lives," said Gracie.

"Ah well I can't help you," said Mr. Olsen hoping Gracie would just leave.

"Harriet is a witch," said Gracie.

"Oh, is she? Most likely a very nice witch," suggested Mr. Olsen trying to be polite.

"Are you related?" asked Mr. Olsen.

"No, just a friend," said Gracie.

Behind Gracie taped on the wall was a wanted poster with her picture on it. It said: "Wanted for murder of magical forest creatures. Anyone caught helping her will be severely punished."

Mr. Olsen's eyes suddenly grew large with horror. Gracie turned around to see what he was looking at. Outside coming up the street were two huge Centaurs.

"Quick, follow me," said Mr. Olsen.

Gracie followed Mr. Olsen into the back of the bakery. He led her to the back alley.

Mr. Olsen whispered in Gracie's ear. "You should be looking for Agnes McDermit. You must find her soon. She is your only chance of surviving here in Broomstick."

Gracie peered at Mr. Olsen as she started to walk down the alley.

"Run, run quickly," exclaimed Mr. Olsen.

One rule Gracie read in the Knotem's Guide to the Magical World was, "Bigger the monster, the bigger the weapon you will need."

Gracie was making her way through town by way of back alleys and small streets. She would stop and look around corners before proceeding.

At one corner was her wanted poster she didn't see in the bakery. "Wanted for murder? Those Centaurs mean business."

Gracie pulled off her backpack. Out of it she pulled out a single shot black powder door buster. Gracie loaded it with the only three-inch iron ball she had carried those hundred miles.

"One shot, Two Centaurs. That is all I got if I get into trouble," Gracie thought.

Gracie went up one street and down another. Gracie didn't know what she was looking for. She just went with her gut feeling of which way felt right.

Eventually Gracie made her way through a quiet neighborhood with old style homes. She stopped in front of one particular house.

"Finally a familiar sight," said Gracie.

The house was dark. The front yard was weeded over in need of care. Gracie stepped up onto the porch. She took off her backpack and tried the door.

The door was unlocked, but the door was hard to open. Gracie gave it a push with her shoulder. She tried a light switch. "No electricity."

Gracie got out her flashlight and headed into the house. A layer of dust covered the furniture. In the living room Gracie picked up a picture frame from the fireplace mantle. Gracie blew the dust off the picture. Gracie carried it into the kitchen and found a dirty towel.

Gracie shook out the towel making a cloud of dust. "Cough, cough," went Gracie.

Gracie held the flashlight between her jaw and shoulder. She wiped off the glass of the picture frame.

"George, where are you?" said Gracie.

The picture was of George and Gracie at a baseball game with Eric and Kizee.

Gracie walked into George's bedroom. She began to rummage through his stuff. "Where is that old book?"

That is when Gracie found the flash drive with the note stuck to it. "In case something goes wrong. Well, George something did go wrong."

Outside Gracie heard the clomping of horse hoofs. "The Centaurs!" exclaimed Gracie.

Gracie realized she had set down the black powder door buster on the porch next to her backpack. Gracie slipped the flash drive into her pocket. Quickly she made her way to the front door. Gracie crouched down and reached out to grab the gun.

Gracie pulled it back in and held it close to her chest. Gracie was breathing hard with panic as her sword and handheld shotgun were still in her backpack on the porch.

"One shot, I have only one shot," Gracie kept repeating to herself.

Gracie crawled through the dusty house to find the back door. "One chance to escape and only one shot," said Gracie.

Chapter Eleven
The Broomstick Scandal

Eric Braun also disappeared that day of the rainstorm. He was sitting in his car on the side of the interstate the next day when he came out of his hazy dreamlike foggy mental state. Eric, the car seat, and the floor mat were soaking wet from the event of the day before.

Eric stood on the side of the interstate where the exit to Shadow Creek Valley was supposed to be.

Eric took a bold step. He climbed over the guard rail leaving his car behind and started walking in the direction of where the road should be to Shadow Creek.

Eric trudged through tall grass and weeds with clinging stickers that were poking through his clothes. Walking was difficult as something was grabbing his ankles.

Eric fell below the tall grass. Long strands of vines wrapped around his legs and arms.

"Help! Help!" Eric called out.

There was no one around to hear him.

Eric was being dragged through the grass and weeds with dirt flinging about. Suddenly Eric was thrown out of the grassy field up against the guard rail at the interstate where he left his car.

Eric lay there by the guard rail scratched and bruised. He raised one arm and pulled himself up into a leaning position against the guard rail.

Eric looked out over the grassy field. "Something or someone surely doesn't want that road to be found."

Eric climbed back into his car and drove away. At a truck stop he cleaned his wounds and thought of his next move.

Eric asked a truck driver, "Where do you exit to get to Shadow Creek?"

"You passed the exit about ten miles back," said the truck driver.

Eric stared at the truck driver, but didn't say a word. "Someone made that exit disappear," Eric thought to himself.

After spending a couple of nights in a roadside hotel recovering from his painstaking ordeal, Eric had a plan. He went to a local hardware store and bought some required items.

Eric made his way back to the place on the interstate where the exit should be. From the trunk of his car, Eric pulled out a heavy jacket and pants with boots and work gloves.

Next Eric pulled out a gas powered weed whacker. He used duct tape to tape a large bottle of weed killer to it.

Over the guard rail, Eric went with determination to push his way through this treacherous grassy field. He started the weed whacker and began to mow his way through. At times Eric would spray weed killer ahead of him to ensure nothing would grab his legs.

Whipping the weed whacker back and forth, Eric moved at a quick pace through the field. After about a half mile Eric saw what he was looking for.

The asphalt road laid in front of Eric like the yellow brick road in the land of Oz. Behind him was the terrible field all grown back where he had cut a path.

"There's no turning back now," Eric said aloud.

Eric dropped the weed whacker and the heavy clothing on the side of the road and started walking.

It was a while before Eric came to a sign, "Witchaven three miles". The Sun was beaming down and Eric was getting thirsty. Eric could see the wavy lines of heat rising from the asphalt road.

"It's only three miles. I can make it," said Eric.

The quietness of the road was disturbed by an off in the distant sound of a diesel engine. Eric turned to see a truck coming toward him.

Eric stood at the side of the road waving his arms hoping the truck driver would stop. The truck got closer.

Franticly, Eric waved and started yelling. "Stop, please stop!"

The truck passed Eric without slowing down. Eric saw it was a tow truck and it was towing his car.

"Hey, that's my car. Wait, that's my car," yelled Eric as he ran after the tow truck.

Eric stopped running as it was no use. Then Eric saw the tow truck had stopped. Eric started running again.

Panting heavily Eric said, "Hey thanks for stopping,"

"I figured after I passed you that this might be your car," said the tow truck driver.

"It is my car," said Eric still panting.

"Well I'll get your car and you to the repair shop," said the tow truck driver.

Eric didn't say anything. He just smiled.

"I also picked up the road maintenance crew equipment that they left on the side of the road," said the tow truck driver making conversation.

Again, Eric didn't comment.

"You're heading to Witchaven or Shadow Creek when your car broke down?" asked the tow truck driver.

"Broomstick actually," answered Eric.

"Ever been to Broomstick before?" asked the tow truck driver.

Eric lied, "No, my first time coming this way,"

"You look familiar. A fellow that looked like you drove the Mayor of Broomstick's car into my repair shop about six months ago," stated the tow truck driver.

"The Mayor of Broomstick's car?" questioned Eric.

"Yep, looked just like you," said the tow truck driver.

"Sorry, it wasn't me," said Eric.

At the repair shop, Eric was told, "It's going to be three days before your new radiator arrives."

For the next three days Eric stayed at a cheap hotel. He tried to phone Gracie multiple times "Still no answer. What could have happened to her?"

Late in the afternoon Eric paid the tow truck driver his price gouging rate for the tow and the new radiator apparently he needed.

"Just keep on this road straight through Shadow Creek until you come to the fork in the road. Stay to your left to head to Broomstick. To your right takes you back to the interstate," said the tow truck driver.

"That isn't what I remember," thought Eric. "Thanks for the directions," said Eric.

"Now why wasn't he telling me the truth?" thought Eric.

In Shadow Creek, Eric stopped for a late lunch. He decided to try asking one more time which direction it is to Broomstick. Eric asked the waitress.

"Excuse me I need to make sure I'm heading in the right direction. At the fork do I go left or right to get back to the interstate?" asked Eric.

"Keep to your left. You don't want to go right," said the waitress.

"What's to the right?" asked Eric.

"It's best you just steer clear of that town. Nothing but trouble comes out of there," said the waitress.

"Well okay then, I'll take your advice. Stay to the left back to the interstate," said Eric.

When Eric came upon the fork in the road he went to the right. After a couple of miles there was a sign, "Broomstick fifty miles". An hour later Eric passed another sign, welcome to Broomstick. A tingly sensation of déjà vu passed through Eric's body.

Eric went straight to his apartment for a long shower and change of clothes. Instead he found someone else living in his apartment.

"I received this letter from you that you had left town and won't be coming back," stated the apartment manager.

"Where are my things?" asked Eric.

"The apartment was empty," said the apartment manager.

Eric left the apartment building and went to the Moonset Four Star Hotel that was in the downtown area of Broomstick.

"Single room, double bed," said Eric setting down a credit card.

"How long will you be staying Mr. Braun?" asked the desk clerk.

Eric stared at the desk clerk for a long moment before answering, "Ah, not more than a week."

Then Eric thought this might be a good time to start asking about Kizee. "Perhaps you could help me with contacting...a young girl by the name of Kizee Wisestone?"

"The daughter of Harriet Wisestone I'm not sure she is still around," stated the desk clerk with hesitation in his voice.

"Did she move away?" asked Eric.

"No, she disappeared in the lightning storm that passed through here a week ago along with a boy. I'm sorry, here is your room key," said the desk clerk.

Eric settled into his overpriced room for the night thinking about the events since the lightning storm.

"What in the world is going on?" questioned Eric with shattered nerves.

Eric turned on the television for background noise.

"We interrupt this program to bring you breaking news. Live on the scene is our reporter Maranda Nymph."

"It appears that two horses had gotten loose and wondered into this house. The occupant of the home panicked and shot one of the horses dead. The shot must have frightened the other horse which may have caused the collapse of the house upon the horse."

Eric shouted aloud, "That's Gracie's house!"

Eric got dressed and ran down to his car. He drove over to Gracie's house only to find Agnes, Harriet and the Sheriff.

On the other side of town, known as the Troll District was a crummy dive called the Root Cellar. This was the place where dirty rotten scum of the magical world went to mingle.

This is what they heard as the breaking news story. "Live on the scene is our reporter Maranda the Tree Nymph."

"Two Centaurs had tracked down the forest murderer Gracie Düben to her house. Gracie Düben shot one of the Centaurs dead. The other Centaur was killed when the booby-trapped house collapse upon him. Gracie Düben must be found before she kills again. There is a ten thousand wizen bounty on Gracie Düben."

Snarls and jeers were heard through the Root Cellar of capturing Gracie Düben.

Gracie was sitting on the floor at the back door. "One chance to escape and only one shot," said Gracie.

The Centaur at the front door picked up Gracie's backpack and sniffed it. He threw it to the street just before he turned around. With his hind legs, he began to kick at the door and frame. Slivers of wood flew through the house with each kick.

Gracie knew the Centaur couldn't maneuver inside the house because of his size. She waited until he was inside to make her move.

When the kick against the living room wall reverberated through the walls, Gracie scrambled out the back door.

To her surprise, the other Centaur was waiting in the back yard. Gracie pushed up against the house wall. She put the butt of the door buster gun against the wall underneath her arm.

The Centaur moved toward Gracie. Just at the right moment, Gracie aimed the large black powder gun at the Centaur and pulled the trigger.

The three inch ball flew out the barrel with a loud report. The ball hit the Centaur square in the chest. Blood, guts and flesh splattered everywhere. The Centaur hind legs buckled. He fell down on his tail just before falling over.

Gracie ran from the backyard past the garage to the front yard. She saw her backpack lying in the street. She picked it up as she ran by and threw it over her shoulder. Gracie continued running. She ran fast and as far away from her house as she could.

Gracie turned her head and took a quick looked back to see if the other Centaur was coming after her. The loud creak and snap followed by the crushing sound of timber rushed out of Gracie's house as it collapsed down on the Centaur.

Gracie didn't stop running. She knew at the very least that gave her a head start of finding a place to hide. Up the street from her house, Gracie came to an intersection. An idea suddenly popped into her brain.

"That it's! This way is to downtown Broomstick. I'll hide in the back alleys," said Gracie.

Gracie slowed down from a run to a steady fast hiking stride. It was about an hour of steady walking when Gracie ducted into an alley.

About half way down the alley Gracie stopped. Behind a big blue dumpster, Gracie pulled out of her back pack a very large black shroud that had a waist rope and hood. Next, she pulled out a bottle of white vinegar.

Gracie dribbled the white vinegar all over the black shroud. Not enough to dampen it, but just enough to have the smell soak in.

"The book Randle gave me said a black shroud doused with white vinegar works as an invisibility shield to all magical creatures. Let's hope the book is right," said Gracie.

The book Gracie was referring to was "Knotems Guide to the Magical World". Hopefully Gracie understood the term magical creatures do not refer to witches, wizards and little magical people like fairies and pixies.

Gracie slid the straps of the backpack over her shoulders then wrapped the vinegar laced black shroud around her. Just in case this didn't work, Gracie pulled out her sword and belted it around her. Gracie slid into the belt her hand held shotgun.

Gracie kept to the back alleys as she looked for a cubbyhole to hide in for the night until she could come up with her next move on finding Agnes.

Gracie found an old storage shed behind an herbal health shop that had an unlocked weather worn lock that looked as if it had been forgotten to be locked for some time. She slipped inside and closed the door tight. From her backpack, Gracie pulled out a flashlight and her sleeping bag. With the black shroud wrapped around the sleeping bag, Gracie settled down for a long night sleep lying on some burlap sacks.

Franklin burst into the house shouting, "Agnes! I'm glad I found you. Something is happening on the other side of town. News is that two Centaurs were tracking Gracie Düben for the murder of magical creatures."

Agnes went to Gracie's house. She found the town sheriff standing in the backyard of Gracie's house that had collapsed.

Lying on the ground was a dead Centaur with a gapping bloody hole where his chest used to be.

"I'm not sure I know how to write this, Agnes. I mean come on I am not supposed to be investigating magical crimes even when a knotem is involved," said the Sheriff.

"How do you know a knotem was involved?" asked Agnes.

The Sheriff pointed at the large wound in the Centaur's chest. "Now follow me."

Eric came up next to Harriet during the conversation. He whispered to Harriet, "What's a knotem?"

"A non-magical person like yourself and Gracie," said Harriet.

"Gracie couldn't have done this, could she?" asked Eric.

Agnes followed the Sheriff over to the back porch. Lying on the porch was the door buster gun Gracie left behind.

"That is not a magical instrument. That is an old fashion black powder gun used at short range to blow locks off of heavy doors," said the Sheriff.

"Why do you think a knotem shot the gun?" asked Agnes.

The Sheriff pulled from his pocket a folded paper. He unfolded it and handed it to Agnes.

"A wanted poster for Gracie Düben for killing magical creatures?" questioned Agnes.

"Do you know who she is?" asked the Sheriff.

"I know her," answered Agnes.

"I also know her Sheriff," said Eric.

"And who are you?" asked the Sheriff.

"I'm Eric Braun and Gracie Düben is my friend," said Eric.

"Your friend is a violent armed psychopath running around Broomstick?" stated the Sheriff.

"No, no she isn't violent… uh, until now I guess. Why do you suppose she shot this Centaur?" asked Eric.

"These two Centaurs are bounty hunters. It appears to me they were after her," told the Sheriff.

"Two Centaurs, where is the other?" asked Agnes.

"He knocked down the house of top of him," said the Sheriff while pointing at the rescue crew trying to raise a portion of the roof.

"Any clues you could give me to find her would be very helpful. I got to take her into custody for her own protection," said the Sheriff.

"I agree we need to find her before any other bounty hunters come, pardon the expression, galloping into town," said Agnes.

"Sheriff," called out one of the rescue workers.

The Sheriff walked over to the rescue worker. At first, they whispered to each other before the Sheriff called out to everyone there.

"Alright suspend the rescue mission. We'll let the magical community clean up their own mess," said the Sheriff.

"What is it Sheriff?" asked Agnes.

"The other Centaur is dead. A support beam smashed in his skull. I suggest you find this woman fast before she really becomes my problem. If one of us knotems is killed, you know what I have to do," said the Sheriff.

"Yes, I know Sheriff," said Agnes.

After the Sheriff and the recue team left, Agnes turned to Eric. "What happened out in that field last week and where have you been?"

Eric described the scene of Kizee and George running out into the middle of the field. "Then she held up her magic wand. George was holding onto the broom. When the lightning struck, the broom turned into a hot air balloon with them inside the basket."

"What happen to you and Gracie?" asked Harriet.

"I found myself sitting in my car up on the interstate where the exit was supposed to be for Broomstick. Only it wasn't there," explained Eric.

"Why are Centaurs bounty hunters looking for Gracie?" asked Eric.

"We won't know until we find her," said Agnes.

Gracie woke up the next morning still wrapped in the black shroud that was laced with white vinegar to hide her from the magical world that she has found herself in.

Gracie pulled out from her backpack the well-worn book "Knotem's Guide to the Magical World". Gracie had read and re-read it many times since Randle gave it to her.

Gracie thumbed through the little tabs she had put in places within the book until she came to the one marked "How to contact someone in the magical world". Two main categories had tabs. The first was "The magic telephone" and the second was "SNARF Mail".

Gracie read, "The magic telephone. You must use a rotatory phone and just dial Q. Q? There isn't any Q on a rotatory phone. Stupid magical world."

Gracie read next the paragraph that discussed the unusual mail service.

"SNARF Mail, Selfish, Nerdy, Arrogant, Rude Fairies that deliver messages around the magical world. To find a SNARF Mail station, look in a garden or in places of business in the preter-normal district. A fairy dressed in wild color clothing will be sitting there patiently waiting for a letter. They don't do packages. Cost is one wizen, which is a magical world gold coin. Knotems have been known to use U.S. mint gold dollars or gold wrapped chocolate coins."

"Great, just walk into a store full of magical people to find a SNARF Mail station. With all the wanted posters with my face on it, I might as well just yell out my name and ask everyone there if they know Agnes McDermit," said Gracie after reading the paragraph.

Gracie packed up her stuff back into her backpack except for the black shroud. She tied the rope belt around her waist hiding her handheld shotgun and sword.

With the hood pulled over her head, Gracie left her backpack in the shed and ventured out into Broomstick in search of food and a SNARF Mail station.

A few city blocks from the alley where the shed was, Gracie found the Ex-Press Coffee Shop where she had worked. No one in the shop paid her any special attention like she would have expected wearing the black shroud, except one.

"Why are you dressed like the Black Fairy? Uh, never mind. What can I get you?" asked the girl behind the counter.

"That was an unexpected question. If the shroud works that way, I'm good with it," thought Gracie.

"A large coffee and a breakfast sandwich with cheese," ordered Gracie.

After getting her order, Gracie sat down at a corner table with her back to the wall. On the opposite side of the coffee shop sitting near the coffee condiments was a small little person with wings.

"I've never seen her in here when I was working," thought Gracie.

The fairy had shoulder length straw colored hair that needed brushing. Her face had round blush red checks that ballooned out with a button nose and a straight lined lip mouth.

Gracie went over to the girl behind the counter and asked, "Is that a SNARF fairy?"

The girl looked over to where Gracie was pointing at. "Yeah that's one of those snot nose, potty mouth, pain in the rear..." The girl was interrupted by a loud voice.

"Hey Katee Greene, I heard that!" said the SNARF fairy as she threw a liquid creamer cup at them.

"Wow, she has a temper," said Gracie.

The SNARF fairy threw another creamer cup at them.

Gracie walked over to the SNARF fairy. "Hey, hey settle down little one."

"Why should I? You heard what she called me," said the SNARF fairy.

"That is interesting. You can see me. You're not supposed to be able to," said Gracie.

"And why shouldn't I be able to see you?" rudely asked the SNARF fairy.

"Because I have a shroud to make me invisible to magical creatures," answered Gracie.

Oh, did the SNARF fairy really get mad then. She started throwing stir sticks at Gracie while yelling, "I AM NOT A MAGICAL CREATURE!!!"

Gracie backed up, dodging the stir sticks. "Oh sorry, I didn't know," said Gracie.

"You're sorry. Sorry, sorry, sorry. Humph," said the SNARF fairy as she crossed her arms and turned away from Gracie.

"Listen I was just asking if you were a SNARF fairy because I need to send a letter to a witch," said Gracie.

"Purple nail polish, red lipstick and Chanel perfume with a sincere apology first," said the SNARF fairy.

Gracie stared at the little fairy with a weird expression. She didn't ask the obvious.

Instead Gracie walked over Kate Greene at the counter. "Um, yeah...I don't suppose you could help me out with ah, what the little lady asked for."

"Just so happens we have that behind the counter just for little Miss nas..." Gracie stopped Katee Greene from saying what she was about to say.

"Please I need her cooperation really bad," said Gracie.

"Here, and you'll need a couple of these as well," said Katee.

Gracie looked at the little items along with the two gold coins. "Are these wizens?" asked Gracie.

"Yeah, it's alright. Maybe you could work a shift or two for me," said Katee.

"Yeah okay, after I clean up the mess I'm in," answered Gracie.

Gracie walked back over to the SNARF fairy. Holding her hand out with the items she requested, Gracie said, "I sincerely apologize for any remarks that offended you. Please accept these gifts as a token of redemption."

The SNARF fairy turned back toward Gracie and picked up the three items. "Alright, now who do you want to send a letter to?" asked the SNARF fairy.

"Agnes McDermit," said Gracie.

Instead of going straight to Agnes with the letter, the little SNARF fairy went to the Root Cellar instead. She sat down the two wizens she received from Gracie.

"Fairy nectar and leave the bottle," said Franzel.

"Now what is a little SNARF fairy doing down here," said a Troll.

"Humph, that Katee Greene and her new friend called me a snot nose magical creature."

"You're pretty steamed about that, eh? What's your name little fairy?" asked the Troll.

"Franzel."

"Franzel, what is Katee Greene's new friend's name?" asked the Troll.

"No one important, just a knotem looking for Agnes McDermit," said Franzel.

"Her name!"

"Okay, okay, you don't have to get rude about it. It is here on the letter," said Franzel.

The Troll opened the letter and read it to his buddies and anyone else that was listening.

> *"Agnes McDermit,*
>
> *I need to meet with you. I am in real danger. I am under a terrible black magic spell. Someone has taken my brother away from me and I don't know why. Help me. I'll meet you on Wednesday at one pm in the park by the statue with the V cut in the top.*
>
> > *Lost in time,*
> > *Gracie Düben."*

"How very touching," said the Troll.

Then the Troll said, "Look boys we know where Gracie Düben will be tomorrow."

"Hey, give it back. I still have to deliver that letter," said Franzel.

"Here, deliver this one instead," said the Troll as he wrote another letter.

Around the town square where Gracie was waiting on Wednesday to see if Agnes would show up was a billboard advertising a new line of clothing. On the ground was a flyer that also depicted a special event of a new clothing store opening.

"Edna's Fashion Boutique featuring Stephan Chambers' new collection? Those dirty double crossing... He said no sooner than Labor Day," said Gracie steaming hot mad rubbing the trigger of her handheld shotgun.

Gracie forgot the reason why she was in the square. She went back to the shed where her stuff was to plot a new plan to get even with Stephan Chamber.

The town square clock bell tolled one. The Trolls were right there on time jumping out of bushes and off of tree branches. They looked around. Gracie Düben was nowhere to be found.

"We been double crossed by that little SNARF fairy," said the Troll that led the mob.

Agnes and Harriet were at the Hidden Quiddity Potion Shop finishing up on deliveries and waiting for information from Mindy and Searat if they had discovered where Kizee and George had gone.

It was about four in the afternoon when Agnes went over to the window where a SNARF fairy was waiting for her. She slid open the window to let the fairy in.

"There is a knotem looking for you," said the SNARF fairy politely to Agnes.

Agnes took the note and handed the SNARF fairy a ten wizen gold coin. "Thank you Franzel," said Agnes.

"Why is it you get treated nicely by those little vermin with wings? And on top of that, you know their names," said Harriet.

"Respect those little magical people and they will respect you," said Agnes as she opened the note.

Agnes McDermit,

> *I am dangerous. Don't use any black magic spells.*
> I will kill more magical creatures unless you meet
> my demands. *I'll meet you on Wednesday at one pm*
> *in the park by the statue with the V cut in the top.*
> > *Magical creature killer,*
> > *Gracie Düben.*

Agnes read the note aloud to Harriet. Then she said, "Franzel! This letter has been tampered with. What was the real message?"

"Um, Gracie is in danger and needs your help. The Trolls changed the message," said Franzel.

"Now what do you think of those little people now, Agnes?" questioned Harriet while staring at the SNARF fairy who was stepping out onto the windowsill getting ready to fly away.

"Not so fast, you little mail snail. Freeze!" said Harriet while pointing a finger at Franzel.

Agnes walked over to the window. "When and where did you get this note?"

"It was yesterday, at the Ex-Press Coffee Shop. She called me a magical creature and gave me two wizens she borrowed from that nasty pixie person, Katee Greene. I didn't know it was time sensitive," said the SNARF fairy frozen to her gold coin.

"Harriet, let her go. If you get any other notes, don't wait. Bring them straight to me no matter where I'm at, is that clear?" said Agnes to the SNARF fairy.

"Yes Mrs. McDermit," said the SNARF fairy just before she flew away.

"I still don't get it. You chew her out and still she shows you respect," said Harriet shaking her head.

"You finish up here. I got to go and talk to Katee Greene," said Agnes.

Agnes quietly materialized in front of the Ex-Press Coffee Shop. Katee Greene had a skinny pumpkin spice latte waiting for Agnes when she walked through the door.

"Good afternoon Agnes. How did your meeting with Gracie go yesterday?" asked Katee.

"It didn't go well at all. We didn't get the message until a few minutes ago. If you knew she was looking for me why didn't you contact me instead of letting her use SNARF mail?" asked Agnes.

"She came in here wearing a black hooded shroud covered with vinegar. I thought she was doing something for you and wanted to hide from magical creatures that would give her away," said Katee.

Katee turned her head over to where the SNARF fairy normally sat. "Humph, maybe that is why she didn't show up today."

"Do you know where I can find Gracie? She is in real trouble," said Agnes holding out the wanted poster put out by the magical creatures that live in and around Broomstick.

"There is one clue I noticed. In her hair was a smidgen of Dragon Nose Hair Ash," said Katee.

"There is only one place that uses Dragon Nose Hair Ash in Broomstick. So how did Gracie get a smidgen of it in her hair? Unless she was sleeping on top of the burlap sacks," suggested Agnes.

"Was Gracie hiding out at Sagan's Herbal Pharmacy?" queried Katee.

"The clue you gave suggest she was somewhere around there," said Agnes as she vanished from the coffee shop.

The small bell tinkled when Agnes opened the old wood door to the herbal pharmacy. The wood floor creaked as she walked to the counter.

Behind the counter was a menagerie of glassware from Doctor Frankenstein's laboratory. On the far side was a wide wood chopping block with an assortment of cleavers and knives.

Standing there in a white lab coat was an elderly man with thinning white hair chopping herbs and tossing them into a bubbling metal pot sitting on a burner.

"Be right with you Agnes," said Sagan.

"A couple more heavy chops with the cleaver on this willow branch. Next, toss it into the metal pot," said Sagan out loud as he picked up an egg timer and set it for twenty three seconds.

"Now what can I do for you, kind lady?" asked Sagan.

Agnes pulled out the wanted poster and held it up for Sagan to examine. "By any chance are you allowing this young woman to reside in the back of your shop?"

Sagan took a long look at the picture. "I wish I were," said Sagan with a chuckle.

"Has she come into your shop in the last few days?" asked Agnes.

"No, no I would remember someone as nice looking as her. What is this about, Agnes?" asked Sagan.

"I'm trying to find her and the only clue I have to go on is Katee Greene noticed she had Dragon Nose Hair Ash in her hair and on the shroud, she was wearing," answered Agnes.

"I suspected someone took refuge in the storage shed in the alley when I found two empty vinegar bottles in there this morning," stated Sagan.

"Would you mind if I took a look in the shed for a clue where she might have gone to or if she might return?" queried Agnes.

"Go right ahead Agnes," said Sagan as the egg timer began to ring. "Oh, I have to tend to this. It's in the back alley if you don't mind going by yourself. You can use the back door to get there."

Agnes walked through the back of the shop to the back door that led to the alley. She found the door unlocked.

Agnes slowly opened the door to the shed. Inside the shed Agnes found Gracie siting there on the burlap sacks of Dragon Nose Hair Ash pointing a shotgun at her.

Chapter Twelve
Now or Never

Kizee stood there with her magic wand at the ready. She was waiting for George to give the word. They waited for the last minute to do this one bit of magic as it will attract the attention of Eric and Gracie.

"Are you sure you know how to operate one?" whispered George.

"My magic will tell me what to do," Kizee whispered back.

"Alright let's do it," whispered George.

Without any warning, Kizee with George ran out of the shed straight into the rain soaked field. Kizee pulled out her magic wand from inside her raincoat. George was holding onto Kizee's left hand with his right hand. In George's left hand was Kizee's magic broom.

In the sky Kizee could see the image of the lightning fairy glowing as she shot out a bolt of plasma. Kizee pointed her magic wand high up into the air. The lightning fairy's bolt hit straight on the tip of the magic wand. Kizee twirled her magic wand and chanted very loudly.

"Phase of the moon, silver spoon, raising a typhoon. I conjure up my broom to expand and consume. Present me with a hot air balloon!"

The wind whipped around the field with torment and vengeance of a hurricane hitting the Bermuda Triangle. Kizee and George were pulled up in the basket. The hot air balloon rose quickly up into the storm.

"How do we get there?" asked George yelling over the roar of the wind.

Kizee grimaced as she told George the answer. "We need to pass through a double rainbow in the most terrible of storms," answered Kizee.

"Which way do we go?" queried George.

Kizee pointed in a very dark direction, "That way into the storm."

George moved the sandbags from one side of the balloon to the other to tilt them in the direction they needed to travel.

"We need to keep a look out for the double rainbow. If we don't pass through them we'll be lost and won't be able find our way back," screamed Kizee over the wind.

"We're not stopping off in the land of Oz, are we?" asked George jokingly.

"No, to get to Oz one must go up through a tornado and pass over the rainbow," answered Kizee being serious.

"Yeah, only a witch would know that," said George.

For three days, the torrent wind whipped the hot air balloon like a junk car in a demolition derby being hit from two directions. George was holding on tight to the side of the basket.

"I have no idea how high we are," called out George.

"We're in between worlds," explained Kizee.

"Look over there, a break in the clouds and two rainbows," called out George.

Kizee grabbed onto sandbags to help George maneuver the hot air balloon toward the double rainbow. "Move those sandbags over to this side and shift all the weight to help," yelled Kizee.

George leaned out of the basket to give even more tilt to the balloon. He swung from one side to the other trying to guide the balloon in the right direction. The wind tossed the balloon through a roller coaster dive toward the double rainbow.

"Pull all the sandbags from that side quickly and put them over here. Whoa, put three back, now lean this way…!" yelled George.

The hot air balloon was on the edge of the right rainbow skimming through the double red edges of the double rainbow.

"Lean left! Lean left!" cried out George.

The wind blew the hot air balloon through the double rainbow straight into a dark storm cloud. Rain was hitting them on all sides. George was wiping the water off his face in an attempt to see where they were going. It didn't help. Everything was pitch-black with the exception of an occasional flash of lightning that momentarily blinded him.

Hours went by as George and Kizee struggled to keep the basket upright. By what George considered would be morning, Kizee's balloon came out on the other side of the black cloud into clear blue skies. The winds calmed down and the basket stopped rocking and rolling.

"Are you alright?" called out George as he looked over the balloon for damage.

Kizee answered, "Yeah, I'm alright. What about you? Oh George, your hands are bleeding!"

George's hands had rope burns and cuts from maneuvering the balloon through the double rainbow.

Kizee pulled a corked bottle from a small pouch she had tied to her waist. "Here, let me see your hands."

Kizee rubbed a healing suave into the palm of George's hands while whispering a healing spell.

"It will take a few treatments to heal them completely. For right now the pain should go away," said Kizee.

The healing suave allowed George to make repairs to the basket.

Looking down, all they could see was dark blue water. "We must be over an ocean," said George.

"We'll take turns on watch to sight land," stated Kizee.

For a full day and a half, they flew with the wind. Kizee made simple meals to keep them fed.

While George was on watch, Kizee handed George a cup of hot chocolate. She stood there next to him as he sipped it.

"I want you to know I understand it was wrong to use sunset flash on you. I'm sorry for that," said Kizee.

George stood there sipping his hot chocolate looking out at the horizon.

"Say something, even if you tell me you hate me. I understand the contempt you may have for me," said Kizee.

"Do you know what hurt more than you using magic on me?" asked George.

"Please tell me," said Kizee.

"The fact that you kept the secret about Maranda the White Fairy from me, after we pinky swore." exclaimed George still staring out at the horizon.

"You don't like magic, do you?" asked Kizee.

"Magic like any other power can corrupt. What assurances do I really have that you won't do this again to me?" said George.

"None I suppose."

"Let me ask you a question and I want the truth. Why are we here?" asked George.

"We are here to save my best friend from a fairy's spell," said Kizee.

"You're still holding onto that wish," said George.

"I have feelings for you as my best friend who accepted me for who I am. I would like them to grow into something more when we are old enough to understand what love really means," said Kizee.

"There wasn't any magic involved in the cemetery when I kissed you then. I just wanted to," said George.

"I was slow in understanding you didn't have any magical powers though," answered Kizee.

George asked, "We are going into a terrible place. Will you be doing black magic?"

"I'll use whatever magic I need to do to keep us safe," answered Kizee.

It was on Kizee's watch when something showed up on the horizon. "George, George, get up! There's something coming up on the horizon," exclaimed Kizee.

George got up and stood next to Kizee staring at the peak of a snow capped mountain rising up as they sailed closer to the magical land of Smether Realm.

"We must have a plan to travel through this land without being detected," said George.

"I can change both of us to look and speak like dark elves," said Kizee.

George asked, "What about hiding the balloon?"

"It is my broom after all, it is visible only to us," said Kizee.

George maneuvered the balloon coming low to the water and drifted in with on shore air flow. George pulled the vent valve on top of the balloon dropping the basket on the soft white sandy beach.

"Grab these ropes and guide the balloon canopy down to the ground as I let out the rest of the air," stated Kizee.

George jumped out of the basket and staked down the basket. Together they rolled up the balloon and stuffed it in the basket.

"You're sure no one will find our balloon," asked George for reassurance from Kizee.

"Absolutely, now let me get us changed to dark elves before someone comes along," answered Kizee.

They headed inland to find someone that could direct them to the cavern on the map. Dressed as dark elves, Kizee and George were both scared.

The trees were thick and over grown with vines and underbrush. The thin trial led away from the beach joined with a more traveled path.

"Do you smell food cooking?" asked George.

"We must be getting close to a village or something," said Kizee.

They came to where the wide path is now made with ruff cut granite. About a mile in front of them was an arch entrance with wide pillars. On top of the pillars were statues of a dark elf with a crown.

Other stone roads intersected at this point with wheeled carts drawn by animals George had never seen before. Dark elves were coming and going through this archway.

George and Kizee kept to the side of the road to keep from being run over. On the other side of the arch was a huge marketplace filled with shops and eateries.

"Where do you suppose, we should start looking for information?" queried George.

"My best guest would be where the not so nice elves congregate. Perhaps a place serving some sort of grog," suggested Kizee.

"We don't have any money," said George.

George felt a heavy weight appear in one of his pockets. He pulled out a small bag. In it were wizen coins with different denominations.

"We do now. All we have to do is watch to see what things cost," said Kizee.

George and Kizee made their way into a place that looked like a pub. George observed the custom of ordering drinks and how much it cost.

After getting two large mugs of whatever they were serving, George and Kizee sat down in a corner with their backs to the wall.

"The best bet would be to ask the tavern bar tender who could help us find this cavern shown on the map," whispered Kizee.

"Are you out of your mind? That would be like walking into a beehive and asking the queen bee, 'Where do you keep your honey? We want to steal some if you don't mind," said George.

"That's just it. They wouldn't suspect anyone to do something that crazy. Just don't start a fight," said Kizee.

George went back up to the bar. He got the bar tender's attention, "Anyone in here know of the caverns?"

The tavern bar tender pointed over to a table where a ruff looking dark elf was sitting, "If you want the best guide of the underground caverns, he be the one to talk to."

George looked over to where the tavern bar tender was pointing. The elf was sitting with three other unscrupulous elves that would rather slit your throat than to look at you.

George saw the bar tender's hand out. He gave the bar tender a twenty wizen gold piece. "Thanks."

George walked over to the table as cocky as he could to look tuff. George stood there just for a short second. He spoke up first as not to have them ask what he wanted.

"I hear you the best one to hire to go exploring the underground caverns," said George in a course voice.

"Who asking?" said the Elf.

Kizee joined George. "Names don't really matter at this point. We just want to buy you and your associates a drink and talk," said Kizee.

"We'll accept your drink offer, but talk isn't free," said the Elf.

With a nudge and whisper from Kizee, George tossed down on the table a couple of hundred wizen gold coins.

"Pull up a chair. My name is Kroger. This is Mocker and they are Weddle and Brock. What exactly do you want to talk about?" asked Kroger.

Kizee sat down at the table while George stayed standing. She pulled out the map.

"I'm Kizee and my associate is George. Do you know where the entrance is to this cavern?" asked Kizee.

The dark elf and his associates studied the map closely pointing at certain aspects of references.

"The language it is written in is very old. Not many know how to translate it anymore," said Kroger.

"I can translate this map. Can you take us to the entrance of this cavern or not?" queried Kizee.

"I can for ten thousand wizen all up front. That's in case you don't make it back out," said Kroger.

"Why shouldn't we make it back out?" asked George standing behind Kizee.

"You're in search of the magic wand. It is protected by traps and monsters. Take note ye been warned," stated Mocker.

"Is that what you read from the map?" asked Kizee.

"Aye, the rest be hearsay from those that barely made it back with thar skin attached," continued Mocker.

George said, "We'll give you three thousand up front and three thousand at the entrance to the cavern. If you're willing to come with us into the cavern another three thousand after we retrieve what we are after. If we make it all the way out safely you'll get another ten thousand."

The elves eyes shifted back and forth at each other not saying a word.

"Let's be clear here, you're after the magic wand," questioned Kroger.

"Yes, we're after the magic wand," said George.

"As soon as we receive that first three thousand we'll be off," said Kroger.

George reached into his pocket and pulled out a leather bag. "Three thousand wizens, as agreed," said George.

"Meet us at the arch and we'll be on our way," said the elf.

After Kroger and his three henchmen left, George noticed a couple of other dark elves were eyeing them. They had seen him pull out the pouch of money from his pocket.

"See those two hoodlums over there? We're about to get punched and dragged out to the back alley," whispered George.

"Go stand by the door and get ready to run," said Kizee.

George stood by the door. Kizee walked over to where two other elves were having a loud discussion. At the right moment, she bumped into one of the elves to push his arm into the other elf.

A push turned into a sheave that led to a swing of a fist. Within a few seconds there was a brawl between the two elves. More elves got into the fist fight.

Kizee made her way to the door where George was waiting for him.

"Let's get out of here before the local authorities to show up," said Kizee.

George and Kizee made their way back to the balloon to retrieve some supplies they needed. With torches and the map in hand, George and Kizee waited near the arch at the entrance to the town for their guides.

"I don't trust these elves. There may be a double cross in the works here," said Kizee.

"Just keep your magic wand out of sight to avoid any suspicion on their part," warned George.

"If they don't show up, the money will disappear," said Kizee.

The dark elves led George and Kizee out of town, through the woods and down a steep canyon trail. It was a long and grueling hike for George and Kizee with the bodies of dark elves.

Back in one of the off shoots of the main canyon, the elves brought George and Kizee to a metal door with a heavy slide bolt and lock.

"I hope you brought a key. Because if you didn't you're not getting the next payment," said Kizee.

Kroger pulled out a ring of keys and began to try each key in the lock. After five keys, Kizee was frustrated with this dark elf.

"Let me see you ring of keys," shouted Kizee.

Kizee grabbed the keys and held them up to the light. She picked one and stuck it in the lock. Kizee jiggled and wiggled the key until the key turned. The locking mechanism popped out and the rest of the lock fell to pieces. Kizee tossed the ring of keys back to the elf with a sarcastic grin.

It took all six of them to push the door open. The metal door squeaked long and loud as they pushed it until it stopped up against the inner rock wall.

Kizee had provided them with magical torches to assist in seeing their way. Kroger was leading the way as they were steadily making their way down into the cavern.

George suddenly stopped when bits of dirt and rock fell off an edge where his foot had stepped. He held his torch down low to the ground.

"This trail is getting narrow. Are you sure we're going the right way?" questioned George.

"According to our map we should go left," said Kizee.

"The map is wrong, it's to the right," said Kroger.

"Hold on here," shouted George as he stared down into the darkness. "Take another look at the map and tell me if you're taking us the right way."

"Does it show a dark shaft?" asked Kroger.

"No, it should be a trial ending in a large cavern," said Kizee.

"If we go to the left you'll drop straight down that shaft I'm talking about," said Kroger.

"This could be a map to make sure no one ever gets the magic wand," said George.

Kizee turned away from the dark elves and stood close to George," Kizee whispered, "It doesn't say anything about a shaft."

Kizee was holding the map while George was moving his torch around to see the trail. That was when the light from a torch shown through to the underside of the map for a split moment.

"Look at this," whispered Kizee.

George and Kizee couldn't believe their eyes of what they saw with the torch light shown through the map. The hidden water mark trail showed up.

"The light shows the correct way through the caverns," said Kizee to the Elves.

Weddle held his torch near the map while Kroger looked at the map as to where they were.

"It has embedded in it a water mark trail. Look, it shows a different direction to take then where you are taking us," stated Weddle.

Kizee turned to Kroger and questioned, "What are you up to?"

"Hey, hey, I just made a minor mistake," exclaimed Kroger.

Kizee wasn't satisfied with that answer, but she didn't pursue the matter any further. Kizee's guard just went on double notice.

They started down the new direction following the water mark trail. Kroger led the way walking cautiously as he did not know where exactly they were going.

The trail ended in a large wet cavern that had calcium deposits of various colors. There were canopies and pillars with stalagmites and stalactites. Around the bottom were pools of clear water that overflowed down into a crevasse that ran deep into the bottom floor.

"Where does the map show is the next trail?" asked Kroger.

"I don't see any way out of here. On the map, it should look like a vertical slit through the cavern wall," answered Kizee.

George carefully stepped across the cavern floor to where the slit should be. He turned his head one way then another. George moved up close and stepped back.

"I need two of you to stand on each side of this wall with your torches held up high," said George.

Weddle stood on one side while Kroger stood on the other side.

"There, do you see it. The deposits have grown over the slit. You can just see the edge that separates the two calcium flows," said George.

"It has been a long time since this map had been drawn," said Kizee.

Kizee palmed her magic wand and pointed her hidden magic wand at the slit. A trimmer vibrated under their feet causing the two calcium deposits to separate and spread open making the opening barely wide enough for them to squeeze through.

George stuck his torch through the slit and poked his head in to take a look around before proceeding. "Careful, it looks very slippery."

It was long, narrow, and tight in some places. At the end, they barely managed to get through. When all had gotten through they stood there staring at a deep abyss that separated the cavern.

Kizee studied the map with the light to see if they took a wrong turn. Where they were standing and the point on the map appeared to be correct. There was writing on the map.

"Can you read what this says, Kizee?" asked George.

The four dark elves mumbled as they read it also. They were rusty in the language. Among themselves, they pointed at certain words while they discussed the meanings.

"Well, can you read it or not?" whispered Kroger getting impatient.

"It's not old elfish. This is witch language. Our translation isn't exact," said Weddle.

"It might be saying take a flying leap," stated Mocker.

"No, it's telling us to take a leap of faith," interjected Weddle.

"You two couldn't translate a pub menu if it was read to you. It clearly translates to fly with faith over the leap," whispered Brock.

Mocker and Weddle abruptly got angry by Brock's insult. They picked up the dark elf by his arms and legs.

"Let's see if your translation is correct," said Mocker.

"No wait, you're taking this too serious. Put me down you morons before someone gets hurt," cried Brock.

With a heave, they threw Brock out over the abyss. Brock was waving his arms and legs as if he was trying to fly. George and Kizee stood there in horror as the screams from Brock faded as it echoed off the walls.

"Do you two want to take a stab at translating it?" asked Mocker to George and Kizee.

"No, you're doing a fine job," said George.

Kizee said, "This one word isn't leap, its step. Which make the translation one should take a step of faith."

George stared at the abyss while thinking of what Kizee had just said. "Kizee do you have a mirror in your sack?"

Kizee put her hand into her sack. With magic, she pulled out a mirror that George requested.

George held the mirror up over his head to reflect the light from his torch out over the abyss. It was faint, but George could see something bridging the gap.

"Kizee, hold the mirror like this and shine the reflected light over there," said George.

George took a step off the edge. His foot planted firmly down onto something that they couldn't see.

"Keep the light in front of me," said George.

Kizee moved the reflected light as George walked across the abyss to the other side.

Weddle started to follow George's path. Then Weddle looked down, lost his balance and fell into the abyss. Once again, the screaming echoed as he fell.

"It's like the map, the path must be lit up by reflected light," said George.

Kizee held the mirror up reflecting the light down in front of Kroger and Mocker. When it came Kizee's turn to cross, she reflected the light right in front of her feet.

"I can see it clearly," said Kizee.

George took a sigh of relief when Kizee was on the other side standing next to him.

From the abyss, the labyrinth of tunnels took them deep in the caverns. Strange and scary noises were all around them.

Kroger was carrying the map now with Mocker next to him studying it closely. "Go and find the magic wand."

Kroger shrouded his torch to make the way in front of him dark. Kroger had led them down to a dead end. He did it on purpose to allow his partner Mocker to forge ahead in an attempt to get to the magic wand first.

"I must have turned down the wrong tunnel," said Kroger.

The next open cavern they entered, water from the upper levels was rushing down like a waterfall into a huge lake.

"Where is Mocker?" asked George.

"We must have gotten separated back there when we took that wrong turn. I wouldn't worry too much, he'll show up," said Kroger.

Kizee pointed over to a small wood raft that was sitting on the shore. Lying on it was a fresh cadaver of an elf.

"Apparently, someone very recently made it this far," said Kizee.

"Look closer. It's Mocker. He was burned to death," said George.

"Burned to death? How could that have happen?" exclaimed Kizee.

George looked around to see if he could figure out what happened. Kroger was standing off and away from George and Kizee.

"What do you know about what happened? Why are you standing over there?" queried George.

"Look! Out in the middle of the lake is a large enough boat for the two of us," said Kizee.

"Apparently Mocker tried to use the raft to get to the boat," said George.

Kizee turned to Kroger. "What's in the water? You know Mocker was trying to move ahead of us and ran into another trap of some kind. Maybe we should send you out on the raft to see what we're up against," declared Kizee.

"Where's the map, Kroger?" demanded George.

Kroger didn't give a response. He turned and ran away back into the caverns.

George examined the burnt corpse of Mocker to try to determine what exactly happened. There in his hand were the burnt remains of the map.

George carefully pulled it out of the dead elf's hand. Flakes of ash fell away from the burnt parchment "I found the map or what is left of it."

"We're lost down here without that map," said Kizee.

Kizee changed back to her normal self. Kizee brushed off the last of the elf hair from her clothes. She also changed George back to his normal self.

""I know it will be tough down here, but I think I we can still get the magic wand and get out of here," said Kizee.

"I was tired of looking ugly anyway," said George.

After Kizee had turn George back to normal, Kizee looked at what was left of the map to see if it showed the way.

"Look, the last of the trail is still intact. We need that boat. Kizee, can you call it to come to you?" asked George.

Kizee stood on the shoreline and held her hands out and closed her eyes. "Numbus cisco rertraw," said Kizee with force in her voice.

Slowly she pulled her hands toward her. The boat didn't move very far. Something popped up out of the water slinging a spray of water up into the air. It was a chain attached to the boat and the out cropping of rocks on the other side.

"Apparently, we must use the raft to get to the boat," said George.

"Alright then, let's get a move on," said Kizee.

George and Kizee pushed the burnt corpse of the dark elf off and pulled the raft into the water. Kizee waded out and stepped up onto the raft while George balanced it. With George and Kizee on the raft, George pushed it toward the boat just before hopping up on it.

Trying not to tip the raft, Kizee and George climbed over the rail of the boat and got in. The rocking of the boat sent ripples down the chain to the rock it was attached to. Kizee noticed the rock and the chain was starting to move.

"I don't think that is an outcropping of rocks as we thought. Look, it's a dragon!" screamed Kizee.

The dragon's red eyes were glaring right at the boat that was attached to it leg with the chain.

"Quick, back on the raft," yelled George.

"No, that is what that elf did and look what happened to him," stated Kizee pointing to the shore where the body was.

"It's too late anyway. The raft has drifted too far away," said Kizee.

"Then we must swim for it," cried George.

"Stay in the boat!" yelled Kizee.

Kizee then composed herself, standing in the front of the boat trying to look unconcerned. Let's all stay calm and think this out before things go sour," said Kizee.

"Get down. Lie low in the boat," whispered George.

From the mouth of the dragon a long stream of fire spewed out. It was aimed directly at the raft. The hot force of the fire pushed the raft back to the shore where it smoldered as the small wave washed over it putting out the fire.

"It wouldn't make sense to burn the boat. The one that commands the dragon would need to use the boat to get to the other side," stated Kizee.

"Who do you suppose commands the dragon?" asked George.

"I'm sure it isn't a dark elf," said Kizee.

"Wizards are the only ones that know the magic to control dragons in captivity," said Kizee.

"You're saying Zweig the wizard put the magic wand in this cavern and put a dragon down here to keep anyone from getting to it," queried George.

"It wasn't Zweig that put the magic wand down here. It must have been Maranda the tree fairy. Stand up and command the dragon to bring the boat to shore," said Kizee.

"Why do you think I can command a dragon?" queried George still lying low in the boat.

"Maranda has a fairy spell on you to retrieve the magic wand," stated Kizee.

"Are you sure of this fairy spell you keep talking about?" asked George.

"This isn't the time to be asking those questions. Now stand up and command the dragon to bring the boat to the shore," reiterated Kizee.

George stood up. He held out his hand at the dragon. "Bring the boat to shore!" he commanded.

The dragon turned its head toward George. The terrifying red eyes of the dragon stared at the boat.

"I'm toast."

Horror was streaming through his mind that the dragon would burn them with it fiery breath.

The boat slowly began to move toward the shore as the dragon pulled the chain link by link. George stayed standing in the boat with his hand held out.

When the boat was firmly up on the shore, Kizee got out of the boat and stood in front of the dragon keeping its attention. George emerged from the boat cautiously. They didn't make any sudden moves just slow steady moves.

"Kizee, pull out your magic wand," asked George.

"I'm not going to kill the dragon," said Kizee.

"I want you to use the magic wand to break the shackle from the dragon's leg," said George.

Kizee pulled her magic wand. She commanded it to glow with fire as she held it up over her head.

"Hurrraaaah," yelled Kizee as she brought the fire down hard upon the shackle.

Sparks and molten iron flew in all directions as the shackle disintegrated. With the dragon freed of its bondage, it moved away from them to uncover the passage.

With glowing torches in hand, they headed into the passage unblocked by the dragon. George led the way using what was left of the map.

The tunnel opened into a gigantic cavern filled with huge crystals. The trail narrowed and ran along the outer circumference of crystal cavern.

"We must very careful not to slip off the trail. Those crystals are pointed and the edges are razor sharp. And watch your hands. The ones on the wall are just as sharp." stated George.

Kizee pulled out her magic wand and spun a web rope around them. She attached the end of the web rope to a crystal up in the overhead.

"This will help if one of us falls," said Kizee.

George was watching closely where he was stepping as they made their way along the ledge. On the other side of the cavern, the ledge stopped at a wide landing. Across the way and up was another landing and the way out of the cavern.

"I could sling a web rope up to the landing and we could climb up," suggested Kizee.

"It's too far up. We don't have the stamina to climb all the way up there," said George.

Kizee looked around and thought of what she would do. "No, that would be too easy," said Kizee.

"Easy is always the best way," said George.

"Well…we are in a cavern and…there should be deep cavern pixies…" stated Kizee slowly as she was still looking around.

"What is it we must do?" asked George.

"We must put out all the torches," answered Kizee.

"And stand here in complete darkness?"

"Exactly, the deep cavern pixies will come out only in complete darkness. Then and only then will they fling their deep cavern pixie dust everywhere," stated Kizee.

"And how does this get us up to that landing?" queried George.

"Then we fly," answered Kizee.

"Fly," said George.

George put out his torch and waited for Kizee to do the same. Kizee extinguished her torch and the cavern became complete dark as octopus's ink. The two stood there motionless waiting for something to happen.

In the far reaches of the cavern a single point of light appeared. One by one, points of light popped into existence. The geode crystal chamber soon sparkled with streams of moving light as it reflected and refracted in and around all the crystals.

The little specks of light began to come together and move about in the cavern. Kizee watched and waited for the deep cavern pixies to start flinging out their pixie dust. The little specks formed into something completely different than Kizee had expected.

"Candle, candle burn bright, give us a strong and lasting light," shouted Kizee as she franticly tried to light her torch.

"What's wrong?" asked George.

"Those are not deep cavern pixies. They're Nezbats and they are coming to kill us if we don't get our torches lit!" cried Kizee as she kept trying different spells to get her torch lit.

As the Nezbats started to swoop down on them Kizee waved her flaming magic wand at them knocking them down. The Nezbats were falling out of the air like little planes going in for a fiery crash. Little screams were heard echoing inside the geode cavern.

At the same time, George saw out of the corner of his eye an unusual sight. Up against the chamber wall was an image that reflected the flaming light of Kizee's magic wand.

"Look, it's a staircase leading up to the landing. Kizee, keep your wand in front of you and lead us up," shouted George.

Kizee kept hitting the last of the Nezbats down as she took one step at a time. "There aren't any rails, so don't slip."

Once they got up to the landing and were in the next tunnel Kizee's magic finally worked to light their torches. Behind them in the cavern, the noise of the Nezbats flying around started up again.

"That wasn't as easy as you thought it would be," said George to Kizee.

"It won't be easy coming back this way once we have the magic wand," exclaimed Kizee.

They followed the crusty rock tunnel that led them in another labyrinth. George had the piece of map out and was guessing the direction they should go.

"Does it seem to be getting warmer?" asked George.

"More like a geyser water chamber. Isn't it strange that even after the dragon we are encountering obstacles?" said Kizee.

"I agree it should be getting easier not harder. There has to be another way. If we continue going this way we'll get boiled like a lobster," said George.

"What does the map show?" asked Kizee.

"I think we are here and it is showing to go this way. There aren't any other tunnels on the map," answered George.

The tunnel opened up to a cavern that had a bubbling hot spring pool about fifteen feet off the ledge where they were walking on. The air was thick with steam.

"Watch your step and keep checking the map for any sudden changes," suggested Kizee.

George came to a sudden stop as he ran into something. It wasn't hard like a rock wall. George poked it. It felt spongy.

"What's in the way?" asked Kizee.

"A very large spongy fabric covered ball that smells very bad," said George.

George jabbed it hard. It moved with a growl.

"Urrorurroullouooo."

"I know that sound. Oh no, back up. Back up. Hurry, we must get back to the entrance to this cavern," shouted Kizee.

"What is it, what is wrong?" questioned George.

"It's an Ogre. A very large Ogre," cried Kizee.

Kizee, followed by George scrambled back to the entrance of the hot bubbling spring cavern. They could feel the ground shake as the Ogre stomped toward them.

"He seems to be too big to fit into the tunnel," said Kizee.

"Can you order him to let us pass or some kind of magic to get rid of him?" asked George.

"Ogres are a strange lot. Magic doesn't do anything to them," said Kizee. Then Kizee yelled out, "Hey you. I command you to let us pass."

Just then a long blade rattled around the tunnel with the Ogre growling. The Ogre had the advantage with the larger area where he could raise his blade and slam it down hard.

"Our only chance is to knock him off balance and have him fall into the hot spring pool," said Kizee.

George went back to the other end of the tunnel where they left the web rope that Kizee had made for them to keep from falling onto the sharp crystals. He tied one end to a broken piece of crystal.

George got back to Kizee carrying the web rope with the crystal tied to one end.

"I have an idea. We have only one chance to make it work. Do you think you can pin the Ogre's sword down with magic and hold it long enough for me to run between his legs and wrap the rope around one of his ankle?" queried George.

"I don't know, I suppose so," said Kizee.

"After I have the rope tied around his leg, I need you to use your magic to make the crystal fly around the sword handle," explained George.

"Yeah, I can do that, but why?" asked Kizee.

"When the Ogre lifts up on his sword to slam it down again, he will pull his leg out from under himself and possible make him lose his balance and fall off the edge into the hot pool of water," stated George.

"Brilliant, if it works," said Kizee.

"Alright, are we ready?" said George.

Kizee stepped out of the tunnel just long enough for the Ogre to swing his sword blade down at her. When the blade hit the ground, Kizee pointed her wand at the sword.

"I don't know how long this will hold it," yelled Kizee.

George ran past the sword to the Ogre's legs. He dropped the end of the rope with the crystal near the handle of the Ogre's sword. George wrapped the other end of the rope around the Ogre's right ankle and tied it with whatever knot he could tie quickly.

Kizee waved her magic wand and the crystal flew around the sword handle wrapping the rope to the sword. The Ogre moved his sword.

George stood behind the Ogre and yelled up at him, "Hey ugly over here!"

The Ogre turned and lifted his sword. When the Ogre swung his sword around, he pulled his right leg out from under him.

The entangled rope twisted the Ogre around and the Ogre fell and rolled off the edge. A large splash echoed off the cavern ceiling along with momentary screaming from the Ogre as he succumbed to the blistering hot spring water.

"ARRRRRRRRRRRRRR!"

"Alright let's get out of this sauna before we pass out," said George.

One good thing about this steamy hot cavern was there was cool water running down the walls for them to collect and keep hydrated through to the next set of labyrinth tunnels.

"I'm just saying it seems there is something wrong here. We shouldn't be running into these many obstacles after the dragon," said Kizee.

"You think that Ogre was recently put there," asked George.

"Yes and those Nezbats shouldn't have been there either. I may be wrong, but I think someone is trying to stop us from getting the magic wand," said Kizee.

The tunnel was the longest one they had transverse. It twisted and turned as it led them down deep into the dark bowls of the realm. The air was getting stale and hard to breath.

Just at the moment George had the thought of giving up and making their way back to the surface, they turned a curve. Kizee's torch reflected back at them from a golden door.

Kizee and George pushed opened the golden door. To their amazement, they stared down into an empty pit.

Rock stairs led the way down to the floor where at the far end was a marble pedestal. On the marble pedestal in a wood stand was a magic wand.

It was long and sleek. The mahogany wood stem was polished to a high gloss. The handle was simple in design made of black quartz.

George started down the stairs when Kizee grabbed him and pulled him back.

"Hold on! We have run into too many traps. Let's think this one out clearly. Don't assume that the magic wand doesn't have a spell on it. Let's walk slowly down the stairs with our eyes open for any trouble. Kroger is still possibly still down here watching us," explained Kizee.

Kizee let go of George. She kept her magic wand out in front of her as she took each step down. George was looking up and around expecting something to rain down on them. Kizee was on edge, not knowing what spells she might have to do.

When they got down to the marble pedestal, George felt a stone move under his left foot. "Kizee Move away from here!" shouted George.

Kizee looked up just in time to jump away from George. A metal cage was falling down, Kizee pointed her magic wand at the cage, but it was too late.

"Run!" yelled Kizee to George.

It was too late. George was trapped by the cage as he stood by the marble pedestal. George started to grab the magic wand.

"Stop!" cried Kizee who was on the outside of the cage. "We don't know what will happen next."

Again, Kizee's warning was too late. George grabbed the wand. He pulled at it to get the wand free. George and the marble pedestal suddenly drop down into a dark shaft.

Kizee cried out, "NOOOOOOOOO!".

Chapter Thirteen
Double Double Double Cross

Eric and Gracie were reunited at the Poison Apple Tavern. Even though Gracie smelt like vinegar, Eric hugged Gracie tight and kissed like he never wanted to let her go ever again.

"I heard your house was destroyed by Centaurs," said Eric.

"Agnes told me all your stuff is missing and you don't have anywhere to live. Oh Eric, what did Kizee and George get themselves mix up with?" asked Gracie as she began to cry in his arms.

"We'll find them. It's only been a week. Their trail isn't cold yet. Mindy is doing spells at the field to figure out where they went."

"Maybe this will help. I found it in George's bedroom with this note."

Eric read the note and looked at the flash drive. "I need to get to my computer at Spell Caster Enterprises. Come with me. There is a gym with showers and I'm sure Mindy can get you a change of clothes."

"Hold on, Gracie just can't walk around town. The magical creatures are hunting her down," said Agnes.

"Also, we have to find who is behind all this. You just didn't disappear and have your lives changed for no reason," said Winston.

Harriet spoke up, "I have a question. Eric, how did you find out about the disaster at Gracie's house?"

"It was on the television. You know, breaking news and the roaming reporter news van," said Eric.

"There wasn't any news van at Gracie's house," said Harriet.

"Sure there was. It was…let me think…Maranda Nymph was the reporter. Check with the station," said Eric.

"Franklin, where did you hear about what happened?" asked Agnes.

Before Franklin could speak, the Tavern Keep spoke up, "It was Maranda the White Fairy that put out the news of Gracie shooting the Centaurs."

"Maranda the White Fairy, and Maranda Nymph the news reporter that is definitely fishy. Our kids gone missing, Eric and Gracie thrown out of Broomstick, and A SNARF fairy suddenly gone rogue. Smells like trouble with a capital M for Maranda," said Agnes.

At Spell Caster Enterprises, Eric was again back at work on the zeppelin project. With the crises of going after Kizee and George, work schedules have been extended to meet the new deadline of getting the zeppelin ready for flight.

Eric and Gracie were sitting at a computer. George's flash drive was plugged into a USB port.

"It seems the files are set up like a day to day diary," said Eric.

Eric started clicking to open the files. Gracie read every word. "If George would have told me what some of the things he and Kizee were doing, I would have taken him right back to the crises counselors."

"Here is an entry of importance. I found a splitting page in the book. When I peeled the page open, it was blank," read Eric.

"What is so important about a blank page?" questioned Gracie.

"It may not have been blank," said Eric.

"Here is a good entry. After we had met with the yellow fairy we ran into Maranda the White Fairy," read Eric.

"What is this fairy really up to?" asked Gracie.

"Ah ha! The blank page wasn't blank," announced Eric.

Eric read, "I placed my hands on the page. Words and symbols began to illuminate showing a map to…(Smether Realm)." Eric was trying to pronounce it. "…where the magic wand is hidden."

Gracie was trying to pronounce the unusual name. "What is that word?"

Mindy happened to come up behind them at that time. "Smether Realm," said Mindy.

Gracie asked, "What is Smether Realm?"

"It is the realm of the dark elves. Their magic is very evil. I don't know why anyone would go there. If the dark elves are connected to this wizard's magic wand, there is certainly something horrific waiting for Kizee and George. And us," concluded Mindy.

Mindy was reading over Eric's shoulder. "Here is the other part we needed to find out. They traveled by balloon through a double rainbows in a terrible storm. Kizee needed the help of the lightning fairy to achieve the power to do her magic spell," stated Mindy.

"When do we leave?" asked Gracie.

"You're not, and neither are you Eric. We didn't know what happened to you and I needed an engineer for this mission. I assigned Dirge Firestorm," said Mindy.

"Well he is a good choice. But I would like to see my Nano-gyro system in operation," said Eric.

"Alright, you can come as a civilian consultant of Spell Caster Enterprises."

"Hey, what about me? George is my brother that your niece manipulated into going along with all this unsavory witchcraft stuff in the first place," argued Gracie.

"Cousin."

"What?"

"Kizee is my cousin. I noticed since the summer solstice you have really resented magic. Haven't you noticed magic has pulled your brother out of his depressional state of mind back to the real world?" Mindy argued back. "You're not going."

Gracie couldn't argue that point. Mindy was right about George accepting the reality of their parents are gone.

"Listen, you know I can fight. I have gone up against some pretty hostel magical creatures. How much experience does your wizards and witches have fighting these dark elves?" asked Gracie.

Mindy knew Gracie was right about the lack of fighting experience with dark elves. "You did take on two Centaurs single handed. Very well, report to Second Lieutenant Xzavier this afternoon for duty assignment. Any questions Private Düben?"

"Yes, when do we leave?" asked Gracie.

"Tomorrow morning at oh seven hundred," said Mindy.

The Zeppelin Raging Queen was staged in the field with all hands standing by to get the ship airborne. Agnes and Harriet along with Winston and Franklin were already on board. Eric was checking some system alignments on the bridge with First Engineer Dirge Firestorm.

Gracie was in uniform with the marine detachment stuffed in the lower berthing compartment.

"Can I have a little room to breathe?" said Gracie to one of the witches she was up against.

There was a crowd to see the Zeppelin Raging Queen off that included knotems that thought this was an advertising gimmick highlighting the town's name with two huge broomsticks on each side of the zeppelin. And there amongst the crowd was Maranda.

"Well well, Agnes McDermit, you're going on this rescue also. I can't let you and your sister, get a hold of that magic wand," said Maranda to herself.

Maranda shrank down and flew over to the right side of the zeppelin. She untied a strand of golden rope that held the broom straw to the handle. "Oh look, the nymphs didn't tie this gold rope very well. It might unravel during your flight and cause all of you to fall into oblivion. Maybe I should tell someone. Oh, it's of no importance."

"Cast off the aft line," Searat called out.

"Aft line off," announced Mindy.

"Cast off the forward line, and proceed to raise the ship with one third speed," ordered Searat.

"Forward line off," called out Mindy.

"Raising the ship," said the helmsman as he moved the handle that tilted the huge broomsticks up.

The helmsman moved the throttle to one third. This signaled the huge broom's magical flying power to propel the zeppelin to move forward.

"Set a course for Smether Realm steering North by north east toward the storm with the double rainbows," ordered Searat.

"Aye, aye Captain," said the helmsman.

The helmsman turned the wheel that controlled the rudder as he watched the compass and looked out the forward windows.

"Level off at fifteen thousand feet and increase speed to full throttle," ordered Searat.

The helmsman moved the handle that tilted the huge broomsticks and moved the throttle to full speed.

"Leveling off at fifteen thousand feet and speed is at full Captain," called out the helmsman.

"First Mate, set the first watch," said Searat.

"Aye, aye Captain, steady as she goes helmsman. Set the first watch," called out Mindy.

The crew of the Raging Queen was new at flying a zeppelin of this special design. What gave them a great advantage though was their knowledge of test flying brooms.

The storm tossed the Raging Queen about as the young wizard at the helm steered straight on keeping the air ship on Mindy's calculated course to Smether Realm looking for the double rainbows. Steady blue flames thundered from the two huge broomsticks leaving a trail of stars behind them.

Below the bridge were the tight accommodations for both the crew and passengers. Mindy was lying in her bunk just above Searat.

Mindy not wanting to share her plan with Searat thought to herself, "When we get to Smether Realm I'll take an armed shore party to look for Kizee. This place will be like walking into a den of hungry hyenas."

Agnes and Harriet with Franklin and Winston were huddled together at the galley table making different plans.

"We're going to a world where witches and wizards are not welcomed, in an air ship that calls out 'come hang me'," said Winston.

"We're going to have to give the local population a reason not to fear us," said Franklin.

Agnes suggested, "We don't want any trouble with the dark elves. We'll make this a trade expedition."

"We are after all, merchants of magic. We'll keep the locals busy while the two of you poke around for information," stated Harriet.

Their conversation was interrupted by a quiet bell ringing and a call from the bridge. "Ding ding, Dog the watch."

Mindy crawled out of her bunk and got dressed. She passed by the galley table on her way up the stairs to the bridge.

"You should get some sleep. It's going to be a long night in this storm," said Mindy.

"Keep us on course," said Agnes with a motherly smile at her middle daughter.

Eric found Gracie when she was off duty. They found a cubbyhole to hide in and talk.

"The Second Lieutenant's orders are to protect the zeppelin and not to engage the dark elves. I can't just sit here and not go after George," said Gracie.

"I'm with you. But I am just a civilian consultant. I doubt if they even give me a weapon of some kind," said Eric.

"Wait, I thought you were a third owner of Spell Caster Enterprises?"

"I am. But the Gold Zeppelin Cruise Tours owns the Zeppelin Raging Queen. They are our customer for these zeppelins," explained Eric.

"Hem, this is a private army and airship navy. Sounds like Mindy and Searat are mercenaries for hire more so than a cruse tour company," said Gracie.

"And you enlisted into it."

"Only until George and I are home safe in San Francisco. I'm going after George first chance I get," stated Gracie.

Eric said, "With my help of course!"

"Of course, with your help, I love you, you know."

Mindy stood the senior duty officer watch with two wizards. One manned the helm while the other maintained the broom propulsion controls.

"Commander, the rainbows are fading," said the helmsman.

Mindy pulled up a solar chart. She charted the course of the storm. Using a protractor and a slide rule, Mindy drew a line from the next Sun rise to the angle of the storm to determine the light refraction through the heavy rain.

"Change course to zero two seven and hold until midnight," said Mindy.

"Aye Commander, change course to zero two seven and hold until midnight," answered the wizard at the helm.

Mindy kept busy by reviewing the armory weaponry inventory that could be concealed under clothing. She also took the time to make up bland clothing for her shore party.

Mindy was standing at the window staring out at the lightning when the midnight watch showed up on the bridge.

"Commander, I'm ready to relieve you," said the Lieutenant.

"Commander?" repeated the Lieutenant.

Mindy came out of her private thoughts to face the Lieutenant. "Yes, ah change course to zero one three and maintain until the first reflective ray of Sunlight at oh three forty. When the rainbows begin to materialize steer toward them to pass between them," ordered Mindy.

"Aye Commander, I understand your orders and relieve you" said the Lieutenant.

Mindy didn't go straight to her bunk. She took a detour down to the armory. "Five XC-49 spell blasters, we'll take one. Ten boxes of freeze gas hand grenades, five each should due. Knives, one for each, except for me, I'll take two."

Searat was awake when Mindy got back to her bunk. He could smell the lubricating gun oil on her clothes.

"What were you doing in the armory?" asked Searat.

"Taking inventory," answered Mindy.

"You're expecting trouble, aren't you," said Searat.

"Most likely preventing trouble," said Mindy.

"By taking inventory of weapons onboard?" asked Searat.

"I am planning to take a covert shore party into town to find Kizee and George," said Mindy.

"I'm going with you," said Searat.

"No, your place is here on board the Raging Queen with a rescue party if things go wrong. It's a magical realm out there. My selected members should be able take care of things with our magical powers. You will need to use old fashion pirate tactics to get us out. I know you can handle that with your experience with Captain Davy Jones.

"Some of his pirate tactics I couldn't bring myself to do. He is a sailor without a heart or soul," said Searat shuttering of his thoughts.

"Love, keep to your morals. Just come to my rescue if I need it," said Mindy holding her hand to Searat face while kissing him.

The Raging Queen was heading directly into the storm. the zeppelin was tossed around like a rubber life raft in the crosswinds of a hurricane.

Morning was too early for some who couldn't sleep through the tossing of the Raging Queen. Coffee was the beverage of the day with the crew.

Searat and Mindy were up on the bridge as the rays of the Sun pierced through the storm to make the double rainbows appear in front them.

"Steer hard left!" shouted the Lieutenant on watch to the helmsman.

"Ten degrees down and follow the curve around the red arc," ordered the Lieutenant.

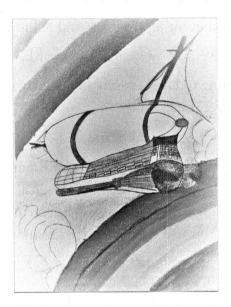

The huge brooms moved pointing down to bring the Raging Queen down toward the double rainbows. Rain was hitting the bridge window hard with massive color surges from the two rainbows.

"Hold her steady sailor!" shouted the Lieutenant as the Raging Queen bounced through the toughest area of the storm.

The wizard that was on the helm was fighting the wheel to keep the Raging Queen pointed in the direction of the rainbows. Mindy jumped in and grabbed the wheel.

"Pull, pull hard left! Come on hold on with me. We can do this… arrgh, hold it, hold it!!!!!" shouted Mindy to the helmsman.

The propulsion control wizard moved his controls to give the starboard broom more magical power and eased off on the port broom. The Raging Queen tipped to the port as it fell through the double rainbow.

"Pull up and level off," shouted the Lieutenant to the on duty crew.

The propulsion control wizard evened out the magic on the two brooms and leveled the Raging Queen. Mindy and the helmsman held the wheel steady as they brought the airship back on their course setting. In front of the Raging Queen, blue sky was seen through the breaking storm clouds.

"Good work Lieutenant," said Mindy to the on watch duty officer.

"Oh, and Lieutenant, you're on my shore party. Make yourself familiar with the XC-49 spell blaster and bring along your engineering snipe with you," said Mindy.

"Aye Commander, and thank you for selecting me," said Lieutenant Whitecastle.

"You may not be thanking me later, Lieutenant," said Mindy.

Lieutenant Whitecastle nodded toward the propulsion wizard. "Thank you, you've saved us from missing that turn back there."

Early in the morning, Searat was looking over the chart that Mindy had used to predict where the double rainbow would be when the sun appeared.

He peered at Mindy's reflection in the bridge window. "I will take this memory to my place of rest when this is over," thought Searat with a sadden heart of love for Mindy.

The Raging Queen was at full throttle flying in the direction of Smether Realm. As promised by Searat, they were closing in on the realm of the dark elves by the next day from leaving Broomstick.

Later, after watch change, Mindy had her shore party down in the armory getting dressed in bland clothing.

"I chose the two of you because of your quick thinking up there on the bridge. Do you think you have the guts to go up against dark elves if things get hairy?" asked Mindy.

"I'm not afraid of dark elves," said Lieutenant Sybil Whitecastle.

"I sure am. I've studied their magic. It's not very friendly at all," said First Engineer Dirge Firestorm.

Searat was up on the bridge when the magical land of Smether Realm was spotted. He pulled out his spyglass and pointed it in the direction the wizard was indicating.

"Captain, straight ahead a snow peak," said the wizard on watch.

Agnes and the rest came up on the bridge to take a look as the Raging Queen sailed past the shore line.

"Slow to one third and bring her down low," ordered Searat.

The zeppelin flew over the town. The area was rough with not too many flat areas. Searat was looking for a place to touch down. He located a field just on the edge of town.

"Over there, set her down easy. Set the anchor detail," called out Searat.

As the Raging Queen dipped down and leveled off about three feet off the ground, two crewmen jumped out forward and after with line and spikes. They hammered in the spikes to the ground and tied off the lines.

Once the two lines were secured, others crew members dropped to the ground and added two more lines on each side both forward and aft.

"Secure from sail detail," called out Searat.

Agnes could see dark elves were coming toward the zeppelin. She grabbed Harriet and they got to work setting up tents and tables of goods they knew the dark elves would be interested in.

Packages of zombied rattlesnake skin were neatly arranged on one half of a table next to colored phosphorous crystals. On another table were glass jars of pickled snodnose troll's eyes with a variety of dipping sauces.

At the last tent were dried bones of ghoulish creatures that the dark elves used for ceremonies and other dark practices.

Winston and Franklin slipped out among the crowd in heavy hooded robes trying to look incognito to the dark elves. On the other side of the Raging Queen, Mindy, Lieutenant Sybil and First Engineer Dirge dropped to the ground and scurried off away from the crowd.

Searat stood on the bridge looking out the window at the scene with the rest of the marines on standby with loaded weapons.

Franklin and Winston went to certain discretionary establishments to find out if they have heard anything of George and Kizee. To say the least they had their guard up and wands at the ready.

Mindy heard a small group of dark elves talking of a private party at a tavern put on by a dark elf by the name of Kroger. Apparently, he had come into a lot of money from an unknown source.

Mindy took her shore party through the back allies to the tavern. Two dark elves that worked the kitchen opened the back door to dump out bags of garbage when Mindy poked one of them in the neck with her magic wand. Lieutenant Whitecastle leveled her XC-49 spell blaster at the other one.

"We don't want any trouble boys. We just want to join the party," said Mindy.

Dirge used golden magical rope to tie their arms behind their backs and sat them down on the bags of garbage.

"Who is this Kroger and what is he celebrating?" asked Mindy.

"He's a local troublemaker," said one elf.

"I heard him boosting about double crossing a couple of elf impersonators looking for a magic wand. He left them to die in the caverns not too far from here," said the other elf.

"Who paid him all this money?" questioned Mindy.

"I don't know," said the first elf.

"I don't know either," repeated the second elf.

"Okay boys, just stay here and be quiet while we go and join the party," said Mindy.

Mindy took point and entered the kitchen. She pointed her wand at the rest of the kitchen staff with her finger to her lips.

Sybil and Dirge stood on each side of the door to the tavern. The tavern keeper came back to the kitchen calling out to the cook. "Hey, where are those fried mermaid tails?"

Sybil poked her XC-49 spell blaster into the tavern keeper's back allowing the door to go close. "Don't make a sound or I'll silence you with a masking spell."

Mindy held her magic wand up to the tavern keeper with her fingers still at her lips.

Out in the tavern Kroger was yelling, "Tavern keeper, where's those mermaid tails?"

Mindy, Sybil and Dirge burst through the door, "Their cooking, so shut up!"

"Who are you?" shouted Kroger as he pulled a knife.

Mindy flicked her wand at Kroger's knife to make it fly off and stick in a wood post with a high pitch echoing 'TING'.

"I have some questions about how you earned your money. Who paid you and where are my friends?" said Mindy.

"Uh, uh," said Sybil as she waved a finger back and forth to one of the other dark elves that made a move for a black powder single shot pistol.

"Who's asking?" queried Kroger.

Mindy shot a bolt of lightning from her magic wand and hit Kroger in the shoulder. "The next one is at one of your knees."

Kroger sat there rubbing his shoulder to ease the pain. "Alright, I led your friends to the magic wand and they left town a day ago."

"Why don't I believe you? I heard you were celebrating a double cross. Now if you don't change your story I'll just have to pour a truth potion down your throat. I'll let you know in advance, it burns all the way down and out while you are spilling your guts," explained Mindy.

"Okay, okay, keep your magical cool, witch," said Kroger. "I was paid by your friends to take them down into the caverns to retrieve a magic wand. Things went wrong. I barely got out alive. As for your friends, they're dead, burned to death by a dragon."

Mindy walked over to Kroger and grabbed him by his injured shoulder.

"Ow oooow ooow," cried Kroger.

"Come on, you're going to take me down through the caverns to where my friends bodies are," said Mindy.

About ten minutes after Mindy and her shore party left the tavern, Franklin and Winston walked through the front door.

Franklin said to the tavern keeper, "We're looking for an elf by the name of Kroger."

"You're too late. He's been taken by a witch and two others. They're headed for the caverns," said the tavern keeper.

Franklin and Winston made their way back to the Raging Queen where Agnes and Harriet were finishing up on their sales. Searat was pacing back and forth on the bridge waiting for any word.

"We found out that a dark elf by the name of Kroger took Kizee and George disguised as dark elves down to the caverns in search of a magic wand. Kroger was taken by Mindy from the tavern where he was celebrating his good fortune," stated Franklin.

"Why didn't she bring Kroger back here?" asked Searat.

"They're heading for the caverns. I bought a map to get us to the entrance to the caverns," said Winston.

"How are we supposed to make our way down through the cavern?" questioned Agnes.

Searat held up the solar chart that Mindy made her calculations on for the double rainbows. "I couldn't help but noticing there were coffee stains on this chart."

Searat held the chart up to the Sun. Through it the coffee stains showed a detailed drawing of the cavern trail.

"That looks like a sailor's hand drawn treasure map. Where did Mindy dig up this information?" asked Harriet.

"Who knows, Mindy, being a collector of pirate stories perhaps helped? I'm sure though she left this hand drawn map in case we needed a rescue plan," suggested Searat not telling what he knew.

"Let's get going Captain. She may need that help," said Agnes.

"To your stations, we're lifting off and going on a rescue mission!" shouted Captain Searat Herzog.

Chapter Fourteen
Lost in the Shuffle

"Come on keep moving," said Mindy as she pushed Kroger forward.

Kroger was very reluctant to, once again, go down into the caverns. He didn't exactly leave it the way he had found it, if you catch my drift.

"What's wrong, why have you stopped again?" said Mindy.

"The door was very hard to open the last time," explained Kroger.

"Who helped you close it?" asked Mindy.

Dirge was feeling the door with his hands and looking strangely at the dark elf. "There's an elf spell on the door."

"Open it Kroger," said Mindy.

The dark elf rubbed his hand over the door before moving the heavy slide bolt and pushing the metal door open.

"There better not be any more surprises waiting for us inside," exclaimed Mindy.

Mindy ensured Kroger went first as she pushed him through the door. Dirge followed behind the dark elf as he demonstrated his ability to detect elf magic spells.

Kroger started down a trail that led to the left. Mindy reached over Dirge's shoulder and grabbed Kroger's clothing.

"If you insist on your tricks I'll push you off the edge and we'll make our own way down," stated Mindy.

"Oh, oh my mistake, sorry I really meant to go to the right," insisted Kroger.

They passed through the large wet cavern that had calcium deposits and the pools of clear water that overflowed down into a crevasse to get to the vertical slit in the cavern wall.

Mindy, with her magic wand, stood there staring at a deep abyss that separated the cavern. She made a mirror appear above the invisible bridge and held out her torch. "Did you destroy the bridge?"

"No, it should still be there," said Kroger.

"Alright then walk across," said Mindy nudging the elf.

"You, you got your mirror in the wrong place. I think the bridge is over here, maybe," said Kroger.

Mindy spied Kroger with extra suspicion. She knew exactly where the bridge should be because of the mirror spell she had put in place. She pointed her magic wand at the mirror and moved it toward where the elf was pointing at.

The flickering light from Kroger's torch caught the mirror and reflected down showing the bridge. Kroger waved his hand like it was there all the time.

"Dirge, any spells?" asked Mindy.

"None that I can detect," said Dirge.

"You and Kroger together walk across the bridge," ordered Mindy.

After Kroger and Dirge were on the other side Mindy motioned with her hand for Kroger to come back across the bridge.

"Come now witch, I proved it was safe to cross, you're safe to come across," said Kroger hesitantly.

"I don't trust you. Get on the bridge," ordered Mindy.

Kroger stepped on the bridge only a short distant. He held the torch up near the mirror. Sybil stepped onto the bridge and started across.

About halfway Kroger dropped his torch into the abyss and stepped off the bridge. The bridge disappeared from underneath Sybil.

"Nooooo," yelled Dirge as Sybil's screams echoed off the walls.

Dirge grabbed Kroger and pushed him down. No amount of magic could stop Dirge from beating the face of that dark elf with his fist.

"Stop Dirge, I order you to stop. We need him alive," yelled Mindy who was still on the other side of the abyss.

Dirge stopped hitting Kroger and yanked him up off the ground. Dirge picked up his torch and walked the elf and him onto the bridge. Mindy proceeded across until the three were standing on the other side.

"If we didn't need you, I would throw you down into the abyss myself," said Mindy to Kroger.

Kroger wiped the blood from his swollen nose onto the sleeve of his shirt. Blood was drooling from his mouth.

Mindy once again pushed the dark elf. "Get going."

The labyrinth of tunnels took them deep in the caverns down to the waterfall and lake where the dragon used to be.

On the lake shore the boat was gone and so was the dragon.

"I see one burnt corpse. And it's an elf where are my friends? What did you with the dragon?" questioned Mindy.

Kroger stared at Mindy wondering what to say. "The young witch let the dragon free from the chain. He hasn't gone too far."

"We need a raft if we're to get over to where your friends are," stated Kroger

Mindy pointed at the shore and began to chant, "Fix a rudder forward and aft. Conjure up a floatable raft."

"Get on and start rowing," said Mindy to Kroger.

On the island Mindy pushed Kroger toward the passage to the giant geode cavern.

In the giant geode cavern Mindy used her magic wand to make the crystal staircase appear. Dirge kept Kroger in front of him out of arm's length in case Kroger had any ideas of pushing him off.

Steadily, the three went as they passed through the hot spring cavern. When the air became stale and hard to breath, Mindy knew they were close to where they were supposed to be.

Mindy knew a treasure chamber she heard of wasn't much father.

Where an entrance should be, Mindy found a wall of gold.

"Take your spell off the chamber or I'll turn my back and let Dirge finish what he started earlier," demanded Mindy.

Kroger put his hand on the wall of gold and mumbled a counter spell. The gold began to move and shrink back to its original size.

The marble pedestal came to an abrupt stop. George almost fell off the small area he was standing on clutching the pedestal and the stuck magic wand with a death grip.

All around George, in a heaping pile below him, were skeletons from centuries gone past of wizards trying to retrieve Zweig's magic wand.

At first George could hear Kizee call out to him. He tried to call up to her.

"Kizee, I'm alright," George's voice would not carry up.

It wasn't too long George stopped hearing Kizee calling out. "She'll think of something. She is a smart witch," George was telling himself.

When Mindy, Dirge and Kroger in tow, entered the chamber they found Kizee lying by the cage whimpering to herself, "George, George…"

Mindy ran down the stone stairs right up to where Kizee was. Mindy grabbed the bars of the cage. "George, George can you hear me?

George heard Mindy's voice. "Yes, yes I can hear you!"

This time George's voice was faintly heard by Mindy. "Don't move. We'll get you out of there." Mindy took a deep breath of relief.

Kizee sat up and said through her tears, "George grabbed the magic wand on the pedestal. It didn't come off. Instead George fell down a shaft."

Mindy nodded to Kizee as she called out to George, "Hold onto the pedestal real tight and let go of the magic wand."

George let go of the wand's handle. With a jolt, the pedestal rose back up to the chamber above. The cage moved back up to the top of the chamber.

George was very shaken up. Mindy half carried him from the marble pedestal.

Mindy asked, "Are you alright?"

"I don't think I'll ever be alright. Why would a fairy send us here just to kill us?"

Kizee moved right to George's side. "This is my entire fault. I'm sorry George, I'm sorry."

Mindy calmed them down. "Before we get out of here, I need to know a few things. Was that the treasure chamber you fell into?"

"I didn't see any treasure. There were just skeletons upon skeletons down there in that pit," said George.

"Then there is still another chamber down here. Tell me exactly what the two of you did step by step," asked Mindy.

Kizee described the sequence of events that caused George to fall down the shaft. George even pointed out the one stone that moved to cause the cage to come down.

"We have to change the sequence. You two stand back there while I try to open the lower chamber," stated Mindy.

Dirge got distracted with the discussion of Mindy trying to open the lower chamber. That was when Kroger took that moment in time to slip away.

Dirge realized just a tad bit too late that Kroger wasn't there. He called out to Mindy, "Commander, the dark elf has taken off! I'm sorry Commander, it's my fault."

"There is only one way out. We know where to find him later," stated Mindy not being too concerned.

"Commander, I should be the one to attempt to open the chamber," said Dirge.

Surprisingly, Kroger made it up to the cavern entrance without falling down into the abyss. He appeared at the entrance to the cavern and was about to escape.

Suddenly Kroger fell down to his knees as he was hit from behind with excess force.

Standing behind Kroger was Sybil holding her broom like a baseball bat. "Come on get up again. I just loved how my broom felt when it hit you in the back."

Searat, followed by a second lieutenant with the ship's marines showed up at the entrance of the cavern to find Sybil holding her broom above Kroger.

"Come on, I dare you to get up," said Sybil.

"Hold on Lieutenant. We'll take him into custody," said the second lieutenant.

Sybil looked up to see Captain Searat Herzog and the marine second lieutenant standing there.

Kroger moved his arm toward Sybil's broom. The second lieutenant stomped on his arm. "You, elf, where is Commander McDermit and First Engineer Firestorm?"

Kroger answered, "Their dead."

Sybil wanted to lash out at Kroger.

Kroger looked up at Sybil, "You fell down the abyss. How did you escape the pending death?"

"I always carry my broom in my pocket. When I was falling into the abyss I pulled it out and was able to fly up and out. I waited here near the entrance knowing someone would show up," explained Sybil.

Searat motioned to the second lieutenant to pick up the dark elf. "Have two of your marines take him to the ship. Everyone else, let's go find our crew members."

Dirge heard stomping of solders coming down the steps into the cavern.

In the back of the formation was Searat holding up the coffee stained chart. "We found your map."

Mindy pushed her way through to Searat. She grabbed a hold of him and picked him up with a great big bear hug kissing him repeatedly. "I love you, you old sea dog."

Mindy suddenly stopped and put Searat down. She stood back straightened her clothes. "Ah well, a good rescue, as I expected you would do, being the Captain."

While everyone was paying attention to Mindy and Searat, Dirge quietly hugged and kissed Sybil.

"I thought I had lost you forever," whispered Dirge.

"You can't get rid of this witch. I am not letting you out of your promise that easy," said Sybil.

Searat asked, "Did you get Zweig's magic wand?"

Mindy pointed on her coffee stained treasure map. "There is another chamber down here filled with treasure. Maybe the magic wand is in there. We were discussing how to open the chamber just before you arrived."

Dirge spoke up, "I was about to attempt..."

"No one is attempting anything. I don't want any killed over some stupid magic wand," stated Mindy.

"How do you attend to open the next chamber?" asked Searat.

Mindy explained what Kizee and George had gone through. "So, I was thinking that with the cage not tripped, the one grabbing the handle of the wand connected to the pedestal might open the other chamber."

Mindy started toward the pedestal. Searat stopped her. "This is my job. If anyone is to be sacrificed, it should be me. I am the expendable one."

Mindy reluctantly agreed with Searat. "Step there and there. Hold on tight to the pedestal so you won't fall off."

Searat followed Mindy's instructions. At the pedestal, Searat grabbed the handle of the wand. Instead of Searat falling down the shaft like George did, the floor opened up. The marines scrambled out of the way.

Huge stone steps slid out from the side of the walls alternating from one side to the other. Torches magically lit up showing the staircase that led down to the next chamber.

Carefully Searat, Mindy and everyone else walked down the stairs. At the bottom of the stairs was a room jam-packed with treasure chests of gold nuggets and clay jars filled with gold dust. All the way down at the bottom was a polished wood coffin.

"Do you supposed that could be the resting place of Zweig the Wizard?" asked Searat.

"There is one way to find out who is in the coffin," said Mindy.

Mindy and a couple of marines lifted the coffin lid slowly. Inside was a preserved corpse wrapped in linen. In the hands of the corpse was a magic wand.

"Close the lid. We'll take him home to perform a proper wizard's funeral," ordered Winston who came from behind everyone.

Franklin, Agnes, and Harriet were observing from the stairs. Eric and Gracie were standing in the back of the rest of the marine detachment.

Mindy oversaw the collection of the treasure back to the Raging Queen while Winston handled the coffin detail.

When everything was stowed in the cargo holds, Searat ordered, "Crew, to your stations! Prepare to get underway."

Gracie asked, "Excuse me Admiral, General, Captain, whatever you rank is. That's it, George and her cousin found this stupid lost magic wand stuffed in a coffin and we are just going to go home? What about this fairy called Maranda who caused all this mess?"

Mindy answered Gracie's question, "We will deal with Maranda in time. We came here to rescue Kizee and George and that is what we did."

Dirge was standing next to the zeppelin with Kroger still tied up. "What should we do with the prisoner, Commander?"

"Let him go. I'm sure he'll be welcomed back by the governing counsel when he gets back to town when they find he killed his friends," insisted Mindy.

"I can't go back there. They'll feed me to the grogs! Take me with you," said Kroger.

Dirge cut the rope and pushed Kroger away. "Go on with you."

Kroger ran as fast as his little legs could carry him. He went straight to the hot air balloon. With a wave of his hand, Kroger had the balloon up and moving away from the beach.

"Kroger stole my broom balloon," cried out Kizee.

"We'll catch up with him. For now we need to relax and take a breath first," said Mindy.

The Zeppelin lifted up and away with two extra passengers, a dead wizard and a whole lot of treasure. The living space was cramped before, now it was like being in a sardine can.

"You'll have to take turns sleeping and eating," said Searat to Agnes.

"Excuse us, Captain. May we have a private word with you?" asked Dirge and Sybil.

"There isn't any privacy here," said Searat.

"Sir, we were wondering since you are the Captain of the Raging Queen, could you... would you marry us?" asked Dirge.

"Oh, we can't keep this private! Everyone listen up. This evening before the ship's bell there will be a wedding," announced Searat.

Cheers and congratulations swirled throughout the ship to the happy couple. Suddenly there seemed to be a lot of room, as preparations for the wedding was being made.

The ship's cook got busy making a beautiful three tier cake. Mindy worked with the other witches of the crew to decorate the bridge.

Sybil cleaned and polished her dressed uniform. She asked Kizee if she would be the flower girl. Dirge also was preparing his uniform as well.

"Commander, I have a problem. I don't have a ring," stated Dirge.

Mindy snickered as she pulled out from her pocket a small box. "Lieutenant Whitecastle told me your intentions. So, I picked this out from an assortment of gold rings from the treasure. I hope you like it."

Dirge opened the box to see a glistening gold ring with tiny diamonds inlaid completely around the band. "Oh Commander, I couldn't. This is too, too…"

"Perfect?" Mindy completed Dirge's sentence.

Dirge smiled, "Yes, perfect."

As if it wasn't crowed enough in the crew's quarters, it was pretty cramped on the bridge for the wedding with everyone attending.

Captain Searat Herzog started, "It has always been a great honor of sea captains to have the privilege to perform marriages. This, for me is all too surprising. Never in my wildest dreams would I have thought I would command such a wonderful ship with a great crew as the Raging Queen has."

"Now I am blessed to wed these two individuals into marital bliss," finished Captain Searat.

Just before the evening watch was about to get relieved Mindy went to the cargo area where Dirge and his new bride were honeymooning. Mindy knocked on the cargo door.

"I don't mean to interrupt. We will be coming up on the storm during the midnight watch. Lieutenant Firestorm, I need you at the engineering controls," said Mindy.

"I'll be there Commander," said Dirge.

After Mindy had left, Lieutenant Sybil Whitecastle, now Lieutenant Sybil Firestorm asked, "Why is she splitting us up? We were a good team on the bridge."

"I'm sure there is another reason. Maybe they're expecting trouble and considered me important. Don't worry my sweet Sybil, we'll be together again," said Dirge.

Sybil shifted her eyes as thoughts spun through her head.

"Sybil, is everything alright? You seem to be in your thoughts more lately since we returned from the caverns. Did something happen in the abyss?" asked Dirge.

"Nothing happened down in the abyss," answered Sybil.

"What then?"

"Nothing my sweet, you better come to bed since you have the mid watch," said Sybil.

The storm was coming up on their port side. Fierce lightning bolts were flashing all around the Zeppelin Raging Queen. Mindy was on the bridge with Dirge at the propulsion controls. Another witch, hand selected by Mindy was at the helm.

Mindy had her solar chart out doing her angle calculation for the morning Sunrise to catch the double rainbow. It was almost six hours away before they could pass through to get home.

"Commander up a head, a balloon," called out the helmsman.

"Good eye, steer towards it," ordered Mindy.

Mindy grabbed a call horn. "I need a lookout and the gunners mate up on the bridge."

The below watch jostled two crew members awake. "The Commander needs you up on the bridge."

When the gunners mate and the other crew member arrived on the bridge, Mindy ordered, "Man the laser wand and standby to shoot down that balloon. You, keep a close eye on where that balloon goes if we have to shoot it completely out of the sky."

Without warning a blast came from the balloon and a shot past the Raging Queen's starboard side. The gunners mate had the balloon in his sights ready to shoot the balloon out of the sky.

"Gunner, aim and shoot one and only one line from the balloon to the basket," ordered Mindy.

The gunner took aim. It was hard to keep the balloon line in his sights as both the balloon and the zeppelin were bouncing around in the storm. Incorporated in the laser sight was the Nano-guidance system.

Suddenly the shot from the laser wand rang out. At the balloon a single line snapped. The basket leaned and shifted the direction of the balloon's travel.

The blast of the laser wand rattled through the Raging Queen, waking everyone up.

Searat was the first up to the bridge followed by Franklin, Winston, and Eric.

"Commander, the laser blast and the lightning lit up a figure leaning out of the basket. It jumped out of the balloon with a huge cape bellowing in the wind. The figure didn't fall, it flew away," reported the lookout.

"Hold your fire, gunner," ordered Mindy.

Mindy stood there looking out the window. The flashes of lightning showed the balloon flying off course and away from the zeppelin.

"Kroger jumped out of the balloon and flew into the storm. I'm sure he'll regret that," said Mindy.

"Kizee was on the bridge in the back. She heard the balloon was flying away. "That was my broom."

Kizee pulled out her magic wand to cast a retrieval spell when Harriet pulled the wand from her hand.

"Your magic won't work here, there's too much magical power being put out by the broom propulsion. Your wand would spark up and burn up like a twig in a campfire," said Harriet.

"But, my broom, I will lose it," said Kizee.

"Does your broom have a homing pigeon spell in it?" asked Harriet.

Kizee nodded yes to her mother.

"Then it will find its way back home," said Harriet comforting her daughter.

"Secure from special operations. Get us back on course," ordered Mindy.

"We're on course," answered the witch at the helm.

From the storm, a bolt of lightning flashed on the starboard side of the zeppelin. The zeppelin took a fast swerve to starboard.

Dirge saw the magic control meter on the starboard broom take a dive. He cut back on the port broom's power and slowed the zeppelin down. However, this caused the zeppelin to be unstable in the storm and the helmsman was fighting the wheel.

"We lost power on the starboard broom, Commander," yelled out Dirge.

Searat was looking out at the starboard broom. He could see the lightning had hit the bindings that held the golden straw to the broom handle.

"The broom is unraveling!" shouted Searat.

"I'll climb out there and tie it down," called out Dirge.

"No, the Captain has the responsible of keeping the ship and crew safe. I won't allow anyone to go out there. I'll do it, and there will not be any argument about it," said Searat.

Mindy stood there as Searat stared at her with determination in his face. Mindy knew she would lose this argument.

Down below three crewmen had helped Searat put on foul weather gear and a harness. They set up a pulley system at the starboard door where Searat would climb out onto the broom.

The Raging Queen was being tossed this way and that as they weren't going through the storm. There were two crewmen on the helms wheel trying to keep the zeppelin steady. The Raging Queen was falling out of the sky into the darkness between realms.

Searat climbed out on the handle of the starboard broom and inched his way down to the bindings. Rain pounded the zeppelin as some of the golden straw was being ripped away by the high winds of the storm. The zeppelin was tilted to the starboard side and the front of the airship was headed down.

Searat untied the rope from his side and began to lash it to the broom. First, he did a chain hitch around the bindings. Searat covered the chain hitch with round lashing. He tied it off with a cat's paw knot.

Searat called to the crewmen at the door, "Have them bring up the power on the starboard broom."

"Captain, we should bring you in first," shouted back a crewman.

"No, I need to see if this will hold first. Bring up the power," Searat shouted back.

Mindy heard the order called up and the reasoning for it. "Bring up the starboard broom magical power slowly," Mindy ordered.

Dirge moved the power lever up while watching the magic meter. "The power isn't rising, Commander."

"Check the magic level," ordered Mindy.

Searat was watching the starboard broom. It sputtered and popped as it tried to emit stars out the ends of the straw. The repair seemed to be holding the broom in place well enough.

Searat notice a couple of strands of straw fly away. Searat had already used up the rope he had brought out there with him and he didn't want to undo the repair and try to tie it again.

"Captain, what are you doing?" cried out the crewman at the door.

Searat had pulled out a knife and cut the rope to his harness. He pushed down farther on the broom and started to tie off the bundle as tight as he could. He pulled the rope tight. At the handle Searat tied a surgeon's knot.

"There, that ought to secure it for good," said Searat to himself.

Searat called to the crewman at the door, "Have them try it now."

Dirge started to raise the power on the starboard broom. Searat could see a stream of stars coming out of the end of the broom.

"Commander, we have power to both brooms," shouted Dirge.

"Bring up the power to full power and get us out of this dive. Get us leveled off now!" ordered Mindy.

Out of a black storm cloud the basket of the balloon slammed against the starboard side of the zeppelin. It slid all the way down to where Searat was sitting on the broomstick.

The basket hit Searat straight on and knocked him right off the handle. The balloon went on past and Searat was seen falling away by the crewman at the starboard door.

The crewman pulled the door shut and secured it. He made his way up to the bridge to Mindy. The crewman whispered in her ear.

"The Captain is lost. He was hit by the basket of that balloon when it hit the starboard side. We could have saved him if he hadn't cut his harness line to re-tie the broom straw," reported the crewman.

Mindy stood there staring into the darkness of the storm. Subdued feelings welled up inside Mindy that she had been holding down for Searat.

The first time Mindy saw him was on a cruise across the equator with Captain Davy Jones coming on board the Wanted Pirate to do shellback day with the paid customers. Mindy felt sorry for that lost soul.

It wasn't that often Mindy had seen Searat, but when she did they had a good time together swapping sea stories and pirating sunken treasure.

When Searat told her he had earned some on land ashore time, it was her idea to bring him home to meet her family. She knew nothing could come of any kind of relationship as he was a member of Davy Jones ship of dead souls. Still, Mindy loved Searat even if it was a lost cause.

Now Searat was lost to her again. Mindy knew she would wind up on Davy Jones' ship for a hundred years.

She hadn't any clue where he would wind up. Most likely she thought, "Maybe he'll go to the eternal paradise he called Heaven. That is where he wanted to go when his time was up."

By this time everyone knew what had happened. The crew was looking at Mindy waiting for orders.

Sybil was standing next to Mindy. "Commander, what are your orders?"

Mindy turned to Sybil. "Maintain maximum power. Let's get back on course to home."

"Aye, aye Captain," said Sybil.

Mindy had to take that in. Sadly, she was the Captain now.

"Lieutenant?" said Mindy.

"Yes Captain?" answered Sybil.

"You're now the First Mate...Commander. I can't have two Lieutenant Firestorms," said Mindy attempting to lighten the atmosphere.

"Alright crew set the watch accordingly and everyone get off the bridge and back to your bunks," ordered Commander Firestorm.

Mindy made her way down to her bunk. She stood there for a moment before she climbed into the lower bunk. She pulled Searat's blanket and pillow close to her. Mindy cried herself to sleep.

Chapter Fifteen
One Hundred Years

Sybil nudged Mindy's shoulder. "Captain, I hate to disturb you, but first light is almost here and we need a new heading."

Mindy turned over and put her feet down on the deck. "Time to teach you realm fraction navigating, Commander."

Up on the bridge Mindy took Sybil through the mathematical equations of the angle of the Sun to the direction of travel of the ship to the relativity movement of the rainstorm.

"In an hour, the rainbows will be appearing here. At that time turn the ship to this course and hold her steady. Once we have passed through the double rainbow use this equation and chart a course to Broomstick," explained Mindy.

"Where did you learn to navigate to different realms?" asked Sybil.

"Being on the Wanted Pirate, we had to sail into different realms that were located within the triangle. I noticed some similarities that led to this magical math formula," stated Mindy.

As predicted the double rainbow showed up and Sybil ordered the course change. They came out of the storm into blue sky with cloud covered mountains right below them.

Sybil charted a course to Broomstick, "Head west two seven zero."

Sybil and other crew members recognized landmarks from when they test flew brooms. Sybil spotted the field to where they were to land.

"Captain, we're about thirty minutes from touchdown. Any orders?" asked Sybil.

"Bring her in easy," said Mindy.

Fifteen minutes later Sybil picked up the ship's horn. "Now set the anchor detail."

The helmsman steered the Raging Queen toward the field as Dirge tilted the two brooms down.

"Level us off," ordered Sybil.

"Leveled off," came back the answer.

"All stop. Set the anchors," ordered Sybil.

Crew members jumped out on both sides and started to hammer in the mooring stakes. The Raging Queen was tied down and the lines were doubled up.

"Stand down from ship detail and set the quarterdeck watch," ordered Sybil.

Mindy stood at the gangplank when Agnes and the rest of the ship's passengers disembarked.

That wasn't the end of Gracie's troubles. She and George was preparing to pack up what was left of their stuff and head home to San Francisco.

Sybil called out an order to the quarterdeck watch. "Hold that private and place her under arrest for attempted desertion."

Assembled on the field was a good size posse with the Sheriff standing there in front with weapons.

"Good work, you manage to bring back my fugitives from justice," said the Sheriff.

Agnes was out in front walking toward the Sheriff. "I told you before Sheriff, this is a magical world matter. Go home," ordered Agnes pointing her magic wand at the Sheriff.

Harriet was standing just arm's length behind her sister with a hard look in her eyes just wanting to do a few spells on those knotem vigilantes.

"Now Agnes I'm the appointed officer of law for the town of Broomstick and laws have been broken by Gracie Düben, including murder of magical creatures," said the Sheriff.

"Sheriff, do you remember what happened with the previous sheriff?" asked Agnes.

"He got involved with a gang of Trolls that tormented the town," said the Sheriff.

"And what part of town did this take place?" queried Agnes.

The Sheriff stood there silent.

"You know I bet I could trace the Centurion bounty hunters back to you. Now isn't it funny, you knew where to be when we returned from the dark elves realm? Almost as if you were tipped off by someone," stated Agnes.

Franklin and Winston were up next to Agnes. "Where is Maranda the tree fairy right now?" questioned Winston.

"Hey all of you, if you don't want to get caught up in the profit scheme the Sheriff here is trying to commit, I suggest you just go home right now," shouted Franklin.

The men of the posse looked at each other and mumbled to themselves. It didn't take them very long to decide. Slowly the guns lowered and together they turned and walked away from the Sheriff.

"Well Sheriff... where is Maranda the tree fairy?" asked Agnes.

"She showed up at my office, but she didn't stay long. All she told me was to be here at this time if I wanted my reward. However, I think you may be right about this just being a magical world problem. I'll just go back to my office and forget this whole matter," said the Sheriff.

Mindy left Sybil and the crew to make repairs to the Raging Queen's broom propulsion system, although she had no idea what she was going to do for a hundred years once she returned to the Wanted Pirate and face Captain Davy Jones.

"Eric, you now own all of Spell Caster Enterprises. Sybil, I am putting you in charge of the Gold Zeppelin Cruise Tour Line and all the treasure from the cavern to be split among the crew as per the pirate creed," said Mindy.

"Wait, we still have to find Maranda," said Sybil.

"Mom and Aunt Harriet can handle that without us. For right now, I have another obligation I must attend to on the Wanted Pirate with Captain Davy Jones," stated Mindy.

Mindy went home and packed her stuff. "I got to get back to work, Mom. I have a couple of things I have to attend to in the triangle." Knowing very well she will be gone for a full one hundred years.

"You're going to have a memorial for Searat?" asked Agnes.

"Yes, I am, Mom. You know I brought him home for all the family to meet a few months ago. I know it wouldn't have been the kind of relationship you would have wanted for me. We had those shellback cruises and this adventure together. I hope that was enough for him."

Mindy broke down and started to cry. "I loved him Mom."

Agnes and Mindy held each other as Mindy cried and Agnes consoled her middle daughter.

A couple days later Mindy was standing on the shore of Montego Bay, Jamaica waiting for the liberty launch back to the Wanted Pirate.

"Where's yer sailor you went off with?" asked the salty old sailor in charge of the liberty launch.

"He didn't make it back from our adventure. I guess I have some explaining to do to Captain Davy Jones," said Mindy as she sat down in the boat.

"Ho, AWOL from Davy's ship? That be a first," said the salty old sailor.

"Yeah, now get me back to the Wanted Pirate before I'm AWOL from her," said Mindy.

When Mindy climbed onboard the Wanted Pirate, the Bos'n was waiting for her at the quarterdeck. Mindy knew she was in real trouble at that moment.

"Captain Bonny wishes you well and needs her navigator to plot a course for the rendezvous with Davy Jones. I'm here to tell you this ship won't offer any help as this is not ship's business that will be conducted," stated the Bos'n.

After Mindy stowed her gear she went to the charthouse and began charting the requested course.

In two days, the Wanted Pirate was tied to Davy Jones ship, Purgatory. A gangplank ran between them. The watch blew his boatswain pipe and rang the ship's bell.

"whooo eeee whooo eeee ding-ding... ding-ding, Captain Davy Jones arriving," called out the watch.

Captain Davy Jones crossed the gangplank to be greeted by Captain Anne Bonny. "Welcome aboard Captain," said Anne Bonny.

"Dispense with the pleasantries Captain, I'm here to see your navigator on a personal matter," said Davy Jones.

Standing not too far away was Mindy in her dress uniform. "I'm here Captain."

Davy Jones walked up to Mindy and said out loud for all to hear, "You lost me my best sailor!"

"He was a brave soul. Searat saved everyone on board our zeppelin," said Mindy in her defense.

"I know the whole story. I won't take away from his heroic action. It's you I am here to deal with. Just like the pirate you are, you left him behind, as per the code," shouted Davy Jones.

"I'm sure Captain, you would know if Searat went to his Heaven. You should be glad of that," said Mindy.

"I do know, and no he didn't! The heroic deed of saving the Raging Queen didn't go unrewarded. He earned his life back," said Davy Jones.

Mindy looked at the old salty Captain of Doom wondering what exactly was he talking about.

"Aha, you don't know Searat whole story do you," said Davy Jones. "I kept him on board my ship to protect him from Maranda. If she knew a long time ago that he was the one that could open the chamber to Zweig's coffin…well she would have that magic wand now," answered Davy Jones.

"And now?" asked Mindy.

Davy Jones peered at Mindy with dark hollow eyes. "And now he earned a second chance, to pick up where he had left off. His time line has been restored. However, you… left him behind to possibly lose his second chance and he will come back to me."

Mindy stood there thinking making quick plans. "I'll go back to the realm of the dark elves and rescue him before it's too late."

Mindy turned away from Davy Jones with plans of getting home and back to Spell Caster Enterprises.

"Not so fast lassie. There is one other matter I have with you. You looted my buried treasure from the bottom of my ocean," griped Davy Jones.

Mindy turned back to Davy Jones. "As per the pirate code, finders keepers, Captain."

Davy Jones turned to Anne Bonny. "Are you going to allow your junior officer talk to me in this arrogant manner?"

Mindy moved closer to Davy Jones. "I had the rank of Captain of the flying Zeppelin Raging Queen!"

"Humph, remember how you got that title lassie. Your restitution is waiting for you on the Purgatory if you fail in your mission," said Davy Jones.

"Get off this ship, Captain. Our business is done," shouted Mindy.

Davy Jones held up his head and started to walk toward the gangplank. At the last moment, he turned to stare at Mindy.

"If you do succeed in saving Searat, you best be keeping him and yourself on land. I'll show no leniency to the two of you if you return to the briny," promised Davy Jones.

From a vertex of salt water, Mindy burst into the house throwing her wet sea bag down on the floor. "I need the Raging Queen. Searat is alive. I mean really alive. He isn't a doomed soul anymore. I have to go after him. Searat is still in the dark elves realm."

"Calm down. The zeppelin will be back at midnight. Sybil is taking her with passengers to the Horizon Line Realm for a dinner tour," said Franklin.

"Has it left yet?" asked Mindy.

"Ah, well I guess not yet, but very soon," replied Franklin.

Mindy arrived at the field just a cat's whiskers too late. The Raging Queen was already gone.

That evening at the Poison Apple Tavern, Mindy met with Eric, "I need a zeppelin to go and find Searat. Davy Jones said he is still alive in the dark elves realm."

"The Raging Queen is booked every day this week for those dinner tours," said Eric.

Mindy questioned, "What about the next zeppelin?"

"It will take Spell Caster Enterprises a couple of months to get the next zeppelin lined up for you."

"Alright I had to try. But I want the Captain's position on the next available zeppelin. This time I'm talking permanently," said Mindy.

"That is not for me to decide. That is what I'm trying to tell you. Sybil has ordered four more and has paid for them all in advance. A zeppelin for you won't be started for a couple of months from now," said Eric.

Mindy was waiting in the field when the Raging Queen landed. She started shouting at Sybil.

Sybil was still up on the bridge when she saw Mindy waving at her from the ground. "Take over here and secure the luggage compartment."

Sybil ran down the gangplank to where Mindy was. "What are you doing here? I thought you had to...well take care of business with you know who?"

"I did. He told me Searat is alive. I mean really alive. His heroic act saved him from...anyway, I need the Raging Queen to recue Searat from the dark elf realm," said Mindy.

"Ah, I'm sorry I can't just leave right now. We have repairs and another realm tour set for tomorrow morning," said Sybil. "You know I would if I could. My crew is tired and I can't afford to lose that much business. I spent my portion of the treasure to get this company going."

"Yeah, I understand. I had to try anyway. I'll figure something out," said Mindy.

Mindy thought, "I could conjure up a balloon, perhaps."

Before Mindy could act, one of the crew called out and pointed up in the sky. "Look, something's coming in."

Everyone stared up to where the crewman had been pointing. The object was coming in fast, almost out of control.

Sybil pulled out her spyglass. "It's a balloon," called Sybil.

Mindy couldn't help to notice on one side of the balloon basket was a harness attached to the basket and the balloon rope. Someone was inside pulling the lever that let the hot air out of the balloon to make it come down.

"It's Searat," shouted Sybil.

Mindy was running with a couple of crewmen with ropes and stakes. "Hammer them in here and tie off the ropes tight."

From the teed off ropes, Mindy had a longer rope extended with the crew holding on each side like a game of tug-o-war.

The Balloon hit the ground hard and was dragged by the wind that was carrying the balloon. When the balloon got to the rope, the crew held it up to catch the basket.

"Pull! Hold it! Grab the basket lines and tie her down," shouted Mindy.

Lying in the basket was a cold shivering Searat wrapped in a very thin blanket.

"Searat, Searat, talk to me. Give me a sign," cried Mindy as she pulled him out of the basket and held him close to warm him.

Other crew members were there with more blankets. Mindy rocked Searat in her arms while rubbing him. "I'm sorry. I am so sorry for leaving you behind."

Searat whispered with a scratchy voice, "I'm AWOL from the Purgatory."

"No, no you're not. You're free and alive," said Mindy holding Searat tightly.

The magical medical staff from the zeppelin showed up with a stretcher. Coming out of a vortex was more medical staff from Broomstick magical medical ward. Searat was transported to the magical medical ward. Mindy held onto the stretcher as they disappeared from the field.

At the far end of the field was Maranda the fairy taking in the event of the late evening. "Well I don't think I can top that. But I'll certainly try," said Maranda with a grin.

Chapter Sixteen
What Now?

Gracie and George were staying in a two bedroom apartment on the first floor of the apartments next to the Ex-press Coffee Shop. Everything was packed to leave for San Francisco.

Gracie tried to get things off her mind as she sat in class as if she never left. "The same homework that was there before..."

"...before George disappeared. How can I just sit here and forget everything I had gone through?" cried Gracie to herself.

Everyone in her criminal law class was curious about where Gracie had been for the last few weeks. Rumors were spreading like a wildfire when a memo came to Gracie.

Everyone popped up their heads from their text books trying to listen or see what this memo was about.

Gracie opened it and read, "When you have a moment come to City Hall- Winston."

Gracie grabbed her bag and headed straight to the ladies room. As she cleaned up the streaks of tears, Gracie looked at herself in the mirror.

"My whole world turned inside out and backwards and I am supposed to just act like nothing happened? Three weeks. Three weeks of torment from this magical world and for what, a lousy magic wand? That's it. I am going straight to Winston Wisestone's office and tell him what he can do with his magical world. I quit. I am going back to San Francisco and fix my own financial problems without any help from this lunatic town," said Gracie to herself in the mirror.

At Winston's office in Broomstick's City Hall, Winston offered Gracie a chair at the round table. "Coffee?" asked Winston.

This time Gracie said, "Yes please, black with sugar, no cream."

"How are the repairs coming on your house?" asked Winston.

"I've gotten a few estimates. The insurance company is stalling because they don't understand how the damage to the house happened. They also keep asking me why I didn't report it right away to the sheriff's department and the insurance company," explained Gracie.

"Do you want me to take care of it for you?" asked Winston.

"No, thank you. I'll let the knotem world work on it," smiled Gracie.

"Anyway, that isn't why I had you come here. I need you to oversee the production of your creations for the New York Fashion Show. Do you have a name for the line of clothing yet?" asked Winston.

"Mr. Wisestone, I have something important to say," started Gracie.

Winston sat down Gracie's coffee and moved to his seat and sat down. "What's on your mind, Gracie?"

"Mr. Wisestone…"

"Please, call me Winston."

Gracie let out a sigh. "Mr. Wisestone, I just can't pick up where I left off. Too much has happened. I want to just walk away from these three weeks of madness. I'm going back to San Francisco and fix my financial problems on my own, and without help from this crazy magical world of yours."

"Do you remember the deal we made about Düben fashions?" asked Winston.

"One hundred and fifty million for twenty five percent of a company at that time was worth less than two million. But now it is bankrupt owing more than I could ever make in a hundred lifetimes," said Gracie.

"You designed a very good line of clothing," stated Winston.

"My designs were ruin by the collapse of my house," said Gracie flatly.

"Gracie, please work with me. I can help you get your designs back. And I can also help you get your life back on track. One single signature here and all your problems will go away," pleaded Winston.

Gracie sat there with all her thoughts flying through her head in a mix up quagmire of decisions not making any sense. Her mind couldn't put any of this in a simple order except one. "Sign the document and all my problems will go away."

"Mr. Wisestone, when something is too simple there is something wrong. It can't be this simple to rid me of all my problems with a stroke of a pen."

Winston put his hand on Gracie's hand. "Trust me. Trust magic. Trust yourself."

Gracie calmed down internally. "Everything will be okay in the future," she said to herself.

Winston removed his hand from Gracie's. Gracie picked up the pen and signed the document.

The pen pricked her finger and blood ran down to the pen point where Gracie signed the document in blood. A rush ran over Gracie like slipping into a hot tub of hot water washing away all of her worries. She took a sip of her coffee not noticing the drop of blood running down the handle of the coffee cup.

"Go over to our factory and look around and come up with a magical name for you line of clothing," said Winston.

"You said the New York Fashion Show. I thought my fashions were for the magical world?" questioned Gracie.

"They are, but where do you think they shop?" laughed Winston.

"Um, so I should give it a crazy name that would let the magical world know it's for them?" asked Gracie.

"Now you're thinking," exclaimed Winston.

Gracie spent the rest of the day at the new factory across town that had a sparkling sign that read "Düben Fashions."

Everything Gracie could salvage from their wrecked home was in boxes waiting to be moved back to San Francisco. They were stacked up to the ceiling in the small cramped apartment.

George was still coming to grips with all that had happened. The Witchdoctor at the Broomstick magical medical ward gave him a complete physical and gave George a suave to heal his rope burned hands.

George was sitting at the kitchen table with Zweig's old magic book nibbling on a protein bar. George rubbed the front cover feeling the book's name, "The Quagmire Journal of Magic. Shouldn't I have gotten some kind of magical powers for my effort," thought George.

George didn't notice Kizee appeared in the apartment. They haven't spoken much since they returned to Broomstick.

"George? If I have wronged you in any way George, I am sorry" cried Kizee.

"You haven't done anything wrong to me. I caused everything by taking this magic book in the first place. Gracie and I are no better off than when we first arrived. It's my entire fault and I am left with nothing," said George.

"You still have me George as your best friend," suggested Kizee.

George made a disgruntled expression. "We're leaving for San Francisco in two days. Gracie called the moving company and bought plane tickets already."

"George, we pinky swore to be best friends forever. And in the cemetery, you even kissed me which sealed it. You're my best friend George... You're my only friend," said Kizee with her voice tapering off.

"I wanted that magic wand to show you I can be a wizard. I'm still nobody in your magical world. What do you call us? Knotems, like it's a curse."

"George, we are not done yet. Aunt Agnes and Mom can't find Maranda anywhere. Their spells, their crystal ball, nothing is giving them any clue where to look. They can't even find Maranda's tree."

"So, what's your point?"

"We can find her. Let's go on a picnic tomorrow," said Kizee.

"Some other time, Gracie and I are busy tomorrow," said George.

Kizee disappointed with George, simply disappeared.

Gracie came home to the apartment after she spent the afternoon at the new Düben fashion factory. She had good news to tell George. She found George asleep at the table.

Gracie picked up the phone and called the moving company. "This is Gracie Düben. I would like to cancel my moving pick up for tomorrow. Oh? They're coming right now? But, wait...It has all been arranged? My house? But...Winston Wisestone. I see, all unpacked while I'm away in New York." Gracie smirked at the phone. "Thank you, goodbye to you too."

George stirred awake to hear Gracie on the phone.

"Is it true? We're staying?" asked George.

"Yes George, it's true. And Düben Fashions is back in business."

Gracie was deep into her clothing design business ignoring both Eric and George. She traveled often to New York leaving George to himself.

Gracie had left for New York, leaving George with Agnes.

Her line of clothing was about to be unveiled. It was called 'Witch Dimensions'.

Agnes arranged for George to stay with Peter Candlewick while Gracie was in New York.

Over a microwaved dinner, Peter told George a story about when the Black Fairy passed through Broomstick causing mischief one November day.

Peter said, "The Black Fairy sent a message through the Ouija board. When someone turned the pad upside down they read 'Hello Katee you are going to find true love this day.' They figured out the last five letters stood for, with love the Black Fairy.

"Then what happened after the Ouija board message?" asked George.

"Nothing, no one saw or heard from the Black Fairy since, and maybe you'll never see or hear from Maranda the White Fairy either," said Peter.

"What about Katee Greene, are you her true love?"

"Mmmm, well who knows," Peter hesitated. "Everyone finds true love someday," answered Peter.

Eric stood on Gracie's porch of her rebuilt home that was once just rubble from the Centaur kicking it down. In Eric's hand was a very large bouquet of red roses. He knocked on the door in his usual manner.

George opened the door. "She isn't going to listen."

"Listen to what? I'm here for our weekly date, George."

"With red roses, she'll see right through them," stated George.

Gracie was coming up behind George. "Eric, we had this discussion many times before."

"Gracie, please," insisted Eric.

Gracie stood there grimacing, not saying a word.

"Gracie, honey, you know I love you and George. I will devote my life to you. And no more magical rigmarole," said Eric.

"Is that a promise you think you can really keep?" stated Gracie.

"Absolutely," said Eric knowing very well he couldn't.

"I would call you a liar, knowing very well that you couldn't keep away from Spell Caster Enterprises. That is your new job now."

"Okay, but I can make you very happy being married to me without any magical influence," said Eric.

"Is this a proposal or an empty threat?" said Gracie.

"Please Gracie allow Agnes and Harriet to help George deal with all that has happened. I'll do anything you want," said Eric.

George said, "Please Gracie just this once."

Gracie finally broke down, "Alright, just this one time. You owe me buster, big time. And next time you talk to me about marriage, you had better have a five-piece orchestra behind you, five dozen flowers, and you down on one knee begging me to love you. You got that?"

Eric stood there with a somber expression on his face. He thought to himself, "If this doesn't work, I'll go on one of those tours to a crazy realm and never come back."

Agnes was distracted and deeply absorbed in a book. Harriet tried to interrupt her sister's reading.

"Mar a dhèiligeas ri sìthichean dona," Harriet read the title of the book out loud with some degree of irregularity. "What does that mean?"

"How to capture bad fairies," said Agnes.

"Anything good that we can use?" asked Harriet.

"This book is really out of date. Some of the ways are not used anymore. I found in other references that most spells they used back then didn't work," said Agnes as she closed the book with frustration.

"I've never seen you like this Agnes," said Harriet.

"I'll be back later. I am going to the Ex-press coffee shop to get a skinny pumpkin spice latte," said Agnes.

"Can you bring me back…"

"No," said Agnes as she disappeared with a hint of campfire sparks popping.

While Katee Greene was making Agnes her skinny pumpkin spice latte, Agnes stood there talking.

"I just can't believe a white fairy could go unnoticed by the magical world while she murders wizards for a thousand years," said Agnes.

"Are you talking about this white fairy that has caused all the trouble in Broomstick?" asked Katee as she handed Agnes her skinny pumpkin spice latte.

"The very same," concurred Agnes.

"Who said the trouble maker was the white fairy? What color are her wings?" said a voice in the far corner of the coffee shop.

Agnes and Katee turned to see who the mystery voice was.

"You can't be the girl with frizzy hair pulled into two pony tails on each side of her head that was skinny and no shape to her torso wearing braces on her teeth," laughed Agnes.

Then Agnes said, "Sammie! What are you doing here in Broomstick?"

"Orange Inc. was bought out by a new company called Spell Caster Enterprises. I'm here to be absorbed integrate into the parent company," answered Sammie.

Katee said, "You asked a very good question."

"Oh Katee Greene this is Sammie, you know, I never knew your last name," queried Agnes.

"It's still just Sammie."

Sammie really had changed since college. She had a very nice smile with polished white straight teeth. Her hair was smoothly pulled back in a single ponytail using her magic wand in a hair barrette to hold it in place.

Agnes asked, "What happen to Simon Norman Lavinsky?"

"He is still hanging around with me," said Sammie as she held out a diamond pendant. "Simon tried to embezzle money from our company Orange Inc. Now he is de-pendant upon me for everything. I told him it was love at first sight and he couldn't get out of it."

Katee again tried to shift the conversation, "Back to the white fairy…"

"Ah, well come to think of it, Kizee my niece was the first to see her…" Agnes trailed off for a moment. "…you know I think Kizee and George are the only ones in Broomstick to have seen her."

Sammie asked, "You've never seen this white fairy? Then how do you know she is the white fairy? What you need to know is what color are her wings?"

"Are you busy right now? I could use your help. If your suspicions are correct, then we have a fairy imposter among us," stated Agnes.

"Still, fairies are hard to catch, no matter what kind of fairy they are," said Katee.

Sammie suggested, "What if she isn't a fairy at all?"

"Let's go with that idea," said Agnes.

Chapter Seventeen
Vanishing Fairy Wings

Agnes and Sammie arrived at the Hidden Quiddity Potion Shop in time to find Harriet and Wendy reading through the various books that Agnes had on dealing with bad fairies instead of making up potion ingredients orders.

Agnes asked with concern, "What are you doing?"

"We found a few spells that we could try when we see Maranda again," said Harriet.

Then Harriet saw Sammie standing next to her sister. "Sammie!" said Harriet as she gave her a hug. "What are you doing here in Broomstick?"

Agnes interrupted with, "She is here to help up with our white fairy problem."

"I heard a strange report that two Centaurs had been killed here," said Sammie. "Um, Agnes didn't you say only your niece and her friend had seen this white fairy?"

"Yes. Harriet, think about it, no one else has seen the white fairy except Kizee and George," said Agnes.

Harriet stood there perplexed. "Didn't we see…um, wait we saw her…oh!?!"

"Oh is right," said Agnes. "We need to talk to Kizee and George about Maranda the supposedly White Fairy."

"Supposedly?" said Wendy.

Sammie spoke up, "Well for one thing, what color are her wings? You may have a fairy impersonating a white fairy, or even worse, a complete imposter."

"Oh I see," said Wendy.

"Can you get Kizee and George here in the next few minutes?" asked Agnes to Harriet.

Wendy said, "I know where Kizee is. I'll get her and George here."

"George, wake up its after ten in the morning," said Kizee standing at the foot of his bed.

George opened one eye and stared at Kizee. "You know this isn't normal you appearing in my bedroom."

"You need to get up. Aunt Agnes needs to talk to us," said Kizee ignoring what George had said.

"Please its Saturday, no more magical adventures for a while," said George pulling the blanket over his head.

"It isn't an adventure day silly. This is important," said Kizee as she pulled the blanket off of George exposing his cartoon print pajamas.

"Okay, okay, I'll get up. Meet me in the kitchen," responded George.

Kizee threw George's blanket back at him as she disappeared from his room. George felt a cold shudder pass through his body while grabbing at his blanket.

In the kitchen Kizee made George a special breakfast. "It's an indigo milk cap omelet."

George was looking at a plate with orange colored eggs with blue speckles, "A what?"

"An indigo milk cap omelet."

George still had a quizzical expression.

Kizee shook her head, "A Lactarius indigo omelet. Oh really, the little speckles are the rare blue milk mushroom. It will help boost your magical powers...oh I forgot, I'm sorry George. Well, it will help you feel good anyways."

George silently sat there and ate the orange with blue dots omelet while Kizee talked.

"Did you know we are the only ones that have seen Maranda the White Fairy?"

"I really never gave it a thought," said George.

"Now come on, Aunt Agnes has questions for us," insisted Kizee.

George wolfed down the last couple of bites of the omelet and washed it down with a glass of milk that he got out of the refrigerator himself.

Wendy was waiting on the porch when Kizee and George came out of the front door. "Are you ready?"

"Ready for what?" asked George.

"We're ready," said Kizee.

Wendy grabbed George's left hand as Kizee grabbed his right. "On the count of three say Whiskers."

When Wendy said three, George said, "Whiskers," in a form of a questioned not knowing what was about to happen.

Together they vanished into thin air leaving a white whispery trail behind.

At the potion shop, George fell to his knees and threw up the now mixed orange egg and blue mushroom breakfast.

"Oh, sorry, I thought you and Kizee had been doing this for a while," said Wendy.

After George was cleaned up and felt better Agnes and Sammie asked questions about their experience with Maranda the White Fairy.

Sammie asked the first question, "What color were the fairy's wings?"

Kizee answered, "I think they were translucent. I couldn't really see them that well."

George looked confused, "I don't remember Maranda having any wings."

"Hem, little or no wings," said Sammie. "Did you see her fly?"

George crinkled his face as he answered, "Maranda more or less just sat on her tree stump except at the cemetery where she was standing at the gate."

"What about you, Kizee?" asked Sammie.

"The one time I ran into her before I met George, she appeared sitting on her tree stump."

Sammie's eyes closed to a slit as her nose cringed, "You have an imposter pretending to be a fairy for some reason."

"That would certainly answer the question why would a fairy want a wizard's magic wand," said Agnes.

Harriet quipped, "If not a fairy, then a wizard or a witch perhaps."

Agnes looked at Harriet with a facial expression saying, "Obviously."

"How do you two usually run into this Maranda fairy person?" asked Sammie.

"We go on picnics," said Kizee.

"Except the one time Maranda showed up at the baseball park wanting to know if I solved a clue to find the magic wand," stated George.

"A fairy showed up at a baseball park? That is very unusual," said Sammie.

Agnes started to bark out orders as if she just came up with a plan to capture this Maranda whoever she was. "Harriet, you make up a picnic basket for George and Kizee. Windy, get your two sisters and meet me back here."

"And what do you want me to do?" asked Sammie.

"I want you to come with me to gather up the Sisters of the Q coven. We have to put a strategy together to foil a dastardly scheme," said Agnes.

Agnes grabbed an empty hollow magic wand from a drawer behind the counter that doesn't have any magic contained within it.

"Now George, I want you to show Maranda this wand and let her assume it is the magic wand we brought back from the dark elf realm," instructed Agnes.

It was a cool afternoon when Kizee and George set out on their picnic in the forest where they had ran into Maranda the fairy.

Near the tree stump where Maranda usually sat, Kizee spread out a blanket. George unpacked the lunch with all the best food.

In one bowl was cold fried chicken. Another bowl had potato salad, while still in another was cut up watermelon. For dessert was a fresh apple pie. Lastly, George filled a glass pitcher with fresh squeezed lemonade.

It wasn't long when they heard a familiar voice. "You still haven't learned. Again, you two are on a picnic and didn't invite me," said Maranda sitting on her tree stump.

"It is hard to invite you when you aren't around to receive the invitation," said Kizee.

"This is a picnic for you," insisted George.

"Well then, can I sit next to you George?" asked Maranda.

"Yes, but not too close," said Kizee.

"Oh right, you still think I will steal away your true love," quipped Maranda.

Maranda sat down next to George. She curled his hair around one finger. "You know George I could have made you a very powerful wizard if only you had brought me that magic wand. I know all about the rescue from the caverns. You didn't find the magic wand before your little witch girlfriend's family brought you back home."

Maranda's nose winced while still curling George's hair around her finger. "You're here for something. What is it you want?"

George looked at Kizee before he said, "Well…" and not saying anything more. George pulled out from a bag, the empty magic wand and held it out for Maranda to see.

"You sly little devil, how in the world did you get it back without that nosy witch Agnes knowing? May I hold it?" asked Maranda.

George hesitated a little, to peak Maranda's interest that much more. "How are you going to make me a powerful wizard with it?"

When Maranda had the magic wand in her hand, she stood up from George and said, "By doing this!"

Maranda pointed the wand at George. "Mediocris virtus faciam voluntatem meam, ut te ab hoc knotem te occidere."

Suddenly out from behind trees and shrubs Agnes, Harriet, with Sammie and the Sisters of the Q coven jumped out with wands sizzling high intensity beams of electro-magic power.

Maranda dropped the wand as she shook, trembled, quivered, convulsed, and jerked from the electrical shock running through her body.

The tips of Maranda's hair were smoking. Her teeth chattered while her eyes rolled up showing only the whites of her eyes.

The witches stopped their attack. Maranda laid there motionless. Harriet pulled Kizee and George away to a safe place trying to cover up the horrendous unspeakable scene of Maranda deathly still body.

"Is she dead?" asked Kizee.

"No, but she ought to be, after using an unforgiving Latin spell trying to kill George," said Harriet.

While the witch's coven took care of the unconscious fairy imposter, Agnes and Sammie came over to make sure Kizee and George were alright.

"When Maranda used Latin to do her killing spell, she gave her true self away. Only a wizardress uses Latin to do their black magic spells. Maranda is not a fairy at all. She is a very dark wizardress using black magic to keep her alive these past thousand years," stated Agnes.

Maranda was locked up in the town's jail. Spells and charms were in place to keep her there when she awoke from the high intensity electro-magic.

Agnes was there when Maranda woke up. Maranda was still unstable as she lunged at Agnes.

Maranda fell into the cell bars. The voltage of electro-magic pushed Maranda away from the bars. She fell back onto the cell bed.

"Just sit there for a few minutes and calm down," said Agnes firmly.

"You can't keep me here. I will get free," yelled Maranda.

Again, Maranda stood up. This time she was more stable. Maranda walked over to the cell bars and began to rub her fingernails back and forth on them causing sparks.

"When you are done, I would like to talk to you," stated Agnes.

Maranda stared hard and deep at Agnes.

"Let me start with a two part question. What is so important about that old magic wand that a wizardress would impersonate the White Fairy and for a thousand years send wizards to their deaths trying to retrieve it?"

"Ha, ha, you think I am a thousand years old. How funny is that!" laughed Maranda.

"Well, I have my suspensions. Being a witch doesn't stop me from knowing and studying ancient wizardressery practices," said Agnes.

"It's still called wizardry even to a wizardress," corrected Maranda.

"If you say so," shrugged Agnes. "You being Zweig's apprentice gave you access to some longevity potions made from the legionary philosopher's stone."

"If you believe in that fairy tale that would make the second funny thing you said so far. And what about your thousand year old wizard, what happened to his longevity?" stated Maranda.

"You have the puzzle pieces that would complete the picture of this story, if you are willing to share with us," said Agnes politely.

"NOT IN TEN THOUSAND YEARS WOULD I TELL YOU ANY OF MY SECRETS," screamed Maranda angrily.

"We thought so. Mindy, Searat, she is all yours," said Agnes.

It took some intense magic by the Sisters of the Q coven to put Maranda the wizardress into a sealed glass bottle. But there she was, shackled in irons sitting on the bottom of the sealed glass bottle in a bag slung over Mindy's shoulder.

Mindy and Searat were standing on the shore where the Wanted Pirate's liberty boat would show up.

"Yer com'in on board as crew or guests?" asked the bos'en.

"We're paying guests this time," said Mindy.

Mindy and Searat booked a crossing the equator cruise specifically to face Captain Davy Jones.

Captain Anne Bonny personally met them at the gangplank when Mindy and Searat stepped on board the Wanted Pirate. "You sure have guts, wanting to see Davy Jones after his warning."

"We have important business with that old sea dog," said Mindy not being polite about Davy Jones.

During the shellback induction of the paid guests, Mindy and Searat presented themselves to Davy Jones.

"I told ye, if I'd ever see the two of you again thar be consequences," roared Captain Davy Jones.

"We came here to make a trade. Our lives free and clear for someone who owes you a lifetime," stated Mindy as she opened the glass bottle and turn it upside down.

From the bottle, Maranda came falling out onto the deck on her knees with her arms and legs shackled.

"Maranda, we met again," said Davy Jones.

Still on her knees, Maranda looked up at Davy. "You knew his magic wand and amulet was rightfully mine when he hid himself away. I did your dirty work just as you ordered. I gave that dying wizard your stupid mine claim. He found it and didn't use it. Then you denied me Captain Herzog who could open his tomb."

Searat whispered in Mindy's ear, "I was just a pawn. When we were in the cavern, I recognized the section of the mine we had worked. Everything else in those caverns was put there well after we had sailed away with our share of the gold."

Davy Jones leaned down just a little and said, "Nay did you do my dirty work. It was clearly yers work yer were do'in. I sees before me an apprentice who stole a piece of the one and only mineral best's be known as the philosopher's stone. Yer got your payment."

"Well do we have a deal?" asked Mindy.

"Yer got yer deal." Davy spat in his hand and stuck it out. Mindy did the same and they shook hands.

Davy turned to two of his crew and ordered, "Take her to the brig."

At the Zeppelin air field, poised with charm were the five beautifully crafted magical broom powered zeppelins hand built by the magical team of Spell Caster Enterprises. This was tourism in the magical world at its best.

Mindy and Searat were reading the names out loud that the crews had selected for the four new zeppelins as they took in the sight of ground crews loading supplies for the different tours scheduled to leave.

Mindy called their names out. "Sky Queen, Realm Rider, Out Worlder."

Then Mindy stopped reading and stared. At the very end of the field was the Zeppelin with the name Eighty Two. And hanging on the gangplank was the Zeppelin's Captain dressed uniform.

Mindy questioned, "Eighty Two?"

"She needed a name that inspires courage, fearfulness, majestic, and poetic" said Searat.

Mindy reluctantly smiled at Searat and gave him a kiss. "Thank you for the complement. What you are really referring to is my 'Get the lead out commanding attitude'," said Mindy with a happy heart.

Searat made a gesture with his hand. There were people coming out of the zeppelin. They surround Mindy and Searat.

Searat got down on one knee. "Mindy McDermit, will you marry this old sea dog and make him happy for the rest of his life?"

Mindy dropped down to Searat. "Yes, you old sea dog, I will marry you and make you happy for the rest of our lives."

Mindy pushed Searat over onto the ground and kissed him repeatedly. Everyone there was cheering loudly.

Chapter Eighteen
Pyre and Stone

The Broomstick wizards gathered for the funeral of Zweig the Wizard at a secret desolate ceremonial area. The stars were bright and twinkled under a moonless night.

Pillars were erected to hold the wood coffin that was brought back from the Smether Realm with the remains of Zweig the Wizard. Wood was carefully stacked underneath and soaked with oil. A circle was scratched into the ground around the wood pile with simple symbols.

"Let this Circle of the Bluestones convocation of wizards, come to order," called out Winston Wisestone. When everyone was quiet, Winston nodded to Dirge Firestorm.

Dirge Firestorm began, "This wizard was found hidden from the magical world. His spirit tucked away in a realm of darkened magic. We don't know Zweig's reasons. Now he is among his fellow wizards once again, protected, honored, and ready to be delivered to what lies beyond. We wish his spirit good journey."

From a crop of rocks, a fiery arrow flew. The arrow hit its mark. The first pillar burst into flames. The fire quickly traveled to the other pillar and the neatly stacked of wood below the wood coffin.

As the roaring pyre burned, the convocation of wizards began to walk around the circle chanting, "Two steps forward and one step back. Two steps forward and one step back..."

The meaning of the chant was the two steps forward represented life must go. While the one step back represented a time to reflect.

As the funeral pyre burned, the wood would crackle sending hot sparks flying into the night air. Above in the night sky, meteors fell as to greet their earth bound counterparts.

One by one as the wizards chanted and walked, each in turned disappeared into the night. Franklin and Winston were the last two wizards to step and disappear.

Left in the darkness with just smoldering embers remaining of the funeral pyre, a very mysterious event happened. One hand holding Zweig's magic wand emerged from the embers followed by a cloaked figure.

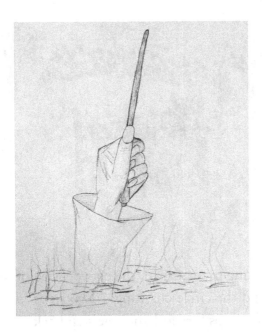

The figure stepped out of the pyre, pulled off his hood and looked up into the starry night sky. Zweig, holding his magic wand tight in his hands, was smiling.

Known only to Zweig was the cryptic secret, hidden within his magic wand next to his magical amulet of power was the philosopher's stone of immortality.

Printed in the United States
By Bookmasters